WINTER'S GHOST

WINTER BLACK SERIES: BOOK FIVE

MARY STONE

To my husband.
Thank you for taking care of our home and its many inhabitants
while I follow this silly dream of mine.

DESCRIPTION

Some ghosts still live and breathe...

Six months ago, on the night Winter Black and her fellow agents took down The Preacher, a mall massacre occurred.

Today, one of the gunmen responsible for taking fifteen innocent lives that night is killed-with a well-placed bullet fired from nearly a mile away. Clearly a professional, either military or law enforcement, the sniper leaves zero evidence, other than a note.

When more suspected rapists and murderers turn up dead, the killer's pattern becomes clear: they're acting as judge, jury, and executioner for a series of cases that were brushed off by the cops. How could a person not cheer a little? Until the spotlight is shone on one of the FBI's own.

Ultimately, it's a matter of right or wrong. Winter knows just where the line is-she learned the night her parents were slaughtered and her baby brother disappeared. After all, that night made her who she is, and she'll uphold the law, even for the scumbags who deserve to die. Even while the ghosts of her past grow closer and closer.

Book five of Mary Stone's breakthrough Winter Black series, Winter's Ghost is an ingeniously conceived psychological thriller that will keep readers enthralled while making sure their door is locked-and pick proof.

1

Tyler Haldane grimaced as the sheriff's deputy fastened the final strap of his Kevlar vest. As he tried to take in a deep breath, his ribs were constricted by the tight binds. Between the vest and the silver shackles that bound his wrists to his ankles, he was surprised he could even move.

Well, he'd been surprised at first. Now, almost six months after he and his friend Kent Strickland were captured, the deputy's gruff motions were part of a routine.

Any time Tyler was transported from his jail cell to a meeting at the psychiatric hospital or the courthouse, the level of security that accompanied him must have rivaled that of a sitting United States president. The irony wasn't lost on him.

Tyler still couldn't believe six months had passed since he and Kent donned their own bulletproof vests, combat boots, and camouflage fatigues. Six long assed months since they'd carried out the plan they'd hatched the summer before.

Toward the end of their junior year in college, Tyler had gone with Kent to visit his father's house in Bowling Green.

In the week of spring break, they had been introduced to the kid Kent's father paid to mow the lawn.

Jaime was a few years younger than Kent and Tyler, but as luck would have it, his school's spring break overlapped with theirs. Their new friend had an intriguing set of ideals, almost all of which aligned with Tyler and his best friend.

Tyler's mother had taken some convincing, but she eventually gave him her blessing to spend the summer with Kent out at his father's acreage. George Strickland had possessed an impressive collection of firearms, and he and Kent went target shooting almost every day.

Once the sun went down, they would gather around a firepit as they discussed their visions for the future of American society. Each time they were joined by Jaime, the high schooler encouraged and reinforced Kent and Tyler's ideations.

They all wanted the same thing—a return to the old ways. A return to the time when a family was comprised of a man, a woman, and their children. When hardworking men could provide for their families, and when they could be *men* without having to worry about the whims of women who overstepped their bounds.

The conversations evolved to plans, the plans evolved to actions, and before the beginning of the school year, Kent and Tyler had crafted a detailed outline of their plans for the Riverside Mall in Danville, Virginia.

Though the obvious choice for a target would have been the nearby metropolis of Richmond, the city was also home to an office of the Federal Bureau of Investigation. In an effort to prolong the response time of well-equipped tactical teams, Tyler and Kent selected a location several hours away from their summertime home in Bowling Green.

Neither Tyler nor Kent expected to make it out of the Riverside Mall with their freedom, but they had been there to send a message, not get away with a crime. The SS armbands had been a last-minute addition, and even though Kent and Tyler didn't necessarily subscribe to the neo-Nazi ideals, they knew the red and black Swastika would draw media attention.

And at the end of the day, that was what they wanted: attention.

The shitty thing was, they would've gotten all the attention they could have ever dreamed of, if it hadn't been for the son of a bitch, The Preacher. It still galled Tyler that their spotlight had been dimmed by an old man.

But how could they have known that the takedown of a serial killer would hog as many headlines as a mass shooting? That fool's victims had been dead long ago...and they all probably deserved it.

Fucking society was messed up.

Although it hadn't gone exactly as they'd planned it, Tyler Haldane and Kent Strickland were still household names across the South, and the event at the Riverside Mall had become the topic of international dialogue. From Virginia to Maine and all the way over to the European Union, everyone was talking about the fifteen deaths in an unassuming Virginia mall.

Perfect or not, Tyler and Kent had made history.

Thirteen people had been killed at the mall, and two more succumbed to their injuries within the next twenty-four hours. The number was lower than he and Kent had envisioned, and before they could make it higher, Kent had been shot in the head. When Tyler saw his friend go down, he thought for sure he was dead.

Tyler had immediately turned his sights to the FBI agent who fired the shot, but he'd only been able to hit her in the shoulder before the air was forced from his lungs as he was tackled to the floor.

When he awoke the next day, he was met with the drab gray concrete of a prison cell. Later that afternoon, the defense attorney in charge of his case had told him that Kent had survived an extensive operation to minimize damage to his brain.

He was in a medically induced coma, and the doctors put his odds of survival at fifty-fifty. But a couple weeks later, he'd been roused from the deep state of unconsciousness. According to the most recent medical estimates, Kent was expected to make a full recovery.

God's sign of approval, if Tyler'd ever seen one.

A cacophonous buzz jerked Tyler's attention back to the present. An armed deputy to either side, their procession started down the hall. The overhead fluorescent lights seemed to sap the vividness from any color they touched. Even Tyler's bright orange shirt and pants looked muted under the harsh glow.

His shackles clattered as they advanced through the first set of doors and to the second. The psychiatric facility was almost as secure as a prison, but no matter the level of security, Tyler knew there would be reporters and onlookers crowded around a chain-link fence in hopes he would respond to one of their inquiries.

And maybe, one of these trips, he would, but not today. He hadn't prepared a statement, and he wanted to wait until he knew the weight of his words were worthy of the harsh reprimand he would receive from the deputies at his sides.

The din of muffled voices grew clearer as the double doors parted to reveal the late-afternoon sunlight. As expected, a hoard of onlookers milled about the perimeter, their cameras and wide-eyed stares fixed on Tyler.

His smirk came unbidden, and despite the discomfort of the metal that bit into his wrists, he felt at ease. Without a doubt, their message was being circulated throughout the country, through the internet, even inadvertently through nationally syndicated news networks.

A change was on the horizon. He could feel it.

Regardless of whether he had to watch the shift from behind bars, he could take pride in his role, could vicariously reap the fruits of his labor. No matter the sentence handed down at his trial, he was only at the beginning of his life. There was much to see, many changes to witness, ideals to spread.

As he inhaled a deep breath of fresh air, he thought he had an entire lifetime ahead of him, but then...*pop*.

Before he could even place the sound, his world went black forever.

2

Glancing around the dusty workspace, Noah Dalton raised a hand to his mouth to stifle a yawn. At quarter 'til eleven, a crime scene was among the last places he wanted to be.

A couple ballistics experts had directed him and Bree Stafford to the six-story apartment building, minutes after they provided a rundown of the trigonometric jargon that had led them to the conclusion. Some type of messy equation about Tyler Haldane's height and the bullet's point of entry in his head was all Noah had bothered to retain.

On the top-most floor, he and Bree made their way from room to room along the side of the building that faced the psychiatric hospital. From three-quarters of a mile away, the facility looked as unassuming as the strip mall across the street.

The light crunch of dust and debris beneath footsteps drew his attention to the wide doorway at his back. White fluorescence caught the face of Bree's watch as she produced a pair of binoculars.

The apartment complex was undergoing renovations, and

electricity had not yet been restored to the building. They relied on a series of industrial battery-powered work lights to navigate their way throughout the rooms.

"You talk to the site manager yet?" Noah asked.

"Yeah." Bree nodded as she handed off the binoculars. "He didn't have anything. Since the place is under construction, there aren't any security cameras around here that would've caught anything helpful. The gas station and that strip mall aren't at the right angles, but we can try them tomorrow. The construction manager said everyone at the work site left before five. In the interest of preventing injuries, no one stays behind alone to do extra work or overtime."

Noah swiped an arm over his sweaty forehead. "And Haldane was shot at closer to seven, of course. Forensics is on their way, but I haven't seen anything out of place. No shell casing, and since this is a construction site, there will be a shitload of prints all over everything."

Bree's dark eyes flicked over to the wall-spanning window. There was no glass in place, so in addition to the litany of fingerprints, the forensics team would have to contend with the elements.

"Well," she said, gesturing to the view of the sprawling city. "What about this? That psychiatric facility is almost a mile away from here, isn't it? And from what Ted told us during that trigonometry lesson earlier, none of the other buildings between here and there would have been the right height for the shot."

Noah nodded as he peered through the binoculars. At the highest zoom setting, he could see the crime scene techs mill about the dark splotch of blood still staining the sidewalk. Somewhere among them was Winter, but he didn't spot her in his cursory examination.

With a low whistle, Noah glanced back to Bree as he passed the binoculars to her.

"That sounds like an impressed whistle." Bree offered him a quick smile before she turned her attention to the window.

"It was. That's a hell of a shot, even for a trained sniper. There are some rifles designed just for shots like that, but they're not cheap, and they can be difficult to get ahold of. Hopefully, they'll find the bullet, so we'll at least know what we're dealing with."

"They'd have to prep for this." Bree was still scanning the building before them. "You don't just find a place to post up for a sniper shot at the drop of a hat. Whoever fired that shot had to have planned this."

Noah agreed. A sniper shot was 99 percent preparation, 1 percent execution.

Distance. Wind speed. Barometric pressure. Even temperature could affect a sniper shot in unexpected ways.

"What are you thinking?"

Bree pursed her lips as she tapped a finger against the binoculars. "For motive? It's got to be something related to the shooting in Danville. I seriously doubt anyone with a personal grudge or an ax to grind with Tyler Haldane would wait to settle their score until *after* he's in police custody with four armed guards escorting him back to prison."

"He and Kent Strickland did kill fifteen people, and I doubt those SS armbands they were wearing made them a lot of fans. We sure as shit aren't going to be lacking for suspects." With a sigh, he crossed his arms over his chest.

"Shit," she spat in agreement.

He glanced over to his partner, reading the confusion on her face. "What are you thinking?" he asked again.

She was tapping her finger against the binoculars again. She often fidgeted when she was annoyed. It was a tell she needed to work on. Even after more than twenty years as an agent, she didn't always hide her irritation. "What kinds of people usually get taken out by a sniper from almost a mile away?"

When she paused for a response, he merely shrugged.

Her finger started tapping again, answering her own question. "The kinds that are tied to a whole bunch of nasty shit, or the kinds who have enemies in some seriously high places. Even back in Baltimore and D.C., the mobsters didn't usually take out their rivals with a damn sniper."

Noah nodded. Bree would know. She'd worked in the Organizational Crime Division for years.

"Some of them did," she went on, "but the shots were almost never from a distance like this. So, either Haldane's got an enemy with a great deal of disposable income, or someone was pretty desperate to tie up a loose end."

"You think Haldane's part of something bigger?"

The thought that there might be a whole club of people with violent tendencies and Tyler Haldane's twisted ideals made him sick to his stomach. But he wasn't surprised. In his years in law enforcement and when he'd been in the military before joining the FBI, he'd learned there were plenty of twisted people with equally twisted ideals.

"I think he might be," Bree replied with a slow nod. "But if he is, then that means they'll probably want Kent Strickland next."

"Strickland's still in the hospital. He's guarded twenty-four-seven."

She snorted. "Just make sure he's not close to any windows."

Sarcasm dripped from her words, and he barely stifled a bark of laughter before he lifted his phone to pass her warning down the line.

Sarcasm or not, she wasn't wrong.

ey, sis. Heard you've been looking for me.

Those eight words hadn't left Special Agent Winter Black's mind for more than a second since she received the email containing them early that evening.

Was it her little brother?

His ghost come to haunt her?

A nutjob with a warped sense of humor?

Someone close to her who simply wanted to torment her?

Winter had scarcely been given enough time to think all her questions through. She'd just forwarded the email to the FBI cyber division, explaining her thoughts in a quick rush of words. Then she, Bree, and Noah had headed out to the psychiatric treatment facility.

As much as she wanted to stay at the office to follow-up on the email from Justin—to find out if it was even *real*— Max had ordered all hands on deck for the investigation of Tyler Haldane's death.

Local news networks had barely been able to cut their live footage as the long-range shot ripped through Haldane's head, spattering the sidewalk with gore. There had been plenty of cameras that caught the carnage, and by now, the video had circulated far and wide. Australian media networks had awoken to news of the brutal footage, and by now, the killing of a mass murderer had undoubtedly been covered by broadcasts across the globe.

A mass shooting in the United States didn't always make international news, but the deliberate, premeditated murder of a mass shooter *did*.

For the time being, Winter had done all she could with the suspicious email from Justin. She wasn't equipped to track the origins of an electronic message, but the cyber division was. If anyone could locate more information about the source, it was the men and women in cyber. Like Autumn had become fond of saying, Winter "didn't have to do everything by herself."

Right now, she had a job to do.

Despite their host of personal misgivings with Tyler Haldane and his extremist ideology, Max wanted the threat of a media circus off their doorstep. According to the SAC, sensationalized cases like the murder of Haldane brought out nutjobs from all walks of life, journalists and civilians alike.

With or without Max's unique brand of encouragement, Winter had no desire to be at the center of a media frenzy. She liked her privacy, and the fewer eyes on her, the lower the likelihood of anyone stumbling upon her sixth sense.

As she ducked down beneath the ribbon of yellow crime scene tape, she nodded a greeting to a familiar forensic ballistics examiner.

"Agent Black," the man greeted, reaching out for a handshake.

She accepted the gesture. "Ted. Where is everyone?"

"Pretty sparse here, yeah. Once we figured out which building the shot was fired from, most of the crime scene people headed that way. Jo and I are still here trying to find the damn bullet, though."

With a shrug, he produced a clipboard from beneath one arm and held it up for her to see.

From a distance, the marks on the lined paper looked like they might have been Chinese, but even when she squinted and leaned closer, she was unable to decipher the rows of numbers and equations.

Knitting her brows together, she looked back up to him. "None of that makes any sense to me. Even if I *could* read your handwriting, I doubt I'd understand it any better."

The harsh glow of a nearby work light glinted off the plastic as he pulled the clipboard away to glance back down to the page.

"Shit," he muttered. "Right. My bad. Well, here's what I've got so far." As he moved to stand at her side, he pointed to a tall building in the distance. "That's where the shot was fired from. Based on where the bullet hit and what we saw from the video, there's no doubt about that. It's the only structure around here that's tall enough for the right angle."

She looked around. "How can you tell?"

"The bullet came from the north, and aside from that building, everything else in a two-mile radius is three stories at the max. That apartment building is six stories. I based my calculations on Haldane's height, factored in how much the bullet would have dropped over that distance, determined wind speed and such. That put our shooter in the sixth floor."

Winter squinted. "Isn't that building something like a mile away?" She had enough knowledge about firearms to know that such a shot was difficult but possible. For an expert, which would narrow their suspect list considerably.

"It's close to a mile, yeah. A little over three-fourths of a mile and the wind was blowing about seven miles per hour from the west." Clipboard in hand, he gestured to the dark shape of blood spatter on the concrete. "We know the shot was through and through, but I'll be damned if I can find that bullet."

When Winter looked up from the splotch of burgundy, she noticed the predicament. Based on the trajectory of the blood spatter, there was a good chance the wayward bullet had continued unimpeded past the corner of the psychiatric building. It could be blocks away, embedded in the asphalt of a parking lot, the side of a car, or even in the trunk of a tree.

Just as she was about to return her attention to Ted, she caught a faint glimpse of red. The glimmer was no larger than a pinprick in the concrete edge of the building, and she figured it was the glow of a security camera or another electronic device.

No, it wouldn't be a camera. The glow was level with the middle of her stomach.

Pushing the sudden rush of excitement down, she cleared her throat before turning back to Ted. In an effort to feign nonchalance, she shrugged. "What if it hit the side of the building?"

He heaved a sigh as his blue eyes flicked down to the paper and then back to her. "There's a slight possibility, if the bullet glanced off the skull in an unexpected way. Guess it's worth checking out before we start creeping through the neighborhood, huh?"

With a slight smile, she nodded. "Definitely. Rule out the easy stuff first."

He looked thoughtful as he scratched his scruffy cheek. When his attention shifted back to her, he returned the nod. "Fair enough. Let's go check it out. It was Jo's turn to go get coffee, but she ought to be back pretty soon. Or at least I hope she will because I sure could use a second wind."

Winter stifled a yawn. "You and me both."

They made the short trek in silence, and as the distance to the edge of the building lessened, the air of anticipation became even more palpable.

Though Winter could already see the red glow intensify, she bit down on her tongue to keep any potential exclamation to herself. Her pulse picked up, and she clenched and unclenched one hand against the cool touch of adrenaline.

When she'd only been thirteen years old, a madman had broken into her childhood home, slaughtering her father and brutalizing her mother. Winter had only gotten a glimpse of the man before he hit her on the head, almost killing her too.

After weeks in a coma, she'd awoken to learn that her baby brother was missing. She'd also learned that the blow to the head had given her special abilities she couldn't understand.

Abilities like knowing where a tiny bullet was hiding.

Now, if only Ted had the same bit of intuitive wisdom.

Pretending to search a farther off section of the brick, she was starting to grow annoyed that it was taking so long when Ted took in a sharp breath.

"That looks like a bullet hole to me," she said, giving him a congratulatory slap on the back when she walked over to investigate with him.

Dropping down to crouch beside the drab concrete, he squinted and leaned in until his face was less than a foot from the pockmark.

"Yeah," he agreed. "Yeah, agent. That looks like a bullet hole."

"You've got it from here, right?" Winter asked after a moment of silence.

Max had sent her to the site of Haldane's death with the understanding that she would take statements from the sheriff's deputies who still lingered at the scene. Discovery of the bullet or not, the SAC would be unimpressed if she returned to the office before she completed her task.

"Hey!" a woman called, snapping her and Ted's attention back to the sidewalk. A paper cup in each hand, the dark-haired woman approached them with a quizzical look on her face. "Did you find something?"

"Sure did, Jo," Ted said as he rose to his full height. "We found the damn bullet."

"Nice!" Although Jo's word was full of enthusiasm, her face carried a hint of bemusement. "Not exactly where I'd have started the search, but I'm glad we didn't have to scour every inch of the next few blocks." She handed Ted his coffee. "I'll go get our kits, and we'll dig that thing out."

Winter realized that Ted was looking at her strangely, and a shiver ran down her back. Did he know of her special abilities? As hard as she'd tried to hide them from the world, she hadn't always been successful. And people talked.

Feeling a wave of embarrassment begin to spread up her neck, she stuck her hands in her pockets. "I'll let you all get to work."

Hurrying away, she still felt Ted's eyes boring into her back. Her unease didn't waver as she made her way to the brown and gold clad deputies. Though engrossed in a conversation she couldn't hear, both men trailed off before she came within earshot.

"Deputies…" She reached into her black blazer, retrieved her badge, and flashed it at the pair as she closed the remaining distance. "I'm Special Agent Black with the FBI. I'm sure you're both aware that Tyler Haldane's case was federal, so we'll be handling the investigation."

The taller of the two crossed his muscular arms over his chest and shrugged. The nameplate on his uniform listed his name as Peterson. "Well, we sure as shit don't want it, so go nuts."

That surprised her. Law enforcement teams were normally very territorial. "You don't want it? Why's that?"

At his side, the second deputy, Ortiz, replied with a dry chuckle. "We've got more important work to do than investigate the murder of some shit bag like Tyler Haldane. No disrespect to the bureau. I mean, someone's got to do it, right? But when you find whoever it was, tell him the sheriff's department says thanks."

Deep inside, she couldn't blame them for their attitude, but still, she kept a carefully neutral face. "I take it none of you were fans of Mr. Haldane."

"Look, agent," Peterson replied. "We've both been doing this for a while, you know. The sheriff's department is almost always in charge of prisoner transport, and we've both been part of that team for more than ten years now. We've escorted some seriously nasty dudes, but that little shit takes the cake."

Curious now, Winter took a step closer. "Is there any particular reason why?" She smiled and watched both men blush a little. "Aside from the obvious, of course."

Ortiz snorted and shook his head, turning his gaze until he was looking over her shoulder. "Couldn't get the little bastard to shut up half the time. Going on about his mission and all the shit he thought was going to happen now that he and his buddy had killed all those people in Danville. I've seen paranoid schizophrenics and dudes high as a kite ramble on about weird shit before, but Haldane was no schizophrenic or meth head. Kid was stone cold sober, and you could tell he wasn't saying all that shit because he was hallucinating."

"Plus," Peterson added, "that's the whole reason he was here today, anyway. He was here so some psychologist could ask him questions and see if he was even fit to stand trial."

"Was he?" Winter asked.

Peterson nodded. "Sure was. Doc said the bastard knew exactly what he was doing. He and Kent Strickland had been planning it for almost a year."

"Did he ever say anything about anyone else? Anyone involved in it other than him and Strickland?"

"No, nothing," Ortiz answered. "If we'd heard anything like that, we would've let y'all know."

"Right." Winter bit back a sigh.

They had the bullet, she reminded herself. And if she was given the choice, she would take a piece of physical evidence over the ramblings of a mass murderer any day.

4

Aiden Parrish knew that Dan Nguyen had only been in possession of Tyler Haldane's body for an hour or two, but he hadn't wanted to sit on his hands in the formative hours of the investigation. And if anyone could give him a useful piece of information after such a short time, it would be the tenured ME.

As Aiden pushed his way through a set of double doors, the medical examiner's dark eyes snapped up from the clipboard he held in one hand. On top of the silver table in front of him, its head a mangled mess of shattered bone and ruined tissue, was the body of who Aiden assumed was Tyler Haldane. Though, with the damage done to the face, he couldn't say with complete certainty who in the hell it was.

"Parrish," Dan said, drawing Aiden's attention away from the gory sight. "Didn't expect to see you here so soon."

"Yeah, well, the bureau's trying to get a jump-start on this whole thing before it spirals into a full-blown media circus. Mass murderer shot in the head by a sniper is going to be one hell of a headline." With one hand, he gestured to the body. "Anything you can tell me about him yet?"

Sighing, Dan placed the clipboard on a metal table to his side. As he produced a pen from the pocket of his white lab coat, he stepped over to the body.

The fluorescence overhead shone on his neatly styled hair, and beneath the jacket was a pastel blue button-down shirt complete with a shiny black and silver striped tie. No matter the time of day Aiden saw the man, he always looked like he was ready for a day at work on Wall Street, not a morgue.

"I haven't cut him open yet." Dan waved the pen over the site of Haldane's fatal wound. "But I think it's safe to say that this is what killed him."

With a groan, Aiden rubbed his eyes. "Thanks, Dan. That's informative."

"You're welcome." Dan chuckled as he pocketed the pen. "Anything else right now is mostly an educated guess, but from what I'm seeing here, I think your shooter was a trained sniper."

Although Aiden thought that was a pretty accurate guess, he still asked, "How do you figure?" He glanced back down to the remnants of the head. The face was gone, and only the bottom portion of the jaw remained intact.

A sniper with a big damn bullet. The man was unrecognizable.

"You see where he was shot, right?"

"It's hard to miss," Aiden replied flatly.

"No, but I'm not being a smartass this time." Dan flashed him a quick grin. "Really, though. I might not be able to tell you the exact point of entry, but I think the shot hit him about right between the eyes, probably a little bit lower. That's the shot they train SEAL snipers to make. With a weapon this caliber, you've just got to hit someone in this general region." He paused to tap a finger against the tip of his nose. "And it blows their brainstem out the back of their head. Instantly ceases all nerve function, and there's not even a twitch afterward."

"That sounds familiar, yeah. I've heard it before." Aiden nodded. He left off from *whom* he'd most recently heard it. The last person he wanted to talk about right now was Douglas Kilroy. Just thinking the name of The Preacher made Aiden's teeth want to grit together. "Any guesses on what he was shot with? Caliber, anything like that?"

Dan shrugged. "Any caliber capable of distance like that will be reasonably high. I don't think it was a .50 caliber round, though. If it was, there wouldn't even be this much of his head left. Could be a .330 Winchester Mag or a .338 Lapua Magnum. We'll find out on closer examination."

"You sound like an arms encyclopedia right now. What in the hell did you do when you were in the Navy?"

"Intelligence," Dan answered with a knowing smirk. "I was here when Haldane was shot, by the way. Just in case you were wondering."

"Why would I wonder that?" There was no accusatory tinge to Aiden's question, only curiosity.

"Because I'm pretty sure you're looking for someone with military or law enforcement experience, my friend. Good training too. Not just someone who sat behind a desk. Whoever made this shot from that distance has done it before, probably more than once. And even though I know it's taboo to speak ill of the dead, I'm glad someone wiped this shit stain off the face of the planet. This little fucker didn't deserve the air he breathed."

"No argument here," Aiden muttered. He was a little relieved to know he wasn't the only person who shared Dan's view of Tyler Haldane. "Any other Navy related knowledge you've got for me right now? Can your firearm spidey sense tell you what kind of weapon it was?"

"Hey." Dan held up both hands in feigned defensiveness.

"Almost twenty years I've been doing this, all right? I haven't seen very many people killed with a long-distance high caliber shot like this, and the ones I do recall are pretty memorable. Assassinations, I think that's what we called them."

Aiden chuckled. "Fair enough. That everything for now, then?"

"That's all I've got, yeah." Even as Dan nodded, Aiden could tell there was another question on the tip of his tongue.

"But?" he prodded.

Seconds ticked by as the ME clearly considered the wisdom of speaking up. Finally, he asked, "You mind if I ask you something? About that case you guys just wrapped up? You know, the one with the mad scientist brain surgeon who dumped her victims in fifty-five-gallon drums after she doused them with lye. That one?"

"Do you even know how to not be sarcastic?" Despite the feigned admonishment, Aiden could feel a smirk tug at the corner of his mouth. In a basement room with a corpse that was virtually headless, he much preferred Dan's off-color sarcasm to a grave tone and a deadpan expression.

"I don't think so, no. That's another thing you can thank the military for."

"Right, the military. That's who we'll blame." Aiden waved a hand like he was swatting away an invisible insect. "All right, the Schmidt case. What about it?"

"How's Autumn Trent doing? I mean, after Nico Culetti tried to kill her." There was a glint of concern in Dan's dark eyes that Aiden hadn't expected.

"She's fine." Aiden fought to keep the look of skepticism at bay. "Why? Do you know her?"

Dan ignored the question and scratched at his temple. "No witness protection?"

"No," Aiden replied slowly, his curiosity growing. "She refused it. How do you know her, anyway?"

Dan shrugged. "She was in a class I taught at VCU Law School years back. I don't teach there anymore, got enough shit to deal with after the promotion here. She was a good student, and I still hear from her now and then. She's up for her Ph.D. in a few days, defending her dissertation."

Though he was unconvinced of Dan's dismissive explanation, Aiden nodded. "Yeah, she is. She's friends with Noah Dalton and Winter."

"All right, well, that's good to hear. They're good people."

Aiden's first inclination was to ask Dan what exactly drove his interest in Autumn Trent, but he bit back the query and merely nodded again. His curiosity would have to wait.

Right now, he had a vigilante sniper to find.

A month earlier, Sun Ming had finally been given the okay to forgo the sling she'd been ordered to wear while her shoulder healed. Though she had regained much of her arm's former strength, her range of movement was still hindered by a sharp pain.

Whenever she raised her arm out to her side, the muscles and tendons felt like they might rip apart from the bone. Her physical therapist told her the sensation was normal, and while it would never entirely disappear, routine exercises could keep the discomfort at bay.

In truth, the therapist's kindness and encouragement were some of her life's only bright spots in the last six or so months. Well, that, and a certain someone she couldn't yet name.

Because her life was mostly shit.

But she guessed it could have been worse.

Her twin brother, Lee, had traveled down from his home in Washington D.C. to visit her, but Lee had enough on his plate. His wife of eight years had filed for divorce only a day before Sun had been called to the Riverside Mall in Danville on that fateful day. He tried to be supportive, but Sun could tell how heartbroken he was, and she'd ended up trying to support him instead.

Sure, Sun had been shot, but the wound wasn't fatal. It wasn't even life-threatening.

From the time the bullet ripped through her shoulder to the point where she laid down on the operating room table, she had even been conscious and lucid for the entire experience. Physically, Sun was fine, or at least as fine as she could expect to be after such a near miss.

Mentally? Well, that was a different story.

She might not have been fine, but she didn't think a few nightmares and a twinge of lingering anxiety superseded Lee's divorce.

Sun had been hurt by the little mass murdering shit, Haldane, but the wound would heal. Lee, on the other hand, had his entire life ripped out from beneath him. The woman to whom he'd devoted all of his adult life had found someone new, had fallen out of love with her husband of nearly a decade.

No matter the sluggish progress of her healing, Sun figured she'd be ready to pitch at softball tournaments before her brother's heartache healed. She knew what he was dealing with. She was familiar with the feelings of hopelessness, of worthlessness that accompanied the failure of a long-term relationship.

As she glanced to where Aiden Parrish sat at the other end of the briefing room, she thought she'd rather take another bullet than deal with that kind of emotional fallout again.

Before Aiden's pale eyes flicked to her, she returned her attention to Max Osbourne and the podium at which he stood.

At Max's side was a less familiar man, one whose name

Sun couldn't recall, although his tall build and expensive suit reminded her too much of Aiden Parrish. Though she'd seen this man around the building, she couldn't remember his role within the bureau.

Max swept his steely gaze over the room before he nodded a greeting to the woman who had just stepped through the doorway.

Why all the strangers? Sun wondered, keeping her expression carefully neutral. *What's going on?* Sun didn't like being out of the loop. Not at all.

"Close that behind you," Max barked.

The newcomer nodded and eased the glass and metal portal closed. Her lustrous chocolate brown hair and jade green eyes should have jogged Sun's memory, but for the second time, she couldn't remember a person's name. This woman was new, though. Sun knew that much.

Apparently, the death of a malignant tumor like Tyler Haldane brought FBI agents out of the woodwork. When Sun pictured the smug little shit, the corner of her mouth twitched in the first hint of a scowl.

She remembered that day so clearly.

Sun had been pissed that she had been called away from the Douglas Kilroy case to work the hostage situation at the Riverside Mall. It had been her luck that she'd only been a few miles outside of Danville when the call came in, and even though she'd wanted to be the one to take The Preacher down, she'd found herself sitting behind a potted plant instead, waiting for her best shot at the murdering little bastards.

And you could bet your ass, she'd been the one to take the shot.

Though she'd landed what she'd hoped was a fatal shot at Kent Strickland, she'd wondered on more than one occasion if she should have aimed for Haldane instead. Maybe she would have gotten lucky, and Haldane would have died from the same wound Strickland had miraculously survived.

It still pissed her off and hurt her pride that the bastard survived. She was better than that.

Just as it pissed her off that some of the Richmond office's best and brightest were gathered in a briefing room to put their various skill sets to use in the search for a person who had arguably done them all a favor by shooting Tyler Haldane.

How much money had the killer saved the federal government anyway? Tens of thousands? *Hundreds* of thousands? Millions?

"All right," Max grumbled as he looked from one agent to the next. "Looks like that's all of us."

Judges had a gavel to begin their meetings, and Max had the phrase "looks like that's everyone." Sun couldn't recall a briefing where the SAC had deviated from his usual opening line.

To her side was Miguel Vasquez, and at the table in front of them was Noah Dalton and Winter Black. Behind Sun and Miguel sat Bree Stafford and another agent from the Violent Crimes Division, though he worked the night shift and they didn't often cross paths. The woman whose name eluded her had taken a seat at the same table as Aiden.

Other than the occasional all-hands meeting, Sun couldn't recall the last time she'd been at a briefing with so many attendees.

"You might have seen Agent Levi Brandt around." Max gestured to the tall man at his side. "He's with the victim services division, and he's here because there's a good chance we'll be talking to a lot of victims."

"All this for Tyler Haldane," Sun muttered to herself.

At least she thought she'd muttered it to herself.

"I'm aware, Agent Ming," Max said, his voice as flat as his

expression. Sun lifted her chin, accepting the reproach with as much grace as she could muster. "But sure, let's start there. We're all here on this lovely afternoon to discuss how to approach the investigation into the murder of a mass shooter. No one in here has any love for Tyler Haldane, but we've still got a job to do. This is going to be a media shitshow."

"Hell, it already *is* a media shitshow," Noah Dalton said, and it pissed Sun off a little more when the SAC only nodded. No death stare for the golden boy.

Max went on. "And, I hate to break it to you, but the only way to get them off our backs is to figure out who killed Haldane. We've got a lot of ground to cover, and each of you will be responsible for covering some of it. But first, let's get through what we already know. Stella Norcott is our new leading expert in ballistics."

As he waved a hand to the woman with the dark hair and green eyes, she nodded. "Nice to meet you all," she said, her green eyes flicking from person to person. "Guess I'll get right to it then. Forensics found the bullet in the side of the psychiatric building where Haldane was shot. If the angle had been just a little more to the side, we probably wouldn't have been able to recover it. But I guess we can save all our thanks for the awards ceremony once we wrap this thing up."

The ballistic expert paused, clearly hoping for a few laughs. When she didn't get any, she went on.

"Haldane was shot from a distance of almost a mile. My colleague, Ted, established that the shooter was on the sixth floor of an apartment building that's currently being renovated. There wasn't much physical evidence there, but the bullet was a good find.

"Haldane was killed by a .338 Lapua Magnum round, and after comparing the striations with what we have on file, I'm almost certain the weapon used was a Barrett Model 98 Bravo sniper rifle chambered for the .338 ammunition."

Sun felt her eyes go wide for a split-second, but she forced an expression of nonchalance back to her face. Ever since high school, she and her brother had competed in marksman competitions, but only she carried on the hobby into adulthood.

Though the Barrett M98B was expensive and military grade, Virginia's firearm restrictions were nil, and Sun had bought one of the rifles for herself years earlier.

"Barrett Model 98 Bravo rifles are primarily used in the military," Stella went on, snapping Sun's attention back to the room. "They're used by snipers in the Army Rangers, to be more specific. There are some law enforcement agencies across the country that use them too. And even though it's not as common as some other high-powered rifles, M98Bs are sometimes used for hunting big game."

Stella was right. The M98B wasn't a weapon typically handled by novices. It also wasn't cheap, Sun knew.

"What can you tell us about that shot?" Max asked, his gray eyes fixed on the woman.

"It was a hell of a shot," Stella replied with a shrug. "The wind was moving that night, not much, but at that distance, you'd have to be an expert to contend with it."

"Expert is right. It's not a shot you just wake up one day and make," Sun put in, then wished she'd stayed silent when all eyes turned on her.

Stella nodded her agreement.

"You have to be really familiar with the weapon you're using. Familiar with the bullet's velocity, with the drop, with everything. And when you throw in even a light breeze, you're seriously impacting all of that." Sun absentmindedly reached to rub her shoulder. "The caliber makes a big difference too. The fact that the shooter was using a .338 Lapua Magnum means they were going for accuracy."

"That's what Dan Nguyen said too." Aiden's eyes shifted from Stella to Max, but he didn't pause to regard Sun.

"The medical examiner?" Sun didn't hide the skepticism from her query. "How would he know that?"

"Dan Nguyen was Navy Intelligence for six years," Max answered before Aiden could respond.

The tenured SAC had a rough idea of her and Aiden's past, and his gravelly tone told her he wasn't in a mood to deal with a squabble between the two of them.

Sun bit off a sarcastic comment and nodded her understanding instead. "I didn't know that," she said, although it goaded her to no end to admit it.

Max stared at her. "Let's move this along."

"Right," Stella agreed. "Well, the striations on the bullet recovered from the scene match the marks from another .338 Lapua Magnum bullet in a different case."

With a click, Max brought the overhead projector to life.

On the whiteboard to his back was a DMV photo of a middle-aged man with a close-cropped salt and pepper beard. His mouth was set in a straight line, and his blue eyes seemed about as enthusiastic as someone at the DMV ought to be.

"Mitch Stockley," Max advised. "Killed about six months ago a little ways outside Norfolk. Ironically, he was out target shooting when he was shot in the head. Same shot that took out Haldane." The SAC paused to tap between his eyes. "Right here."

"It's a precise shot," Aiden added. "That's another thing I got from Dan Nguyen. It's the same shot they train military and law enforcement snipers to make. It takes out the brainstem, so there's not so much as a twitch when the person dies. Keeps them from pulling a trigger or a detonation switch, anything like that."

"I'd have someone ask the BAU what that meant, but it looks like we're in luck."

Sun didn't miss the dry sarcasm in Max's offhand comment. Apparently, the tenured SAC was about as thrilled to spend his time investigating the death of a mass murderer as Sun was.

"You are," was Aiden's flat response. "It means that whoever we're looking for very likely has experience in either the military or law enforcement. Based on the fact that they took the shell casing with them, I'd say they've got some familiarity with forensic investigations. They probably wanted the bullet to go a little bit off to the side so we wouldn't find it as well."

"What about the second victim, Mitch Stockley?" Winter asked, her dark blue eyes shifting from Aiden to Max and then back. "What do we know about his murder?"

Sun grated her teeth together at the sound of the woman's voice.

She knew there was more between Winter and Aiden than just a professional familiarity, and despite the two and a half years since Sun and Aiden's split, their bond left a bad taste in her mouth.

Winter had already captured the attention of Noah Dalton. What in the hell did she have over Aiden too? And *why*? Biting back a groan, Sun crossed both arms over her chest.

"Not a lot," Max replied. "Local LEOs handled it at the time. They didn't realize they were dealing with a precision sniper. I think they chalked it up to a hunting accident or something. But same as this one, there wasn't a shell casing. No trace evidence, just a bullet in the trunk of a tree.

"Agent Ming, Agent Vasquez." Max turned his intent stare

to her. "You're looking into Stockley. The sheriff's department outside Norfolk already sent everything they've got over, and they'll be here to drop off the physical evidence in an hour or so. You can talk to them when they get here. Find out if Stockley has anything in common with Haldane. Maybe he's a distant relative, or maybe we're dealing with an expensive hitman, and they've never even met."

Straightening in her chair, Sun nodded.

"Agent Dalton, Agent Black, you're going to the hospital to talk to Kent Strickland. He's been under armed surveillance ever since Haldane got shot. Ask him if they've got any co-conspirators that might be trying to tie up a loose end, someone who might've been worried that Haldane would talk."

Even if he was irritable about devoting his unit's time to Tyler Haldane, Max's laser focus had returned.

"Agent Brandt," the SAC went on. "You and Agent Stafford talk to the victims of the Riverside shooting. Agent Weyrick, thanks again for coming in on such short notice. I know this is something like three in the morning for you, so once you're in later tonight, I'll have you following up on what Agent Stafford and Brandt found."

"Copy that," Brandt replied.

"All right, everyone. That's it. I already sent you all everything we've got so far. Let's figure out who in the hell shot Haldane so we can get the media off our doorstep."

6

During her brief tenure with the FBI, Winter had come face-to-face with a handful of cold-blooded killers—Scott Kennedy, Heidi Presley, Catherine Schmidt, and of course, Douglas Kilroy. But as she and Noah stepped into a pristine hospital room to flash their badges at a man in a tailored suit, she realized Strickland was the first mass shooter she'd encountered.

As much as she hoped he'd be the last, she knew how naïve the thought was.

A mass shooting was any event where more than four people were shot. The bureau only handled the worst of them: those involving a sniper, a high body count, or military grade weaponry. Thanks to Tyler Haldane, she could officially check off all three requirements in just one case. Maybe she would update her resume when she got home that night, she thought bitterly.

"Mr. Strickland," Noah said as they returned their badges to their jackets. Winter didn't miss that the usual cheer and amiable air had vanished from his demeanor. He must have been as thrilled to tick off the boxes as she was. "I'm Agent

Dalton, and this is Agent Black. We're with the Federal Bureau of Investigation."

From where he was seated on the hospital bed, one arm shackled to the side while a handful of cream-colored blankets covered his lap, Strickland shifted his dark eyes from Noah to Winter and then back.

As he glanced over to the well-dressed lawyer, the older man nodded his bald head.

"I'm Kent's attorney, Harold Lisman. What can I help you with?"

"You?" Noah raised his eyebrows at the man. "You, probably not much. It's your client we're here to talk to, Mr. Lisman."

"You're not going to violate my son's constitutional rights," said a woman seated to Strickland's side. The dark shadows beneath her eyes were pronounced, and her fair skin was tinged with an unhealthy pallor.

The corners of Winter's mouth tightened. *I guess that's what life is like when your son is a mass shooter*, she thought to herself.

"We're not here to violate anyone's constitutional rights," Winter returned. "We're here because, less than twenty-four hours ago, a sniper shot and killed Tyler Haldane."

"That boy was always trouble," the woman huffed as she pulled her gray cardigan tighter around herself.

"Tyler's dead?" Strickland blurted, his mouth agape. "How? A sniper? What does that mean?"

"Sorry." Noah shook his head. "Can't discuss an ongoing case. We're here to ask you who might've wanted your friend dead. Aside from, you know, the obvious."

"What?" Strickland's mother exclaimed. "What the hell does *that* mean?"

"Mrs. Strickland," the lawyer began, holding up his hands. "I—"

"It means your son doesn't have a lot of fans, Mrs. Strickland." Noah's response was flat, and for a second, Winter wondered if he was Noah at all.

Maybe the man at her side was Aiden Parrish, and she had officially lost her damn mind. He *sounded* like Aiden Parrish, not the younger Texan.

"Haven't you people ever heard of 'innocent until proven guilty?' *Habeas Corpus*? Any of it?" the woman snapped, her gold and green eyes alight with ire.

"I sure have, ma'am," Noah shot back.

Winter marveled at how his Texan drawl could sound so condescending and folksy at the same time.

"That's not what we're here for," she interjected before Strickland's mother could respond. "We're here to find out if your son knows of anyone who might've wanted his friend dead. And yes, ma'am, that does extend to co-conspirators. Here's the deal, all right? There are literally hundreds of eyewitnesses, including plenty of federal agents and other law enforcement personnel who saw your son at the scene."

The lawyer shot to his feet, but Winter went on.

"There's absolutely no doubt that he was there, but we aren't here to argue over who pulled the trigger or why. Your son was there, and so was Tyler Haldane. The event was planned, *meticulously* planned, and we want to know if your son is aware of anyone else who might've known about it. Anyone who might've wanted to make sure Haldane didn't say anything to the authorities."

"He wouldn't," Tyler's mother said, her face growing pale as death. "He couldn't. He—"

Winter lifted a hand. "Before you go off on another tirade, Mrs. Strickland, let me just phrase it this way. If that's the case, if the person who killed Tyler Haldane wanted him dead because he or she is worried that they might be implicated, then it stands to reason that they'll be after Kent next.

And from what we've been able to gather so far in our investigation, whoever this person is, if they want someone dead, there isn't much that can stop them. So, Mrs. Strickland, you've got two options."

Winter paused, waiting to see if the woman was really listening to her. Several seconds passed before the older woman met her eye. And nodded.

Winter raised a finger. "You and your son can help us, or…" she raised the second finger, "you can keep being obstinate and prevent us from doing our job. In this case, that means that you'll just be making it easier for whoever killed Tyler to get to your son too. I'll give you a few seconds to think it over, but honestly, we're pressed for time, so you'd better make it snappy."

Hazel eyes wide, Strickland's mother opened and closed her mouth before she finally glanced to her son and his lawyer. From the corner of her eye, Winter saw Noah flash her an appreciative glance. As much as she wanted to offer him a smile in response, she was on a roll, and she didn't want to risk a crack in the steely veneer she had donned.

As Strickland glanced back and forth between his mother and the lawyer, he started to shake his head, slow at first before gaining speed. The silence had grown so thick and pervasive that Winter felt like she would have to hack away at it with a machete if someone didn't speak soon.

Rather than answer her and Noah's question, Strickland leaned to whisper in his lawyer's ear. She doubted the softly spoken words were audible to Noah, but Winter heard him as clearly as if he'd addressed the entire room.

"No, there wasn't anyone else," Strickland murmured to the man at his side.

"Are you sure there wasn't anyone else," the lawyer asked, and Winter couldn't blame him for needing to ask the question.

"Have you received any death threats in the past few weeks?" Winter prodded.

The lawyer was shaking his head before she finished the question. "Anything we've received, we send straight to the FBI."

Regardless of whether or not she had hit her stride, Winter knew they wouldn't get any more useful information from the three people in the hospital room.

"Keep doing that, then," she said as she reached into a pocket for a business card. "Here's my card. If you think of anything, call me or send me an email. Otherwise, we'll be in touch if anything changes."

Without another word, Winter looked to Noah before they strode by an armed guard and into the quiet hallway. Two more black-clad men stood to either side of the doorway, and they nodded as Winter and Noah made their way past.

Winter held in her resigned sigh until she had closed the passenger side door of the sedan.

"Hey, you did a damn fine job," Noah said as he turned the key over in the ignition. "Seriously, you were great. All I wanted to do was swear at those two idiots for thinking that kid's some innocent fucking bystander."

"Isn't it usually the other way around when we go to talk to people?" she asked. A grin spread over her face as she glanced to him.

A faint smile on his lips, he nodded. "Maybe. Either way, I bet my ass they won't be giving us anything useful. Even if they've got anything to begin with."

"Yeah, I got that feeling too." She pushed a stray strand of long hair behind her ear. "What a waste of time."

"Honestly, darlin', if it wasn't for this other guy, this Stockley guy, I'd say this whole damn thing was a waste of time. We're investigating the murder of a neo-Nazi mass shooter. I mean, for just Haldane, our line of suspects would look like the line waiting for a Six Flags rollercoaster on a Saturday in the middle of June."

Winter looked at him curiously. "What are you thinking?"

"Stockley either narrows it down, or it just means that the rifle changed hands in those six months. It's an expensive weapon, so I wouldn't rule that out just yet. Could be that the first killer decided to sell it instead of scrap it after he offed Stockley."

Winter nodded. "You're right. That's a real possibility. But why would they sell it without at least trying to scrape the barrel and make the next round more difficult to trace?"

"Good question."

"And based on that look on your face, you've got a good answer," she quipped.

The entire day had been strained and weird, but the air of discomfort slipped away when his slight smile brightened to a grin. From the creases at the corners of his eyes to the way the shadows played along his jaw, she loved everything about that smile.

"It's acceptable." Attention fixed on the road, he shrugged. "But I think the reason they didn't alter the barrel was because they wanted it capable of making the shot that killed Haldane. And when you get to distances like that, every little detail matters. A screwed-up barrel might knock your aim off by just enough for you to miss your target."

"Good point."

Truth be told, in that moment, her mind had wandered far away from the subject of the military-grade rifle used to kill Tyler Haldane. At just the sight of Noah's smile, Winter was drawn back to the night she'd fallen asleep with her head on his chest. She could almost feel the warmth of his body, the faint beat of his heart, the slow cadence of his breathing.

When she thought that she might never wake up like that again, her throat tightened.

How did she even begin to broach the subject? Last time she had tried to express her feelings, she came within an inch of ruining their friendship.

She didn't want a hasty kiss in the middle of her kitchen, she reminded herself. She wanted dialogue, but she didn't have the first idea of how to open that dialogue. What in the hell did she even want from him? A cuddle buddy? How old was she, thirteen?

If she couldn't form a coherent question or make a request that made sense, then she would be wise to keep her mouth shut. She could feel the yawning chasm open in her mind, could feel herself slipping down into the swirling void of what-ifs and anxiety.

What if that had been it? What if that had been her last chance? What if he'd changed his mind?

No, damn it, she told herself, clenching one hand until her nails bit into her palm.

Noah wasn't going anywhere, and now she could say without a doubt that *she* wasn't going anywhere, either. Not as long as she could help it. There would be a time for her to bring up the new flurry of emotions that had begun to whisper through her mind when she looked at him, when she saw him smile or heard him laugh.

But right now, at the start of a case that would likely devolve into a media free-for-all before the end of the week, wasn't the time. On the trip back from a visit with a mass murderer wasn't the place.

Their workday wasn't even half over, and neither of them needed the distraction if they wanted to make any headway in the venture to find the sniper who had shot and killed Tyler Haldane.

Or was Haldane's murder just a convenient excuse for her to remain silent?

Damn it, she thought.

If she didn't find a new focus for her racing thoughts soon, she would undoubtedly succumb to the mounting panic attack.

"So…" She didn't know how long they'd been quiet, but she felt like she had just interrupted a moment of prayer at a funeral. "What do you think about this whole thing? About investigating the murder of a neo-Nazi mass shooter?"

Tapping a finger against the steering wheel, he blew out a long, slow breath. Though they'd known one another for well over a year, she had only recently noticed the tic. When Noah tapped his finger against something—the steering wheel, a glass of water, a tabletop—he was in the midst of contemplation.

"I don't know," he finally replied. "It's not really what I expected to be doing when I joined the bureau. I mean, don't get me wrong. When I was in the Dallas PD, we'd investigate the murder of drug dealers and shit, but…"

When he didn't go on, she prompted, "But…?"

He shrugged. "It's different, you know. Most drug dealers, when you get right down to it, are just people who'd been dealt one shitty hand right after the other. They started down at the bottom, and they didn't have any way out, so they did what they had to do."

"So…you sympathize a little?"

Another little shrug. "In a way, I think I understand what they did, why they did it. For most of them, it was all they'd ever known. They didn't grow up with parents who made their money working in real estate or managing a grocery store. Their parents dealt drugs, did drugs, and they just followed suit. Not calling it an excuse, but it's an explanation. And when you think about it, it makes sense."

Winter worried her lower lip. "And now?"

"Now, no matter how I spin it in my head, Tyler Haldane and Kent Strickland don't make a damn bit of sense. They came from middle-class backgrounds, they were college students. So, I don't know. I'm not trying to focus on who the victim was, I'm just trying to keep myself focused on the idea that there's a lunatic out there with a Barrett M98B sniper rifle taking out civilians from close to a mile away."

With a half-snort, half-laugh, she nodded. "When you put it that way, this case actually makes a lot more sense."

7

Though Bree Stafford and Levi Brandt had done the heavy lifting to sift through the list of Tyler Haldane and Kent Strickland's victims to rule out suspects, Noah and Winter had been tasked with verifying the various alibis.

Noah didn't envy Bree and Levi, but reaching out to confirm whether or not a person was where they said they were on the eve of Haldane's death was tedious. By the time he took a seat in the briefing room for their evening meeting, he felt more like a telemarketer than an FBI agent.

Max looked over the gathering—the same as earlier in the afternoon, minus Stella from ballistics—before he eased the door closed behind himself.

"Everyone's here, so what've we got?" the man said as he made his way to the front of the room.

Bree and Agent Brandt exchanged resigned looks before Bree shook her head. "Nothing, sir. We made it through everyone on the list, and we ruled them all out. If they had a reliable alibi, then they weren't capable of making the shot that killed Haldane."

"Well, that seems like par for the course for today," Max muttered. "Agent Dalton, Agent Black, what about you?"

Now, it was Noah's turn to shake his head. "Nothing. Strickland said there wasn't anyone else in on it."

"And you believe him?" Max's query wasn't accusatory but hovered closer to a deep weariness.

Noah spread his hands and leaned back in his chair. "I trust that little shit as far as I can throw him, but I don't think he knew anything useful. Until we got there, it looked like he didn't even know that his buddy was dead, much less that he was taken out by a professional sniper."

To his side, Winter nodded. "Yeah, he didn't know anything."

"Ming, Vasquez." Max's gray eyes shifted over to the two agents. "Please tell me you've got something other than nothing."

Sun coughed into her hand to clear her throat. "We do, sir, but it's not...I don't know if it's good news."

"Of course it's not. Let's hear it." The SAC leaned against the whiteboard and crossed his arms.

"We looked into Mitch Stockley." Miguel Vasquez shook his head. "Mitch Stockley was a real estate broker in Norfolk. He lived in the 'burbs, divorced, two kids both living with their mother. As far as we can tell, the custody battle was vicious, but..." He glanced over to Sun.

"I think we know why," she finished for him. "Aside from a DUI from ten years ago, Stockley's record was clean, but that didn't mean *he* was clean. He'd had his fair share of run-ins with the cops in Norfolk, but they never had enough to press charges. He was suspected in the disappearance of a few girls from Old Dominion, but none of their bodies were ever found."

As if they'd practiced their speech, Miguel picked up the story, "About eight years ago, there was a college girl who claimed she escaped while Stockley was trying to knock her out and kidnap her. But Stockley denied it, and there wasn't anything to corroborate the victim's statement, so they couldn't do anything with it. Or, at least, that's what they said. She'd been drinking that night, and honestly, I think the cops over there might've rushed to judgment."

Sun nodded vigorously. "But when a girl went missing a few months later, and then another one about a year after her, they started to think that the first victim might've been onto something."

The distaste on Sun's face was as plain to see as the color of her shirt. Normally, Noah thought she was too harsh when it came to her interactions with other law enforcement departments. But this time, he was inclined to agree with her. He could only hope she'd given them an earful when they handed her the files on Mitch Stockley.

"Fortunately for us," Miguel went on, "the Norfolk PD kept their records nice and pristine. I think they were hoping that they'd nail him one of these days, but then he turned up dead. The guy was heavy into coke, so for the past six months, they've just assumed he crossed the wrong dealer, maybe a cartel, and got his head blown off."

"We could be looking for two people," Noah put in. "Ballistics said the weapon was a Barrett M98B, and those things aren't cheap. Instead of scrapping it, whoever killed Stockley might've decided to sell it instead. The M98B is made for precision, so they wouldn't have tried to alter the barrel. If they'd altered the barrel, it would have thrown off the aim and defeated the purpose of the entire rifle."

"Great," Max muttered. "Got any thoughts, Parrish? Any idea what type of person, or *people*, we're looking for?"

"That depends." Aiden's pale eyes flicked to Noah. "Agent Dalton makes a good point. If Stockley and Haldane were each killed by a different person, then it's hard to say what their motives might have been. Could be a cartel that took out Stockley and a pissed off bystander that took out Haldane."

"What if we're only looking for one killer?" Winter asked.

When she looked over at Parrish, Noah thought he saw a different glint in her eyes. The fleeting look wasn't the same reverence, the same attraction, with which she had regarded him during the hunt for Douglas Kilroy.

Though she and Aiden had a pointed conversation several days earlier, Noah hadn't prodded her for the details. He knew the topic had involved Autumn, but he knew little else.

"If we're only looking for one person," Aiden said. "Then we have to look at what Stockley and Haldane had in common."

"We looked into that too," Sun jumped in. "They aren't related, and from what we could tell, they've never even met. Tyler Haldane hadn't ever even been to Norfolk. He and Kent went to Virginia Tech, not Old Dominion. So, as far as similarities go, they—"

"They're both pieces of shit," Bree suggested.

In the silence that followed her casual observation, every set of eyes in the room shifted to her. She was either unperturbed by the sudden spotlight, or she didn't care.

Why should she care? She was right.

"Agent Stafford," Max said, breaking the spell of quiet. "You're suggesting that we're dealing with a vigilante, right?"

In response, Bree nodded.

"It makes sense," Aiden put in. "If there's nothing else that the two of them have in common, then it makes sense. Stockley was a real estate broker, late forties, lived in the suburbs. Haldane was a college kid from a middle-class household, young enough to be Stockley's kid. Neither of them look anything alike, and they didn't even live in the same geographic area."

Max nodded. "And what do we know about the killer so far?"

"We know that there's a good chance they've got military or law enforcement training," Aiden said. "No one fits the profile of vigilante quite like a pissed off, disillusioned cop."

"You know what?" Max glanced back and forth between Bree and Aiden. "I've been with the bureau for almost thirty years, and I never thought I'd say this…"

"Say what?" Bree prodded when he didn't immediately elaborate.

With a mirthless chuckle, Max grabbed a blue dry-erase marker. "I hope we're dealing with a cartel."

"Me too," Noah muttered.

"Based on what we've got so far," Max pulled the cap off the marker, "we've got a few different angles we can work. First," he raised his arm and started to write, "we've got the vigilante theory for both victims. That Haldane and Stockley were killed by someone because they're both killers. Second, we've got the idea that there were two different killers."

He scrawled out Haldane, then Stockley, and drew a line beneath each. "For this, there are two likely possibilities for Haldane, and only one for Stockley. If Stockley and Haldane were each killed by someone else, then right now, we're thinking that Stockley was deep into the drug scene and he pissed off the wrong dealer. Does anyone have any other theories on who might've wanted to kill him?"

Beside Noah, Winter propped her elbows atop the table and leaned forward. "A pissed off victim, or a pissed off victim's family. Might be that one of his victims was related to someone with law enforcement or military experience. Since the cops couldn't, or wouldn't, do anything about her disappearance, they took matters into their own hands."

With an approving nod, Max scrawled "pissed off victim/vigilante" beneath Stockley's name.

At the sight of the stoic SAC writing such an unprofessional observation, Noah could barely suppress a snort of laughter. That was Max's humor—he struck when his audience least expected it.

"Now, what about Haldane?" Max asked. "We've got co-conspirator, but we're in the process of ruling out pissed off victim, right?"

"Right," Bree replied. "We're close to being done with the list, and so far, we haven't found anyone feasible."

"That leaves us with co-conspirator and vigilante," Aiden surmised.

"Here's what we're going to do, ladies and gentlemen," Max said, waving the marker at the gathering. "The top one, the theory that the same vigilante killed both of them, we're going to put a pin in this until we eliminate everything else. Because statistically speaking, an unknown, unrelated third party taking out Haldane *and* Strickland is the least likely scenario. Dalton made a good point about that weapon. A Barrett anything is expensive if you're buying it legally, and if you're looking for one on the black market, it's *really* expensive."

"Plus," Aiden put in. "If it was bought on the black market, it stands to reason that the person who bought it would be familiar with the process enough to sell it."

"Agreed," Max replied. "So, for right now, we're going to look at Haldane and Stockley as two different cases. Divide and conquer, agents. Black, Vasquez, you've got Stockley. You take the cartel hit angle. Brandt, Ming, you take the pissed off victim angle. Stafford, you and Brandt have done a lot of the groundwork for the Haldane murder already. Weyrick, Stafford, and Dalton, you divvy up what you've got left to look into for Haldane."

Everyone shuffled in their chairs, ready to get to work.

Everyone except Max. He wasn't quite finished yet. "I'm

shifting a couple of you around so we've got fresh eyes on each case. I doubt I've got to say it, but I will anyway. Give priority to any victims or family members with military or law enforcement experience. Parrish and the BAU will be helping you, so don't leave anything off the table."

8

Aiden looked from Cassidy Ramirez to Max Osbourne and then back before he took his seat in front of the ADD's polished desk. He and Max were fresh from the briefing with the agents involved in the Tyler Haldane case, and Aiden suddenly wished the work environment at the FBI was more akin to the office in *Madmen*. Then, at least, he wouldn't have to wait until he returned home to pour himself a stiff drink. He hadn't smoked a cigarette in close to fifteen years, but right now, he would have accepted one if it was handed to him.

Maybe the theory was far-fetched, but he was stuck on Bree's casual statement.

They're both pieces of shit.

Well, she wasn't wrong.

A vigilante was enough to deal with on its own, but a vigilante with a military or law enforcement background was a damn nightmare. As soon as word worked its way to the press, they'd all drown in cameras and microphones before they could ever solve the case.

They needed to get a handle on the Tyler Haldane investigation, and they needed to do it soon. He could only assume that was why ADD Ramirez had called him and Max to her office so they could update her.

Damage control.

"Evening, gentlemen," Ramirez greeted as her dark eyes shifted from him and over to Max. "Thanks for staying late to meet with me. I appreciate it."

"It's no problem," Aiden replied.

It'd be better if you had a bottle of bourbon to pass around, though.

Even though he knew Cassidy well enough to be sure she would chuckle at the remark, he kept the sentiment to himself. He wasn't in a humorous mood.

"Yeah, no problem," Max seconded.

"You two look like you just got back from a funeral." Cassidy leaned forward as she folded her hands atop the mahogany desk.

Max leaned forward in his chair, mirroring her position. "We think we're looking for a vigilante."

Aiden nodded as the man's gray eyes flicked over to him. "It seems just as likely as the alternative."

"And what's the alternative?" Cassidy asked, one sculpted eyebrow arched.

Aiden shrugged. "A cartel hit *and* a vigilante."

There were so many possibilities for their perpetrators, he wasn't sure which direction to pursue in his head.

Of all the feelings that had been thrown at him over the past couple weeks, uncertainty was by far his least favorite. He was a decision maker, he picked a course of action and stuck to it. His decisions were made with confidence, and he didn't waver.

Normally.

But between Autumn Trent and the level of enigma asso-

ciated with the Haldane and Stockley cases, he was swim-
ming in a treacherous gray sea of indecision.

He couldn't fucking stand it.

Seven o'clock had not yet rolled around, but he was
already confident he would manage little sleep that night.
Not unless he drank himself into a stupor.

"What do you mean? A cartel hit *and* a vigilante?" Cassidy
pressed. "Is this something we'll have to hand off to organized crime?"

Max heaved a sigh as he shook his head. "I don't know.
We don't know much of anything right now."

"Well, let's start with what you *do* know." She turned her
scrutinizing gaze from Max to Aiden and then back. "Theories, evidence, all of it. We've got half the press in the entire
country breathing down our necks right now, stalking the
damn FBI so they can get a little tidbit of information for
their story about Tyler Haldane." She snorted. "I just got
done watching a little bit of CNN, and they're already specu-
lating on whether or not we're going to see an outbreak of
violence directed at the perpetrators of mass shootings. The
ones that don't kill themselves at the end of their rampage,
anyway."

"Can't say I'd be opposed to it," Max muttered.

In what had become an increasingly rare occurrence,
Aiden agreed with the SAC. "It'd save the Bureau some time
and effort."

"Like all the time and effort we're putting into finding out
who killed Tyler fucking Haldane," Max grated. "You know
there are real victims out there, right? Victims who could
actually use the bureau's help, people like the men, women,
and children that Tyler Haldane and his neo-Nazi buddy
massacred six months ago."

Though Aiden half-expected to see a flicker of annoyance
pass over Cassidy's face, she merely frowned. The look of

exasperation was insincere, and the feigned ire didn't reach her eyes.

She was trying to be their boss, but when it came to Tyler Haldane, even the perpetually level-headed Cassidy Ramirez was hard-pressed to maintain a poker face.

"We don't get to pick the victims, Max," she replied. "I'm about as fond of Tyler Haldane as you are, but we've still got a job to do. What about co-conspirators? Other neo-Nazis in Strickland and Haldane's inner circle?"

"Based on what we've got so far, it's unlikely," Max advised. "Agent Black and Agent Dalton went to talk to Strickland today, and they seemed pretty confident that he didn't know anything about other members of their neo-Nazi brigade."

Cassidy's dark eyes shifted to Aiden. "Parrish?"

Aiden kept his expression blank. His mind was a mess right now, but Cassidy and Max didn't need to know about his mental turmoil. "We're not going to get anything from Kent Strickland. He's been lawyered up since he came out of a medically induced coma a few months ago. He's been shackled to a hospital bed ever since, and when Dalton and Black showed up, his lawyer and his mother were both there.

"He's got the wool pulled over both their eyes, from the sound of it. He's probably looking to use his condition as a defense in his trial, something to get a more lenient sentence or avoid the death penalty. There's no way he's going to compromise that now to cooperate with the Feds."

Lips pursed, Cassidy flexed her fingers but didn't unfold them from where they lay on her desk. "We could offer him leniency if he gives up his co-conspirator. *If* we're certain there is a co-conspirator."

Max had already begun to shake his head before she finished. "No. We aren't giving that piece of shit anything. And it isn't just me you'd have to convince. The US Attorney for this case is a take no prisoners Texan, so good luck trying to convince her not to stick a needle in Strickland's arm."

Aiden was nodding. "Not to mention it'd be a publicity nightmare. I'd rather deal with the press being stuck on a vigilante than them fixating on how the bureau made a *deal* with a neo-Nazi mass murderer. That trial is going to be a nightmare enough as it is. Strickland's parents have money, and they're throwing a hell of a lot of it at their only son's defense."

"And what about the other victim, Mitch Stockley?" Cassidy pressed.

Aiden and Max exchanged glances before the older man launched into a recap of their most recent meeting. They took turns to explain the various angles at which they viewed the men's murders, and they gave a rough outline of what the agents assigned to the investigations would evaluate.

To her credit, the ADD maintained a neutral expression.

"All right." She didn't look pleased. "I understand your reasoning for keeping the single killer theory until after you've ruled out all the theories that are more likely, and I agree. It's what I would've done. But for a second, let's just suppose that we're looking for the same shooter in both cases. What exactly does that mean for our investigation? We're all but certain that Haldane's killer had military or law enforcement experience, so what does that mean, exactly?"

"It means we're probably looking for a pissed off cop or a pissed off soldier who just so happens to be an expert marksman," Max answered before Aiden could open his mouth to respond.

"A pissed off cop or soldier who can hit someone between the eyes from almost a mile away," Aiden added.

"This is a really specific profile, gentlemen." Ramirez ran

a ballpoint pen along the fingers of one hand as a contemplative look spread over her face.

"You'd think it'd make our job easier," Max muttered. "But so far, it's had the opposite effect."

"We had a really specific profile for the Catherine Schmidt case too," Aiden reminded them, his voice flat. "That's the problem with really specific profiles, or just generally when we're dealing with a suspect who's an expert in something. Whether they're a brain surgeon or a sniper, it means they're skilled. And if they're skilled, it means they're even better at eluding law enforcement."

"Especially if they *were* law enforcement," Max added.

As she tightened her grip on the pen, Cassidy's expression turned grave, almost haunted. Aiden knew that look. It was a look reserved for only the darkest moments of her work, a look he hadn't seen in over a decade.

"It means we can't rule anyone out. *Anyone*. That includes FBI agents. This office was called to the Riverside Mall, and Mitch Stockley was in *our* backyard. If there's going to be a pissed off cop who's got a grudge against Stockley *and* Haldane, there's a real possibility it's someone in this office."

9

Sun Ming had been hesitant to leave the FBI office that night. She had done an admirable job of keeping the metaphorical devil at bay, but by the time she closed and locked her apartment door, she knew the façade had come to an end.

Swallowing against the bile that rose in the back of her throat, she squeezed her eyes closed and massaged the site of the months old gunshot wound. It was a terrible reminder of her many failures.

It pissed her off and scared her simultaneously.

If her aim had been off by just an inch or two, her shot would have missed Kent Strickland entirely. He would have finished his reach for the trigger of his rifle, and Sun would have been done. She wouldn't have even been given a chance to make a miraculous recovery like Kent Strickland: she would have been dead.

What kind of poetic irony would that have been, anyway? An FBI agent shot and killed while a mass murderer was saved by some of the most skilled surgeons in the country.

Once upon a time, Sun had been an adamant believer in karma.

After all, she was an important part of the karmic circle, wasn't she? She made sure that the scumbags who hurt other people got what was coming for them. She kept the karmic ideal alive, brought killers and rapists to justice.

But what kind of justice had saved Kent Strickland from a shot to the head—a shot that *she* had fired, a shot she intended to be *fatal*—when two of the man's victims had succumbed to their injuries in the same damn hospital?

What if *she* had aimed a couple inches to the right?

What if she had put the round between Strickland's eyes, just like the shot that had killed his friend six months later? Would one of the two victims have won their battle in the intensive care unit if she had taken another split-second to perfect her aim?

Don't be stupid, she told herself.

That wasn't how the world worked. That had never *been* how the world worked.

With a shaky sigh, she finally stepped away from the front door and made her way to the kitchen. Though she hadn't managed to eat more than a couple crackers since breakfast, she went straight for the bottle of vodka on top of the fridge. She retrieved a pint glass from the cupboard beside the sink, but before she poured any of the liquor, she twisted off the top and took a deep drink.

Grimacing as the alcohol burned its way down to her stomach, she filled the bottom fourth of the glass, dumped in a few ice cubes, and finished with cranberry juice. She wasted no time before she sipped at the beverage in an effort to cool the fire in her throat.

Vodka and cranberry used to be her drink of choice when she went out to a bar, but anymore, she could hardly stand to be around a group of more than four people she didn't know.

Aside from cranberry juice, beer, and leftover Italian takeout, her refrigerator was bare.

Sun loved to cook, even just for herself, but she couldn't summon up the mental fortitude to venture out to the store. On the rare occasions she convinced herself to go somewhere larger than a gas station, she went at one or two in the morning.

As she replaced the bottle of juice, she lamented that necessity would soon dictate that she undertake just such a trip.

The Fourth of July had been a nightmare. The sound of fireworks had renewed her hyper-awareness, and weeks passed before the tension dissipated. With each pop and crack, she had seen an innocent person's body drop to the floor of the Riverside Mall.

During the start of the Presley case, Sun and the reaper had crossed paths for the first time. On the polished tile in front of a boutique clothing store at the mall, she had her second real brush with death.

Sure, she'd been in her fair share of risky scenarios before then, but she'd never stared death in the face like she had on the California coast. And when the challenge presented itself all those months ago, she had frozen. Like some brand-spanking-new recruit fresh out of Quantico, she'd completely locked up, mind and body.

Though she had been bound and determined to redeem herself in her own eyes—and in the eyes of her colleagues at the bureau—she had not anticipated her opportunity would come so soon. She had been called in to help Danville authorities with a situation at the Riverside Mall, but when she received the call from Max Osbourne, no blood had yet been spilled.

In the time it took her and Bobby Weyrick to get to the mall, the scenario had devolved into a hostage situation.

Haldane and Strickland had a strategic position near the host of computer monitors that displayed footage from each security camera set along the perimeter.

If they saw any law enforcement personnel try to enter the building without their explicit permission, they would kill a hostage. By the time the tech teams had accessed each camera to set it on a loop, the first civilian was shot and killed.

Eleven more died before she, Bobby, and the rest of the tactical response team got to them, and one officer was shot in the head in the ensuing scuffle.

Another law enforcement agent was hit with a shot that nicked his femoral artery, and he didn't survive the night. A stray bullet caught a frightened teenager in the stomach, and she clung to life for only another fourteen hours.

In those same fourteen hours, one of the most renowned brain surgeons in the entire country had performed the surgery that would ultimately save Kent Strickland's life.

With a sharp intake of breath, Sun jerked herself back to the dim kitchen. As she raised the pint glass to her lips, she spotted a slight tremor in her hand. Without pausing, she drained the rest of the potent cocktail.

Sun should have been a better shot. Kent Strickland should have died.

Karma demanded it.

ASIDE FROM A REMARK about the dreary weather as they pulled out of the parking garage, neither Winter nor Noah spoke on their journey back to their shared apartment complex.

On a normal day, Noah would have made a good-natured joke about the lack of leg room when she drove them to work, or he would have asked her when she finally planned to buy a "grown-up" vehicle like the rest of her coworkers.

Until the silence settled in between them, however, she hadn't realized how much she looked forward to the exchanges.

His green eyes were fixed on the windshield, but his stare was vacant. He was lost in thought, and the more Winter tried to decipher what those thoughts were, the tighter the knot in her stomach became.

Finally, after they were more than halfway home, she broke the eerie quiet.

"Are you all right?" she blurted, glancing over to him as she came to a stop at a red light.

He blinked as he turned his head to offer her a nod. If she didn't know any better, she would have thought he'd just awoken from a trance.

"I'm fine," he replied.

No sarcastic comment. No smile. No laugh, no joke, no tirade about the most recent episode of *Game of Thrones.*

Just *I'm fine.*

As she opened her mouth to prod him for a real answer, a sudden realization dawned on her. Rather than the planned question, she forced a smile to her lips. The look was strained, and she doubted it conveyed any sort of reassurance, but it was the best she could do.

"Okay." It was the only word she could manage.

Damn it.

Was this how he'd felt every time she had pushed him out to arms' length? All this trepidation, all this *sadness*—had the same feelings struck him whenever she uttered those same two words in response to a genuine inquiry into her wellbeing?

The thought that she might have put him through the

same heartache on more occasions than she cared to count almost brought on the sting of tears.

She couldn't cry, not now, not in front of him. She wasn't worried about displaying a so-called weakness, nor was she concerned that he would think less of her.

But she knew he wasn't *fine*. If there was enough weight on his mind to prevent even a strained smile, then the last thing she wanted was to force herself into the spotlight by bursting into tears. She wanted to be as good a friend to him as he had always been to her.

As they pulled into a parking space, the only sound was the tinny song that played through the speakers, which was weird inside the little Civic. Ever since they had started to carpool, they'd established a rule that dictated who got to pick the music for their morning and evening commutes. The edict seemed straightforward enough: whoever drove was in charge of the radio.

Winter hadn't expected the decision to extend to their trips for work, but when she thought back to Noah's defensive spiel about order and chaos, she felt a smile tug at the corner of her mouth. She could only imagine the wide grin that would split Grampa Jack's face if she told him country music had begun to grow on her.

Well, the type of country music Noah listened to had grown on her, but she still couldn't stand most of the tunes played on the popular stations. Not unless it was Chris Stapleton, anyway. Grampa Jack was a steadfast fan of artists like Merle Haggard and Johnny Cash, but Winter suspected even he would like Chris Stapleton.

"Hey," she said as they neared her door. She wanted to prod him for more information about what was on his mind, but she bit off the query as his green eyes flicked over to her.

"Yeah?"

"Do you want to, uh, have a drink or something? Watch

another episode of *Game of Thrones?*" She wanted to sound nonchalant, but she sounded hurried and weary.

He pulled his gaze away as he shook his head. "It's been a long day. I think I'm just going to shower and space off to a History Channel show about aliens or something."

"You could do that here." She waved to her door for emphasis.

"And have you catch me drooling on myself? Nah, thanks anyway, darlin'." His smile seemed a little brighter, and for the first time since they left the office, he sounded like himself.

She didn't pause to think the act through before she closed the distance between them to wrap both arms around his shoulders. Rather than appalled at her emotionally charged decision, she was content. As she nestled her head against his chest, she felt the warmth of his touch on her back. She tightened her grasp and took in a steadying breath.

This wasn't a friendly embrace or even an embrace to offer comfort. She knew it, and she knew he knew it too. She wanted the closeness, the familiar scent of his clothes, of his skin, and she didn't want to let it go. She didn't want to let *him* go.

As she brought one hand to rest on the side of his face, she gently pressed her lips to his other cheek.

When he met her gaze, there was a look of dumbfounded awe behind his eyes. "What was *that* for?"

With a wistful smile, she dropped her hand back to his shoulder. "I know you're not fine," she said, her voice as hushed as his. "I know something's bothering you, but I can tell you don't want to talk about it. And that's all right. Really, I mean it. You need time to...to...what does Autumn call it?"

"Think?"

Rolling her eyes to feign exasperation, she balled her

hand into a fist and landed a playful punch to his chest. "No, smartass."

"Hey, that was funny, all right? She'd laugh if she was here," he shot back with a knowing smile.

"You know what," she said, her tone as matter-of-fact as she could manage. For emphasis, she punched him again. "I was trying to be all nice and shit, and you had to go and ruin it by being a smartass. This is why I'm never nice to you."

His laugh sounded more like a snort as he nodded. "Whatever you say, darlin'."

"Now, what's *that* supposed to mean?" Try as she might, she couldn't keep her smile at bay.

"It means," he said, brushing a wayward piece of ebony hair behind her ear. At the feathery touch, she felt like a pleasant breeze had flitted down her back. "I think you're plenty nice to me."

When she smiled up at him this time, the expression was genuine. Between the sarcastic comments and the pleasant touch, she had almost forgotten what she had intended to say.

"If you don't want to talk about what's on your mind, that's all right," she assured him. "But whenever you want to, I'll be here, all right?"

A warm smile crept to his face as he nodded. "All right."

As he turned to make his way to his apartment, there was an unfamiliar twinge of longing in her chest. Sure, she'd dated before, but this feeling—a cross somewhere between trepidation and anticipation—was new.

She didn't know if she should welcome it or run from it.

10

Before she stepped into the hallway to await the committee's decision, Autumn Trent had shaken hands with each of the three members. Her smile grew wider with each, and she knew before she pushed open the door that the presentation had been a success.

But still, as she started the fourth game of Minesweeper on her phone, a series of "what-ifs" started to claw at the edge of her thoughts. Her rational mind insisted that the fifteen minutes she'd waited on the uncomfortable wooden bench was to be expected, but the spiral of anxiety never paid attention to what her rational mind knew.

More often than not, dissertation committees requested a handful of revisions before they officially awarded the candidate with their doctorate. Based on her brief physical contact with the three professors, she was confident her presentation had been successful, but she didn't know the level of revision she would be required to make.

She could tell them that the SSA of the Behavioral Analysis Unit at the FBI had already helped her to elaborate in a couple spots, but she doubted the Fed's stamp of approval would negate their request for changes. Besides, forensic psychologists were not profilers, and profilers were not forensic psychologists.

When the door to her side creaked open, she almost leapt from her seat. As her pulse picked up and her breath caught in her throat, she was reminded that she had come face-to-face with a mafia hitman a week earlier. Apparently, she was still on high alert.

Autumn had shot and killed a man, but no matter the different angles at which she analyzed the scenario, she couldn't find within herself the capacity to feel guilty.

At first, she'd been worried that the lack of remorse might have been a façade, that one day she would wake up with an insurmountable mountain of regret at her feet, or that she'd see Nico Culetti in her damn dreams. But so far, none of the concerns had come to fruition. The confrontation with the contract killer felt as distant and dulled as the host of traumatic events from her childhood.

Maybe she'd file away Nico Culetti with the rest of her biological family. She'd tuck Nico into the same crevasse as every miserable, drug-addled friend her parents let into their house, into their daughter's life.

And maybe, one day, all the memories would coalesce into the unrelenting grasp of posttraumatic stress.

And maybe, one day, she'd drown beneath that crushing wave of guilt, shame, and regret.

But as she returned the smile of the middle-aged professor who had stepped into the hall, she pushed the notion to the back of her mind.

Whatever had happened to her brain when her father knocked her into the edge of that coffee table had made her resilient. He was gone. Her mother was gone. Her younger half-sister, Sarah, was gone.

But Autumn was here. Alive. Thriving.

Autumn knew she would always wonder what might have been, but she had been blessed with a new family long ago, and now she had friends. For the first time, she felt like the life she'd envisioned for herself was within reach.

Despite the eight years of intense study and the hundred grand she'd dumped into tuition expenses, as she walked back down the long hallway to face the people who had control of her future, she realized that she never truly thought the pursuit would pan out. After all, nothing ever went right for Autumn Trent, did it?

She gave herself a mental shake. Her old, negative way of thinking was creeping back into her mind, just like the ghosts of her past. But right now, she couldn't seem to shake the negativity.

She shivered.

She didn't know what she'd expected, but she knew she'd expected *something*. Whether it was a freak hurricane to wash her out into the Atlantic or maybe the apocalypse, she had expected a monumental obstacle. She had expected rejection, but instead, she was greeted with the warm smile of a tenured psychology professor at Virginia Commonwealth University.

Holy shit, she told herself as she followed the woman back into the classroom. *This is real.*

"Thank you so much for waiting, Ms. Trent," Dr. Monahan greeted.

Autumn nodded and dropped down to sit at the circular table. "Of course."

To Dr. Monahan's side, Autumn's advisor, Irene Harris, slid a piece of paper across the polished wooden surface. "Congratulations, Autumn."

As Autumn glanced down to the document, she expected a caveat.

Hell, she was *ready* for a caveat. She had even set aside

time over the next couple weeks to make the revisions requested by the committee. But according to the bolded text at the top of the paper, she needed to change her plans.

"That was one of the best presentations I've seen in a while," Dr. Monahan said. When Autumn looked up, his smile matched Irene's. "Well done, Dr. Autumn Trent."

Autumn wanted to make a lighthearted quip in response, but all she managed was an awestruck smile that threatened to break her face.

There was no caveat. This was real.

"And…" The woman from the hall, Dr. Laura Santiago held up an index finger as she reached into the pocket of her black cardigan. When she produced a business card, she set it beside the sheet of paper. "This is the contact information for a colleague of mine. He's the co-founder of a threat assessment firm here in Richmond, and based on your presentation, I think you've got a skill set he'd be interested in. I'm sure you've got other interviews lined up, but in the event you want to stay in Virginia, give him a call."

"I would," Autumn managed, swallowing down the desire to squeal in pure delight. "I would love to stay in Richmond. Thank you, Dr. Santiago. I will definitely get in touch with him."

"I'll let him know to keep an eye out for it," the woman replied.

A Ph.D. *and* a job prospect? This wasn't Autumn's luck.

Was the sky going to fall when she walked outside? Would she be struck by lightning? Or would another hitman chase her down while she walked her dog or took out the trash?

Honestly, she thought she could deal with the disappointment. Disappointment had been the name of the game since she was able to walk.

Once Autumn's father taught her mother to shoot up, that had been the beginning of the end of her childhood.

But she wasn't a child any longer.

Although Autumn was well-versed in pain and disappointment, as she stood to shake the hands of each professor for the second time, she realized she was ill-prepared to deal with success.

11

If there hadn't been other people nearby, Noah would have dropped his head to rest in his hands. Instead, he kept his unseeing stare fixed on the white glow of his computer monitor. He reminded himself that his job afforded him the autonomy to leave if he was under the weather or to work from home if he needed peace and quiet.

Though he wasn't physically ill, he couldn't focus on any one item for longer than thirty seconds before a whirlwind of unease tore his attention away.

For the first half of the day, he and Bree had sorted through the information they'd gathered on all the victims of Tyler Haldane and Kent Strickland's bloody rampage. Of the fifteen who were killed, four had an immediate family member with military experience, and one had a family member who worked in law enforcement.

All five had airtight alibis for the time Tyler Haldane was shot and killed.

They'd expanded their search to everyone who had been present at the shooting, law enforcement personnel included.

The Danville police officers had been easy to exclude.

Even if their alibis weren't airtight for the precise time of Haldane's shooting, there was enough to show that they couldn't have made the trip to Richmond and back in time. The same could be said for most bystanders, and by the time they reached the end of the list, the likelihood that Haldane had been killed by a victim in search of revenge seemed slim.

The night before, Bobby Weyrick had finally gotten in touch with Kent Strickland's father. George Strickland owned an acreage north of Richmond, and according to Bobby's handoff notes, the man sure liked to rant and rave about conspiracy theories. The piece of paper was decorated with doodles of aliens and UFOs in the margins, and Noah wondered how long Bobby had suffered through the rantings and ravings before he finally threw in the towel.

But regardless of Bobby's valiant effort to withstand an extended conversation with George, the older Strickland had been another dead end. Haldane had stayed with George and Strickland over the summer, but other than befriending the kid who mowed George's lawn and meeting up with the occasional high school friend, Haldane and Strickland kept to themselves.

Noah and Bree had run headlong into another dead end, but the lack of progress wasn't the driving force behind the unease simmering beneath Noah's thoughts.

He had double and triple checked his work, but only after he came to the conclusion that he was half-assing the investigation. Though he was disappointed in himself for the lack of effort, he found it more and more difficult to justify *any* effort as he went through the list of victims and family members.

All these people's lives had been irreparably damaged by the lunatic whose murder they now sought to solve.

Why in the hell did they even *want* to find the killer? So they could offer them a medal and a handshake?

Noah hated the persistent buzz of doubt with which he'd contended since the start of the case, and he hated how damn ambivalent he had become.

Neo-Nazi mass shooter or not, Tyler Haldane had been murdered, potentially by the same person who had murdered another man six months earlier.

Haldane and Stockley were, as Bree had so eloquently put, colossal pieces of shit. But they had been *murdered*. Shot with a military-grade sniper rifle by a man or woman who had likely been trained by the United States government to kill people.

A person who had given themselves permission to be judge, jury, and executioner.

He knew he shouldn't have to justify his own damn job, and in truth, he figured that was the reason for the knot in his stomach. He expected more from himself, and he could only assume that his friends and coworkers expected more too.

Whenever Bree made a callous observation about Stockley or Haldane, he bit his tongue to keep his less than flattering sentiments about the two men to himself.

Sympathizing with a victim shouldn't have been a prerequisite for him to find a damn murderer, but here he was.

If they never found the killer, how would he look back at the Haldane case ten years from now? If an innocent person turned up dead at the hands of the same person who'd shot Haldane and Stockley, what then?

With a quiet groan, Noah finally succumbed and leaned forward to cover his face with both hands.

Maybe he could find a way to get himself unassigned from the investigation. He could fabricate a conflict of interest or play hooky for the next month. Or maybe he could slip away in the night and start a new life down in

North Carolina or Florida. Hell, maybe he'd go all-out and settle down in Iceland or Sweden.

They got a discount on the Rosetta Stone software through work, so he could buy the program before he disappeared. After a few months of dedicated study, he would be fluent and could interact with the locals like he belonged.

Until the light tap of knuckles against hardwood jerked him out of the fantasy world and back to his desk, he didn't realize he had begun to drift off to sleep.

Shit. He really did need to call it a day.

"Hey," Winter's quiet voice greeted.

In all his contemplation, he hadn't even made it to Winter. Any time his thoughts ventured too near the warm embrace from the day before, he stuffed down the memory and reminded himself he had a job to do. A job he had only half-assed so far.

Rubbing his eyes with one hand, he turned to her and tried to force a smile to his face. He was sure his effort was an epic failure.

"Hey," he managed.

"Did you sleep at all last night?" she asked, eyebrow arched.

"I think so," he answered. For emphasis, he stifled a yawn.

"Come on," she said as she stepped away from the cubicle. "Let's go get you some caffeine. We've got work to do." There was a glimmer of contentment in her blue eyes, and his curiosity only intensified.

"Work." Noah practically groaned the word. "You seem, I don't know, *happy* about that."

"Oh." She shook her head as her lips curled into a smile. "No, not *work*-work. When's the last time you looked at your phone?"

"I don't know," he muttered, patting his black suit jacket to assure himself the device hadn't disappeared. "Why?"

"Autumn defended her dissertation this morning."

His eyes widened. He'd forgotten about that. "Oh, shit."

"Oh, shit is right," Winter chuckled. "She's officially Dr. Autumn Trent now, and she said we're invited over to have pizza and beer with her tonight to celebrate. She's not going to the commencement ceremony, and she told me she just wants to keep it low-key. So, me, you, Bree, and Shelby probably. Us and pizza, beer, and a game called Superfight."

With a nod, he brushed off the front of his jacket. "I've heard of that game. If you get the right people together, it's pretty damn funny."

Winter took another step backward and motioned for him to follow.

"Where are we going?" Noah asked, pushing himself to his feet.

"This is basically Autumn's graduation party, so we need to go buy her a present. Haldane and Stockley will still be dead tomorrow."

He barely managed to stifle an unflattering snort of laughter. "Jesus, darlin'. You're terrible, you know that?"

She grinned. "Really, though, we hit a dead end. We've been at it for almost two days straight, so it's time to step away for a second and give ourselves a break. It's a little after two now, so let's just call it a day and go do something fun for a little bit."

His smile widened as he nodded his understanding. Six months ago, she would have run herself ragged chasing down any and every lead on a case. In fact, she *had* run herself ragged during the search for The Preacher.

But now, she was the one who had pulled *him* away from the frustration of one dead end after another. She was here to remind *him* that there was life outside of the FBI office, to remind him that no matter how frustrated he might have been with himself, there were still people who cared.

As they stepped out into the parking garage, he turned to look at Winter. The afternoon sunlight caught the shine of the ebony braid she'd tossed over her shoulder, and her already vivid eyes seemed even brighter.

"Thank you, Winter. You're a good friend. I don't know if I tell you that enough."

When she smiled up at him in response, he would have wrapped her in a bear hug if they hadn't been in the FBI parking garage.

"What did you have in mind to get Autumn, anyway?" He asked the question as much in an effort to pull himself away from the thought of yesterday's warm embrace as anything.

"Well," she wrinkled her nose, "I'm not a great gift buyer, so I texted Shelby to ask what she thought Autumn would like. I just want to make sure I give credit where it's due, you know?"

With a chuckle, he nodded. "Roger that. What'd Shelby say?"

"Well, Autumn really likes to cook, but since she's a broke college student, Shelby said she hasn't been able to buy a lot of the cool kitchen gadgets she wants."

"We're going to get her kitchen stuff? Isn't that more in the 'wedding present' department?"

"See, Noah, you can't box yourself in like that." She flashed him a matter-of-fact look as she raised an index finger. "You've got to get your friends the stuff they want, not the stuff that tradition says is okay to give them."

"Oh, okay, I see what happened there." He paused at the driver's side door of his pickup to fix her with a knowing smile. "That's what you said to Shelby, isn't it? About the wedding present? And then she told you not to pay attention to tradition?"

Winter waved a hand like she was swatting at an insect. "That's beside the point. Autumn wants a stand mixer."

"Like the KitchenAid stand mixers they're always using on *Iron Chef*?" he asked as they climbed into the truck.

"You watch *Iron Chef*?"

"I'm a man of many interests," he replied, resting a hand over his heart. "And yes, I watch a number of different cooking shows, including *Iron Chef*. Alton Brown is my boy."

When Winter burst into laughter, he joined her in short order.

Within the span of ten minutes, his day had gone from absolute shit to a moment he was sure he would remember fondly for years.

12

To Sun's relief, Levi Brandt wasn't a chatty man. He was friendly and quick with a smile, but unless his conversational partner made it clear they were interested in a dialogue, he kept quiet.

His slate gray eyes remained fixed on the road as he tapped a finger against the steering wheel in time with the beat of the song on the radio. Sun wasn't sure she wanted to strike up a conversation, but they had sat in silence for almost the entire trip to Norfolk. The lasting quiet felt *off*.

"Do you like this song?" she finally asked.

His eyes flicked to her and then back to the road as a slight smile touched his face. "Who *doesn't* like Tom Petty?"

She nodded. "Good point."

Sun's musical preferences were eclectic, but there was some merit to Levi's response. Even after she'd discovered hip hop and industrial rock, she had always kept a spot in her playlists for a handful of Tom Petty tunes. And as she raked through her mind, she couldn't recall meeting a person who disliked Tom Petty. Even her brother, a diehard metal fan, loved the man.

Though she expected Levi to pose another question, he remained quiet as the song drew to a close. He must have been able to read Sun's dislike for small talk. Then again, the man was an agent with the victim services division. Aside from the BAU, victim services agents dealt with the nuances of human behavior more than any other department.

Dealing with and putting people at ease was Levi Brandt's job, and as far as Sun could tell, he was damn good at it.

She had volunteered to go alone to talk to the woman who had escaped Mitch Stockley all those years ago, but for the first time, she was glad that Agent Brandt had insisted he accompany her.

As the opening guitar riff for the next song sounded out through the car's speakers, Levi groaned. Arching an eyebrow, Sun glanced over to him.

"Not a fan of Van Halen?" she asked.

Shaking his head, he reached out to change the station. "I can't stand them. I'm pretty indifferent about most '80s hair bands, but for some reason, this one just grates on my nerves."

"I thought I was the only one," she chuckled. "They were simply too popular for my tastes."

"Very true." He shook his head. "I can't stand a lot of stuff that other people love. My friends in college would call me Buzz Killington."

For the first time in weeks, Sun's laugh wasn't forced or strained. "No one ever called me that, but I'm the same way."

"I'd always ruin stuff that's just universally loved. Like *Harry Potter*. I don't hate it, but I never understood the draw. I tried to get into it because all my friends were, but I couldn't get past the first book."

"I made it to the second," she replied. "But I'm more of a *Dresden Files* person, myself."

"*Dresden Files* is great," he agreed with a nod.

She relaxed back into her seat. "I don't like superhero movies, either."

"Me either, and it's weird because I love over the top action movies. Anything with Jason Statham in it, I'll at least watch."

"*John Wick*. That's a comic book movie, but I don't think you can classify it as a superhero film."

"No." He grinned. "Definitely not a superhero anything."

For the next twenty minutes, she and Agent Brandt listed off popular franchises, filmmakers, and musicians they both liked and disliked. To her surprise, she and Levi held many of the same unpopular opinions about their media preferences.

If any more road trips were required during the remainder of the case, Sun knew who she would choose to accompany her.

Their conversation trailed off as they pulled into a residential neighborhood near the outskirts of Norfolk.

Following the directions provided by her smartphone's GPS application, Levi pulled over to the curb in front of a modest, two-story house.

Most of the other homes in the area were similar, and Sun figured most of the occupants were working-class families. They weren't far from a large naval base, and she had spotted a few Navy stickers on the rear windshields of the parked cars they passed.

Though a few weeds had sprouted throughout the front yard, the lawn was well-kept. A bed of flowers rested beneath a picture window to the side of the door, and the pleasant scent wafted past as she and Levi made their way to the porch.

If Sun had a house, she thought she would keep a similar garden. For the time being, however, she would have to settle for her saltwater aquarium. The tedium of maintaining appropriate PH levels in the water, cleaning the tank on a regular basis, and even feeding the finicky fish was calming to Sun.

When she and her brother were young, they made a tradition of helping their father with the vegetable garden in the backyard. Decades later, he still maintained a robust, albeit smaller, patch of plants and flowers. The climate in Florida was a stark difference from their native Washington, D.C., and Sun could still remember how excited he had been when he learned of all the new plants he could grow.

As Levi rapped his knuckles against the wooden door, Sun pulled herself from the reverie. A slew of barks followed the knock, and she thought she heard someone mutter to the dog before the excited outburst tapered off.

"Who is it?" a woman's muffled voice called.

"FBI, ma'am. Agent Brandt, we spoke on the phone earlier today." He held his badge up to the peephole, and Sun followed suit.

"Oh, right. Just a second."

After a brief pause, a couple metallic clicks were followed by a light creak as the door swung inward. With her free hand, the woman held the collar of a German Shepherd, though the dog didn't move from where it sat back on its haunches.

"Good girl, Ripley." The woman's amber eyes flicked back to the shepherd as she released her hold to scratch behind one pointed ear. "Sorry, agents. She's not quite two yet, so she can get pretty excitable. She's a good dog, though. You've got nothing to worry about. Come on in."

Levi flashed her a smile as he tucked his badge back into his suit jacket. "My family had a German Shepherd when I was growing up. Retired service dog, super smart."

"They're very smart dogs," their hostess replied as she eased the door closed behind Sun. "I have a couple cats too, but I doubt they'll come out. They're pretty shy."

"Is it just you here, then?" Sun asked, glancing around the space as they made their way to the living area.

"Yeah, just me, Ripley, and the cats." She waved a hand to the couch. "Have a seat. Do either of you want anything to drink?"

Sun and Levi shook their heads. "No, thank you," Sun answered.

As the woman dropped down to sit, she forced a smile to her face and brushed a piece of strawberry blonde hair from her forehead. The dog sat beside her, head up, on guard. Though the German had done nothing threatening, Sun knew that could change at any moment.

"I know we talked a little on the phone, but I'm Agent Brandt, and this is my partner, Agent Ming. Thanks again for meeting with us on such short notice, Ms. Timson. We're trying to sort through this case as quickly as we can."

"Of course," she replied with a quick nod. "You can call me Anne, or just Timson. I've been in the Navy for almost eight years, so Ms. Timson just sounds odd."

"No problem, Anne." Levi offered her a smile, but the tenseness in her posture didn't dissipate.

"What do you do in the Navy?" Sun asked, trying to ease the woman's trepidation. The desire to do so was surprising, mostly to herself. Maybe some of Noah's friendly demeanor was rubbing off on her. God, she hoped not. "Have you been stationed here for very long?"

"I work on guided missile systems and anti-mortar tech. I'm an engineer. I just moved in here a couple months ago. I was overseas in the Middle East until May, but before then, I was stationed in Hawaii. The only reason I was willing to come back here is because I found out that Mitch Stockley was dead."

Stockley had been killed *six* months ago, and Anne Timson had been in Iraq or Afghanistan at the time. Alibis didn't get much more airtight than military service in a different country.

"You didn't want to be in Norfolk while he was alive?" Sun asked. "Were you worried he was going to try to hurt you, or kill you?"

"Of course I was." Anne laughed, but the sound was dry, almost brittle. "He killed those other girls, didn't he? And they hadn't even had the chance to try to go to the police, but *I* was stupid enough to try. Obviously, I know better now, but at the time I thought I was doing the right thing."

"You did the right thing." Sun's reassurance was hushed, and she met the woman's amber eyes before she went on. "You didn't know how it'd turn out. And just because it turned out shitty doesn't mean you did anything wrong."

"Two more college girls went missing *after* I told the cops about him," Anne said, her gaze shifting from her to Levi and back. The dog bristled, looking from Anne to both agents, trying to understand the tension he was clearly feeling. "Two more, agents. I tried to tell them, but they wouldn't believe me until they had, I don't know, *hard evidence*? Whatever in the hell *that* means. Apparently, it means they needed more than just the word of some dumb, drunk college girl who claimed she'd been sexually assaulted."

Sun grated her teeth together, but her frustration wasn't directed at Anne. She was frustrated with the system that had failed this woman.

She could only assume the injustice was thanks to the same fucked up cosmic force that had saved Kent Strickland's life while a seventh-grade girl went into cardiac arrest on an operating room table. The same force that had granted that mass murderer a complete recovery while Sun would never regain the full range of motion in her left arm.

"It's great, though," Anne said, blowing out a breath. "Great that someone's finally looking into it now that that prick is dead. But you're not even looking into him, are you? You're trying to find who killed that piece of shit. No one gave a damn when I swallowed down all that shame to 'do the right thing' and report him to the police, but by god, now that *he's* dead, everyone's interested in solving it."

Sun understood the woman's fury. Matched it. She didn't even attempt to stop her from venting whatever she needed to say.

"You know, agents. I didn't kill him. That's pretty easy to prove. I was in Afghanistan trying to keep some Navy SEALs from getting blown up by mortars while they slept. I can't give you their names since that's classified, but I was there, and my personnel record will confirm it. I'm not close to any of my family, so I seriously doubt that any of them decided to kill Mitch Stockley to defend my honor. The only reason I'm back here is because one of my friends got stationed in Norfolk. And before you ask, they were with me in Afghanistan."

"Look, I get it." Sun held out her hands. She dropped them back into her lap when the dog growled. "More than you know, I get it. You weren't in the States when it happened, but I'm sure you've heard about the shooting at the Riverside Mall in Danville. About Tyler Haldane and Kent Strickland, right?"

Lips pursed, Anne nodded.

"I was there. Tyler Haldane shot me in the shoulder." For emphasis, Sun patted the site of her injury. "And I got to watch his asshole friend Kent Strickland make a miraculous recovery after I shot him in the head. All that while a thir-teen-year-old girl died in an operating room just down the hall from him. I'm sorry that the system failed you. I'm sorry that you had to go through any of that. And I'm sorry that all I can do now is say 'I'm sorry.' Because you're right. The only reason we're here is because Mitch Stockley is dead. Otherwise, who knows if the Norfolk PD would have ever brought the bureau into their case."

Connecting with witnesses on a personal level had never been Sun's strong suit. After all, that was why Levi was here in the first place. But Anne Timson was different. Sun and Anne shared the same righteous indignation.

With a sigh, Anne shrugged and patted the dog's head where he'd laid it in her lap, clearly trying to comfort his mistress. "It's done and over, I guess. Or it was, at least, until someone blew Stockley's head off. Honestly, agents, I hope you find whoever killed that asshole so I can shake their hand."

13

Winter couldn't remember a more informal graduation party than the get together at Autumn's apartment.

The atmosphere suited Winter just fine. She had never been keen on formal event celebrations. Her attendance at the commencement for her own graduation had been more for her grandparents than anything.

As luck would have it, Autumn and Winter shared the same love for German chocolate cake. When she spotted the rich dessert, Winter could hardly contain her excitement.

Bree had picked up the cake from the same bakery she had used for Winter's return to the FBI office several months earlier. The place was family owned and operated, and Bree and Shelby had commissioned them to make the cake for their upcoming wedding.

Once the pizzas arrived, the five of them shared a champagne toast, but even the formality of the fancy drink was downplayed by the mismatched glasses they all held. Shelby and Bree brought the bottle, so Autumn let them use the only two wine glasses she owned. Noah poured his into a plastic

Spiderman cup, and Winter and Autumn's cups both featured all the members of the Avengers.

The first time they raised their drinks for a toast, Noah had burst into laughter, and Autumn followed suit in short order.

When they touched their cups and glasses together for the second time, Winter thought that Autumn or Noah might spit out their champagne as they took the first drink. They held themselves together, but then it was Winter's turn to succumb to a giggling fit. The sight of Noah's amused smile was such a relief from the past twenty-four hours that she hardly knew what to do with her giddiness.

Giddy. Her. Winter Black.

It still amazed her that she could feel anything other than the oppressive darkness that had pressed on her shoulders for so long.

The ghost of her brother.

And now, the ghost of the man who had haunted her every waking hour for years.

No, she said to herself. *Don't think of either of them right now.*

There were still shadows of uncertainty that threatened to engulf her in darkness, but that night, surrounded by the laughter of her friends, she felt for the first time that everything might pan out.

She still wasn't sure what "everything" entailed, but based on the pitter-patter in her chest whenever her eyes met Noah's, she could safely say it involved him.

No matter what her future held, she *wanted* it to involve him. As a friend or more, she wanted him there.

She didn't know what that meant for her relationship with Aiden, but tonight wasn't the time to deal with those lingering doubts. The lighthearted atmosphere in Autumn's apartment was a much-needed reprieve from the stress and tension that had abounded in the FBI office over the last few days.

Ever since Tyler Haldane was shot and killed, they'd been in a race against the clock. As each hour, each minute ticked by, more speculation about the nature of Haldane's death circulated throughout national and international news networks.

Was Tyler Haldane's death just the start? Would others around the United States take the killer's lead and execute other mass murderers?

The country's political climate was strained almost to its breaking point, and there was no shortage of those who clung to and sensationalized Haldane's death to capture the attention of their audience.

But that night, neither Tyler Haldane nor Kent Strickland were mentioned, not even in passing.

When Winter and Noah presented their joint graduation gift, Autumn wrapped them each in a bear hug. Shelby and Bree's present was an unassuming envelope, inside of which was a gift card to a department store Shelby swore by.

"It's for two hundred and fifty," Shelby said with a wide smile. "Figured you could use a little boost to help with the wardrobe changes you'll have to make after you get this job."

Autumn's eyes widened, and Shelby's grin only brightened.

"Oh my god," Autumn managed, tears causing her eyes to gleam. "Well, now I guess I really *have* to nail that interview tomorrow, huh?"

Shelby waved a dismissive hand. "That was a given."

"Okay, well," Autumn laughed. "We're going to have to have another one of these get-togethers again soon so I can thank you all for these awesome gifts. I'll show off all my new clothes and make us a bunch of food in this super sweet stand mixer."

"You could make a German chocolate cake," Winter suggested with a grin.

"I could, and I will. We'll have cake for dinner, as long as everyone's okay with that."

"I could eat cake for every meal of the day," Bree put in, rubbing her belly for emphasis.

"I'll make each of you your own cake." Autumn's eyes seemed brighter as she glanced to each of them. "Winter gets a German chocolate cake, obviously. Noah, what's your favorite flavor?"

The smile on Winter's lips didn't waver as she looked to where Noah sat at her side. When his eyes met hers, a mirror of her warm expression made its way to his face.

"Pineapple upside down," he answered. "Unless we're counting cheesecake, then cheesecake. Doesn't matter what kind, just cheesecake."

"Everyone loves cheesecake," Winter agreed. "But we've got to give regular cake its credit. It's still delicious."

"You're not wrong." Autumn knelt down to scoop up the fluffy little dog with the underbite. "Even Toad likes cheesecake. And speaking of, I should take him out. You guys think you can hold down the fort while we're gone?"

"I'll go with you." Winter pushed to her feet. "You guys all sort through your opinions on cake, all right?"

With a snort of laughter, Noah nodded.

After Autumn clipped the retractable leash to Toad's collar and grabbed a plastic baggie, she and Winter set out into the balmy evening.

The persistent dampness of humidity still hung in the air, but with the slight breeze came the first hints of the changing seasons. In a month, there would be Halloween candy in stores, people would have hung up their pumpkin decorations, and pumpkin spice everything would be available in coffee shops and restaurants alike.

Even if the change in weather wasn't as dramatic as it had been in Albany, Winter still looked forward to the shift. As much as she liked the warmth and sunshine of the summer months, by the end of August, she was ready for a new season.

And this year was already different.

This year would be the first seasonal shift where The Preacher, where *Kilroy*, wasn't front and center in her mind.

She was glad the man was dead, but what did that mean for her future plans? After all, the entire reason she was here was because of Douglas Kilroy.

Without him, where did that leave her?

It leaves me as an FBI agent with plenty of other scumbags to put away, she reminded herself. Before the uncertainty took over, she decided it was time to change her train of thought.

"Hey." She glanced over to Autumn.

"Yeah?" Autumn asked as she met Winter's curious gaze.

"I don't think I got a chance to ask you about it, but how did that, that *thing* with Aiden go?"

Even as she posed the query, Winter wasn't sure what had sparked her curiosity. What puzzled her even more was her sudden hope that Autumn's face would brighten as she regaled her and Aiden's renewed friendship.

Then it dawned on her.

She wanted her old friend to have an interest in Autumn so he wouldn't be hurt or angered when he discovered that Winter was getting over her teenage crush and hero worship of him.

Even though she'd known Aiden for thirteen years, she couldn't honestly say she knew his "type." Hell, she didn't even know if he *had* a type. But regardless of the host of question marks, she suspected that a woman with a doctoral degree in forensic psychology ought to be right up his alley.

Winter had never played matchmaker before, but she thought she ought to brush up on the skill set.

Autumn shrugged as Winter pulled herself away from the moment of contemplation.

"It was fine," she answered. "He wasn't a dick, so I guess that's progress. He sent me a text this afternoon to say congrats, but I still don't think I'd call us friends. Besides, something tells me I'm not quite the right type of person to be friends with that guy."

Furrowing her brows, Winter looked over to Autumn. "What do you mean?"

"He's too…" she paused to wave her hand as she searched for the term, "polished, I guess. Put together. It's like he's got all his shit together, and I most definitely don't. I tried to date a guy like that, and I guess it went all right for four years, but then it crashed and burned like a Michael Bay explosion. So, based on that, I'd say it probably extends to friendships too."

As the next thought popped into her mind, Winter could hardly suppress a chortle. "You think you'd be a bad influence on Aiden if you guys were friends?"

The corners of Autumn's eyes creased as her lips parted in a grin. "You know what, yeah. We'll go with that."

Toad trotted from a patch of grass to the sidewalk, and Winter and Autumn took their cue to return to the apartment building.

"How about that whole Nico Culetti thing?" Winter asked as she pulled open the heavy glass door.

"Haven't seen anyone creeping around here, and believe me, I've been looking. I'm hoping that the mob looks at failed hits like that the same way you'd look at a failed business venture. Hopefully, they're pissed at whoever hired Nico, and not so much at me for, well, you know. For actually killing him."

"If there isn't any money in it for them, I doubt they'd come all the way down here from D.C. just to put themselves on the FBI's radar by antagonizing someone who was under the bureau's protection."

Thoughts of both Nico Culetti and Aiden Parrish were abandoned as Winter and Autumn made their way inside and joined their friends around the stone surfaced coffee table.

They resumed the discussion about cake, and Winter learned that Bree's favorite flavor was lemon while Shelby's was red velvet.

When eleven o'clock rolled around, Shelby and Bree bade them farewell. Bree proclaimed her role as designated driver, and Winter realized that neither she nor Noah had taken on the responsibility. No one was flat-out drunk, but based on the overall air of chattiness, no one was sober, either.

By the time they decided to take an Uber back to their shared apartment complex, it was almost midnight.

For the duration of the trip, Winter contemplated whether or not to bring up her idea to try to set Autumn up with Aiden. She knew Noah wasn't a fan of the man, but she also suspected that he viewed Aiden as a sort of competition. Whether that competition was driven by friendship or something more, she was less sure.

If his concern was based in friendship—if he thought Aiden was a bad person and worried he might hurt her somehow—then Winter didn't want to broach the subject. But if the concern had more to do with jealousy, then a casual mention of her plan to set Aiden up with *someone else* would be a source of relief for Noah.

Despite the weightless sensation of the alcohol's buzz, she couldn't summon up the fortitude to broach the subject by the time their driver pulled up to their building.

As they stepped out of the sedan and waved goodbye to

the young man, Winter was overcome with a sudden bout of nervousness. Her heartbeat hammered in her ears, and she licked her lips against the sudden dryness in her mouth.

The night air was still, and in the late hour, no other residents of the complex milled about the area. In that moment, she was pointedly aware of how alone she and Noah were.

She wanted to say something charming and complimentary, but as the seconds of silence passed, she couldn't put together a string of words that sounded more compelling than what a third grader might say to their crush.

When his green eyes flicked over to hers, she abandoned the effort altogether.

Would this be the last time they had a moment like this?

Life was chaos, and who knew where they'd be a week from now. Maybe he'd meet the woman of his dreams on a trip to the grocery store, or maybe he'd decide to request a transfer to Dallas or Houston—some city closer to his family. Maybe an old flame would surface, and Winter would be all but forgotten.

The thought made her stomach drop, and she was sure the mental image spurred on her next question. "Do you want to have another beer and maybe watch an episode of *Game of Thrones?*" she asked before she lost her nerve.

As soon as the words left her mouth, she wanted to vacuum them back up. He was smart and observant, and more than that, he knew her better than almost anyone. If he didn't pick up on the real nature of her query, she would have been more than surprised.

But they had been here before, hadn't they?

Not long after she first moved to the apartment, they'd gone out to a bar together for a long night of drinking. When they got back to the door of her home—the same spot where they now stood—they had both been three sheets to the wind. She had made the same offer then, and months later, she still felt like a jackass.

There was a wistful tinge in his smile as he shook his head. "I don't think that'd be a great idea, darlin'. It's past midnight now, and we've got work tomorrow bright and early. I don't need to be hungover while we work on this dumpster fire of a case, you know?"

"Right," she agreed quickly. "Yeah, good point. As long as I drink a bunch of water right now, I don't think I'll be hungover tomorrow. But you're right, if I keep drinking, I probably will be."

"Exactly." He grinned as he tapped his temple. "See, you can drink on a work night, you've just got to be a little smart about it."

Winter liked to think she knew Noah as well as he knew her, and she was confident that the hangover to which he referred wasn't an actual hangover.

Shit.

Even as she offered him a smile and a departing hug, she knew she wouldn't sleep well that night.

She'd toss and turn as she tried desperately to think of a way to curb the awkwardness she knew loomed on the horizon.

BEN ORMUND and Mitch Stockley shared so much common ground that I was almost surprised to learn they were two different people.

The men looked nothing alike, but they shared the same predatory characteristics: they preyed on young, vulnerable women. Ormund and Stockley both stalked their victims on college campuses before they lured them into a vehicle to abduct and sexually assault them. Where Stockley had used his profession in real estate to attend seminars and scope out future victims, the college campus was Ben Ormund's home turf.

Once upon a time, Ormund had been a counselor. Allegations of sexual misconduct with clients led to the revocation of his license to practice, but no criminal charges were ever pressed.

As best as I could tell, Ormund had used a few of his connections in the world of psychiatry to sweep the entire debacle under the figurative rug.

When he returned to Christopher Newport University as a faculty member in the psychology department, it was like nothing had ever happened.

After a couple years as a professor, Ormund made even more money than he had as a private counselor. And now, twenty years and countless victims later, I watched him flick off the light in the foyer before he strode into the kitchen.

The miserable son of a bitch lived by himself in the house, and his property was all alone on a plot of land near a rocky portion of the coast.

I'd been inside a few times, and as much as I hated Ben Ormund's existence, I could admit that the interior was tasteful. But I was also sure Ormund hadn't been responsible for the modern décor.

The east side of the house was comprised mostly of glass to showcase its unique, modern architecture. Apparently, Ormund didn't think he had much to worry about in terms of security.

Maybe the glass was sturdy, but I doubted it was made well enough to withstand a .338 Lapua Magnum.

Huddled in a rocky outcropping a couple hundred yards from the expensive house, I peered through the lens of the long-range scope as Ormund pried open the stainless-steel refrigerator.

I could have broken in again. I could have waited in the shadows until he stuck his head in the fridge to search for dinner, and then I could have stabbed him in the back with a hunting knife.

I could have, but by now, I knew the Feds would have realized that the same rifle I held in my hands had been used to kill Mitch Stockley *and* Tyler Haldane.

Whether or not they'd drawn the conclusion that I was the only killer, I still wasn't sure. But if they hadn't figured it out yet, they would know by the time the sun rose into the sky the following day.

And tomorrow, I'd make sure they knew this was only the start.

Though I had no personal vendetta with the Federal Bureau of Investigation—they were a force for good, after all —I wanted them to know that the same person had wiped Mitch Stockley, Tyler Haldane, and Ben Ormund off the face of the planet.

I wasn't under any illusion that I was about to start a revolution—I knew that the sleazy underbelly of society was here to stay. I knew the men I killed were only a drop in the bucket, but I'd be damned if I didn't do *something*.

No one had looked out for the women and girls Ormund and Stockley had brutalized, and the ideals espoused by men like Haldane emboldened the creeps to act on their perverse impulses.

But for as long as I was able, I would make sure some of those men paid for what they had done.

And in my world, there was only one price I would accept.

I wanted their lives.

14

Other than their usual morning greeting, Noah and Winter spoke little on the short trip it took to the FBI office. Like he'd anticipated the night before, he wasn't hungover, but thanks to the litany of "what-if" scenarios that had flitted through his head as he tried to sleep, he wasn't well rested, either.

They'd Ubered back to get his truck since he didn't want to stuff himself into Winter's little Civic, which had caused her to roll her eyes. Stifling a yawn with one hand, he flicked on the blinker with the other. "I don't know about you, but I need coffee," he said.

From the corner of his eye, he caught Winter's nod. "Me too. I slept like shit."

"You too, huh?"

"Yeah." Her voice was quiet, even strained.

He pulled up as close as he dared to the last car in line. When he went to run a hand through his hair, he stopped the motion short of his forehead. Since he'd become so negligent in visiting a barber, he had figured a few weeks ago that he ought to at least style his hair, lest it turn into a shaggy mess.

At least five days out of the week, he wore a suit and tie to work, and a haphazard mop of hair didn't accompany the professional air that federal agents were supposed to exude.

Then again, if he'd ever remember to get a damn haircut, he wouldn't have to bother.

"I'm sorry." Winter's sudden apology was hurried, almost weary.

Her voice snapped his thoughts away from his sense of fashion as he turned to look at her. Fidgeting with the hair at the end of her braid, her blue eyes darted back and forth.

"What for?" he asked.

"Last night." With a sigh, she shook her head. "I didn't mean to, you know, make anything weird. I've got a knack for doing that, don't I?"

As much as he wanted to know more about her motivation for the offer, he bit his tongue and gave her a quick smile.

In all honesty, his uncertainty about her motivation was the main reason he had turned her down in the first place. They'd established that neither of them was drunk, but at the same time, he didn't want to risk an act that either of them might regret. He didn't want to risk an act that would drive a wedge between them.

He had only recently begun to feel like their friendship was on steady ground.

Before, he'd wondered almost every day if she would up and disappear like she had at the end of the Kilroy investigation. He never doubted Winter's convictions. Loyalty and duty to those for whom she cared came before almost anything else, but those ideals had taken a back seat to her desire to find Douglas Kilroy.

Both Winter and Aiden had played the people around them like a set of pawns on a chessboard, but in the end, each of their master plans fell apart.

When he thought of the Machiavellian tactics she'd pulled out of her hat during the Kilroy investigation, he realized they had still not talked about those dark months. And as much as he didn't want to bring up the painful memories, he knew they'd have to have the conversation one of these days, especially in light of the idea that their friendship might become more than platonic.

But if he was going to rip open that old wound, he needed to be damn sure there was a good reason. Though he wanted to think that she was interested in the same type of relationship development as he, he wasn't about to hazard another guess.

He wouldn't make another emotional confession unless she was the first to reveal her feelings.

In the meantime, the last thing he wanted to be was the creepy friend who kept pushing boundaries. The start might have been rocky, but he valued their friendship, and he respected Winter too much to turn into the guy whose advances she had to turn down twice a week.

"Nothing's weird, darlin'," he finally managed. "Don't sweat it, all right?"

"This might sound weird, but," she paused to sigh again, "I think I like it when you fall asleep on my couch. There's something comforting about waking up with your best friend so close by. It's just, working this job, putting as many hours into it as we do some weeks, it feels isolating sometimes. But when you're around someone you care about in just some of those little places, like when you wake up in the morning, it makes you feel a little less alone. At least that's how it feels for me, I guess I can't say the same for you."

He kept his expression nonchalant and thoughtful as he shrugged.

The words were among the last he'd expected to hear

from her, and he knew he'd need more than just a few seconds to parse through the meaning.

"I think I'm used to living alone," he said, choosing his words carefully. "But I see what you're saying. It's keeping that connection, right? It's easier to keep it if your friend is actually there, if you can actually see them."

"Right," she replied with a nod. "Yeah, I think that's it. Almost like it's a reminder or something. A reminder that I've actually got a friend. Or friends."

"Maybe you need a roommate." He chuckled. "You should see if Autumn's planning to move to a new place once she nails this interview and gets that job."

"Are you kidding?" When Winter chortled at the remark, the tenseness and uncertainty seemed to vanish from the air. "I looked up how much money private forensic psychologists make. Even when they're new, they can make more than a SAC, unless the SAC has been there forever. She's going to be *loaded.*"

"So? Then you can mooch off her. Shit, maybe we should all be roommates. I'll live in the basement."

"Oh my god." Winter's laugh made him smile even bigger. "She's pretty sharp. I think she'd catch on, and I don't know how much she'd appreciate a couple FBI agents freeloading, even if she *is* raking in the cash."

"Now, I never said anything about freeloadin'," he proclaimed, raising a hand. "I'll cook, and I'll clean the pool."

"So, you're a pool boy now, huh, Dalton? You know, I think right now we're getting pretty close to the intro to some cheesy romance novel or a Lifetime movie."

"Easy way to avoid that," he said with a dismissive wave. "I'll just put on some coveralls whenever I go out to clean it. That way neither of you ladies has to worry about drooling on yourselves." He turned to offer her an exaggerated wink.

"Well, that's boring," she scoffed. "Here we were on the

cusp of a reality show that'd land us a gig on MTV, and you had to go and ruin it by putting a shirt on."

"What?" His face was beginning to hurt from smiling so much. "I don't know how I should take that. You think people would pay money to see me without a shirt on?"

The little smirk on her lips was just short of wicked, the glint in her eyes mischievous. He'd never seen her wear such a look before. In fact, he realized he'd never seen any remotely flirtatious side of the stoic woman at his side. Until now, he wasn't even sure she knew *how* to come across as playful, but he liked it.

He *really* liked it.

He and Winter hardly had enough time to get settled at their desks before they were summoned to a meeting with the Associate Deputy Director, Cassidy Ramirez. On their way up to the woman's office, they were both quiet, and Noah could only assume that the same litany of scenarios was running through Winter's head too.

"Probably one of the people we got in touch with over the past few days," he suggested, his voice an octave lower than usual.

Winter's blue eyes snapped over to him, and she nodded. "Probably."

"But being called up to a meeting with the ADD isn't exactly my preferred way to start the day," he muttered as an afterthought.

"Could be something to do with the press too," she put in. "Maybe the media coverage of this thing is ramping up, and the bureau needs someone to look pretty for the camera."

"Man," he said with a quiet snort of laughter. "You're really on a roll today, aren't you?"

As a light chime sounded out, she flashed him a knowing smile.

The rest of the journey was made in silence, and as soon as they neared the doorway of Ramirez's office, any air of amusement that might have survived was snuffed out by the woman's grave countenance.

To the side of her polished mahogany desk, Aiden Parrish stood with his arms crossed over his chest. As his icy blue eyes flicked from him to Winter, the man's irritation was plain to see.

Whatever the purpose of the unscheduled meeting, Parrish was none too happy about it.

"Agents," the Associate Deputy Director greeted with a slight smile. "Close the door behind you, please."

Nodding, Noah eased the glass and metal door closed behind himself. When he turned, Ramirez waved a hand at the two squat chairs in front of her spacious desk.

"Have a seat."

He and Winter exchanged glances before they accepted the offer. There was so much strain in the air, Noah almost thought he could taste it. If Ramirez or Parrish didn't start talking soon, he was sure he might lose his mind.

"Thanks for coming on such short notice," Ramirez finally said, folding both hands atop the desk in front of her. "I'm sure you've already been able to pick up that the reason you're here isn't necessarily one that's chock-full of joy."

When neither he nor Winter replied, a ghost of a smile passed over Ramirez's face as she nodded. "Fair enough. Let's just get right down to it, then. You guys have been working for Max for a while, so I'm sure you're used to his no-nonsense approach to meetings. He and I started with the bureau around the same time, and I can tell you he's always been like that."

She paused, seeming to expect some comment. "Yes, ma'am," was all Noah could think to offer.

It seemed to be enough because she went on. "He was a Marine before he joined the FBI, I don't know if you two knew that or not. We worked together for quite a while before we took on our respective leadership positions, but he never mentioned any more about his service than that." She paused, pursed her lips, and then laughed quietly. "I'm sorry. I just said I wanted to get right down to the point, and then I went off on a spiel about something else."

Noah forced an agreeable expression to his face.

Someone needed to say something. *Now.*

"It's about our case," she said. "And I'm sure neither of you are real optimistic about a surprise meeting with your ADD, so I'll nip that in the bud right now and tell you that neither of you have done anything wrong. This isn't a reprimand. Actually, it's pretty much the farthest thing from a reprimand."

Noah relaxed. "That's good to hear."

Ramirez smiled. "You two have done excellent work in the short time you've been here. I know you've heard me say that, and I don't doubt you've heard it from Max too. You've been working hard on this case, the Haldane and Stockley case, and that's why you're here."

Noah's ball sac tightened. They were getting to the point, and the point wasn't good. Shit. What had happened now?

Ramirez didn't make him wait for long. "This morning, a housecleaner arrived for work at the same place she'd been working for the last six years, and she found the homeowner dead."

"And you think it's related to Haldane and Stockley?" Winter surmised.

The ADD nodded. "We know it is. It's the same weapon, and based on the trajectory of the bullet, or at least what they've been able to analyze so far, he was shot from a distance of about a half-mile. No one heard it, so there's a possibility they used a sound suppressor. Then again, the house was pretty isolated, so that's not necessarily set in stone."

Noah nodded his understanding, but he knew they wouldn't be in a meeting with the ADD just to go over a new crime scene, even if the scene *was* affiliated with the same person who had killed Haldane and Stockley.

Teeth grated together, a forced countenance of neutrality on his face, he waited for Ramirez to drop the bombshell. To tell them why they were *really* there.

"I know what's been established about those shots," Ramirez advised. This time, her dark eyes flicked over to Aiden. "That the person who fired them had to have been trained by either the military or law enforcement. And, Agent Black, Agent Dalton, that's why you're here. You're here because we think the person responsible is involved in law enforcement."

Jaw clenched, he merely nodded. He'd known all along there was a real possibility that the killer of Tyler Haldane and Mitch Stockley was a disillusioned law enforcement agent. The bombshell was close, but that wasn't it.

"When we consider that, and we consider that all three of the victims we've got now are local to the state of Virginia and that Stockley and Haldane's crimes fall within our jurisdiction, we can't rule out agents in this office." For emphasis, Ramirez jabbed her index finger at the surface of the wooden desk.

"This office?" Noah echoed. "Like who? You think one of *us* might've done this?"

The ADD nodded slowly. "Look at the shot that killed Haldane. It was made from a distance of over three-fourths of a mile in a light breeze. The weapon used was a Barrett

Model 98 Bravo sniper rifle. I know I don't have to tell you two that's a military-grade weapon. There aren't even very many law enforcement agencies that use M98Bs, but when they do, they're usually handled by a designated marksman."

"A sniper." Noah managed a quick glance to Aiden Parrish.

The look of distaste on the man's face had only deepened. What the hell kind of announcement had they walked into, anyway?

"A sniper, right." Ramirez tapped her fingers on the desk. Just once, then she appeared to catch herself and folded them together again. She was nervous, Noah realized. He'd never seen her nervous before. It caused his own anxiety to rachet up.

She cleared her throat. "We have several skilled marksmen in our tactical team, but other than them, that only leaves a few others who are capable of the kind of shot that killed Haldane. You were in the military, weren't you, Agent Dalton?"

He kept his expression blank as he nodded. "There was always more math involved in that sort of thing than I cared for." Was he a suspect? Sweat bloomed in his armpits as he forced a lazy drawl to his voice. "Lot of off-the-cuff trigonometry. Not exactly my scene."

"Don't worry," she replied, the faintest hint of mirth in her dark eyes. "You weren't on the short list. No, other than the tactical folks, there're only four others who have a documented history of being able to land a shot like that. One in organized crime, but we can rule her out because she's been out in Chicago for the past few weeks. Another in white collar crimes, but he was here when Haldane was shot, so that rules him out too."

Beside him, Winter leaned forward. Noah could practically hear her heart beating.

"Then there's Agent Weyrick in Violent Crimes. He works the night shift, so aside from this case, you might not have had a lot of previous interactions with him. He was in the military for six years before he joined the bureau, and I remember one of his recommendations mentioned what a skilled marksman he was. But he was here when Haldane was killed, and he was here when our most recent victim was killed too. That leaves us with one."

When Noah dared another look at Aiden Parrish, he swore he could almost hear the man's teeth grind together. "Agent Ming," he grated.

"Sun Ming?" Noah echoed, furrowing his brows. "I knew she'd won a lot of awards for marksmanship, but you really think she would've up and killed three people?"

"It's not a matter of what I think, or even what I feel," Cassidy replied with a shake of her head. "It's a matter of where the evidence leads us. And at this point, a great deal of it is pointed in Agent Ming's direction."

Winter looked as stunned as he felt. "How so?"

Ramirez glanced at Aiden, but he didn't open his mouth.

With a look of consternation, the ADD spelled it out. "First, Agent Ming doesn't have an alibi for the Haldane murder, and she was in Norfolk yesterday to follow-up with a victim. The man who was shot last night was in Newport News."

The silence that settled in seemed to permeate every crack, every crevasse, every pore. It was suffocating, and the only reason Noah spoke was so he would not drown under its leaden weight. "What else?"

"The most damning at this juncture is how vocal Agent Ming has been regarding what she considers to be a grievous miscarriage of karmic justice that both Kent Strickland and Tyler Haldane lived while so many perished or received a permanent injury, including herself."

Noah swallowed the bile that wanted to backtrack up his throat. He had no love for Sun Ming, but she was a fellow agent. He hated this. "Why us?" he asked.

"You know Agent Ming well enough, but at the same time, neither of you are friends of hers. You're close enough to her to pick up on any little cues or oddities, and you're far enough away from her that you won't be biased by your own perceptions." Ramirez laced her fingers together. "I'm not saying with one-hundred-percent certainty that the killer *is* Agent Ming, but what I am saying with one-hundred-percent certainty is this..."

Blood roared in Noah's ears as the ADD leaned forward.

"We can't rule her out. She might be one of us, but we've known from the start that was a possibility. And until we can rule her out as a possibility, I need you two to be on your toes."

15

The calm air and the cozy scent of coffee and baked goods was a stark contrast to the wariness that simmered in Aiden's mind.

He still didn't know why Cassidy Ramirez had called on him after she'd parsed through personnel records to establish the likelihood that Sun Ming was involved in the deaths of Mitch Stockley and Tyler Haldane. Did Ramirez think that he held a grudge against Sun and that his distaste would lead him to take a particularly critical view of her actions? Did she think he wanted revenge?

To be sure, the end of his and Sun's relationship was far from amicable. There had been plenty of four-letter words and threats, but in the end, Aiden and Sun were professionals. Their vendetta with one another had not bled over to the FBI office, even when their dynamic was at its worst.

And now, after more than two years, enough time had passed since the messy split that he could say with some confidence that he was indifferent toward Sun. Whether or not the attitude was shared, he was unsure.

He doubted that Ramirez had been motivated by such a

petty sentiment. Cassidy Ramirez was also a professional, not an angsty teenager. The ADD had needed an expert in human behavior, and that was why she had called him, not due to a lingering misgiving about Sun Ming.

And now, *he* needed an expert in human behavior.

Sun Ming had not gone rogue; he was sure of it. Or, at least, he *wanted* to be sure of it. She was ambitious, but he knew that becoming a vigilante wasn't on her list of job prospects.

As he took a tentative sip of the chai latte he'd ordered, he glanced up to where the newest patron pushed their way through the glass double doors.

Some of her hair had been pinned back with a shiny clip, and the rest fell over her shoulders in loose waves. Though it had been less than a week since he last saw her, he could tell that her hair was a darker shade of auburn.

He'd never fully understood people—men and women alike—who dyed their hair, but when he thought of Autumn's response to the question, he felt the faintest hint of a smile tug at the corner of his mouth.

"Why does anyone do anything for their appearance?" she had said, fixing him with a matter-of-fact look as she held her hands out to the side. "For vanity, duh. Why do you always dress like you're headed to the Oscars? Seems like a band t-shirt and a pair of cargo shorts would take a lot less effort. You'd cut twenty minutes off your morning routine, easy. Not to mention all the money you'd save at the dry cleaners."

With the same hand he now raised in greeting, he had tipped an invisible hat to her logic.

He had gone on to speculate about how he should handle casual Fridays at the FBI office, much to her amusement. Self-deprecating humor wasn't in his usual sarcastic repertoire, but it never ceased to elicit a laugh or a smile from her.

She waved back before she gestured to the counter and the barista.

At half-past eleven in the morning on a weekday, there were only a handful of people seated throughout the open space. He'd picked a table in the far corner, well out of the range of any curious listeners.

As he waited for her to receive her drink, he checked his phone for any new communication.

Winter and Noah were on their way to Newport News, and Winter had assured him she would keep him updated with any pertinent details as they arose.

He had considered calling off the last-minute meet up with Autumn in favor of personally viewing the newest crime scene, but he'd shot down the idea almost as soon as it formed. He was the SSA for the Behavioral Analysis Unit, and there was much more to a murder investigation than just the examination of physical evidence.

If Ramirez wanted to label Sun Ming a suspect, then he would leave no stone unturned, no avenue unexplored.

Not because they had a history—if anything, their sordid past would have dissuaded him from making the effort—but because she was a tenured federal agent who had taken a bullet in the line of duty. The victims so far might not have warranted going above and beyond the normal investigative expectations, but the ADD's alleged suspect was a different story entirely.

Pocketing the smartphone, he snapped himself out of the contemplation as Autumn picked her way across the room.

For only the second time since he'd met her, he didn't feel overdressed. The light green of her patterned, button-down shirt matched her eyes, and the gray cardigan matched her flats. He pulled his gaze away from her black slacks, away from where the fabric clung to her hips and offered her a smile.

"Hey," she greeted.

He didn't miss an unfamiliar wariness in her eyes. Was it hesitance, or suspicion? Or was it lingering nerves from the interview she'd only just finished?

"Hey," he replied. "You seem edgy. How'd the interview go?"

There was only one way to approach Autumn Trent, and that was to be straightforward. Any time he had tried to subtly prod her for information, she had seen right through the words.

As she sipped at her drink, she nodded. "It went well."

"Seems like a pretty fast turnaround. You just got your Ph.D. like five minutes ago, right?"

"Well." She paused to look thoughtful. "Not really. A lot of Ph.D. candidates have jobs lined up before they even graduate. They did the interview so quickly because they need someone soon. Their work is really specialized, so it can be hard to find replacements on short notice."

"Replacements? So, you're replacing someone?"

Her eyes flitted away from his as she shrugged. "Yeah, they lost one of their people recently."

"Lost?" he echoed. "As in?"

"They died."

"Wait, what?" he managed. She had explained the risk of a career as a forensic psychologist while she had been under the protective supervision of the bureau, but even though he believed her, he hadn't expected the dangers to hit so close to home so soon. "One of the psychologists at this firm was killed recently, and now you're going to take their spot?"

She was already shaking her head before he finished. "No, not murdered. She killed herself."

He felt a pang of guilt for the relief that came with the short explanation.

Though he hadn't figured out what to do with his affinity

for this redheaded beauty, he couldn't deny its existence. Even in the limited time since they had been introduced, he had discovered more common ground with her than anyone he'd met in recent memory. Hell, she even shared his secret love of Code Red Mountain Dew. Unlike him, however, she openly admitted it.

At the absolute least, he hoped she would be a long-term professional colleague. Aiden had worked damn hard to get where he was, and that included all he'd learned about psychology and criminology, but he could admit when someone knew more than him.

Autumn Trent had been granted her Ph.D. without the usual request that she revise or otherwise change parts of her dissertation. Between her unquestionable intelligence, her intensive field of study, and the unnerving ability she had to see straight through someone, he figured he couldn't ask for a better consultant for behavioral questions.

"I'm not going to get murdered," she said, breaking a spell of quiet. He wasn't sure how much time had passed since he spoke, but her green eyes were back on him.

With a slight smile, he took a drink of the chai latte. "I know. Someone already tried and failed."

"But," she took a sip of her drink, "they did offer me the job. I haven't told anyone else yet, but I filled out the regulatory hiring paperwork before I left to come here. I also got a chai, and you're right. It's delicious. Thanks for the recommendation."

In truth, he wasn't surprised by the announcement. She was brilliant, and any employer would have to be inept to turn her away.

"In that case," he said as he extended a hand to her. "Let me be the first person to say congratulations, Dr. Trent."

As he had hoped, a wide smile brightened her face, but

the expression seemed to dim when she accepted the hand-shake. "Thank you."

"You're welcome. For that, and for the chai recommenda-tion. Just so you know, though, not every place makes good chai. You've been warned." He pushed her sudden wariness out of his thoughts and offered her a quick smile before he straightened in his chair.

"Fair enough." She chuckled, but he thought the sound didn't hold the joy it usually did. "So, what's up, Aiden?"

"What do you mean?"

"Why did you want to have coffee, or chai, I guess, with me?" She arched an eyebrow and took another long sip of her drink.

"To tell you congratulations. I mean, you just got a Ph.D. That's a pretty significant event, isn't it? Seems like some-thing worthy of a drink. I would've made it alcoholic, but we're inundated with work right now." He feigned an inno-cent look and shrugged.

Christ, it really was pointless to try to be anything other than straightforward with her, wasn't it?

"Uh-huh." The corner of her mouth moved into a hint of a smile as she rolled her eyes. "A congratulatory meetup where I've got to buy my own latte. Seems legit."

"I can give you five dollars," he replied with a smirk.

The joy in her laugh was back. "No, it's fine. I'm fine, thank you."

He slowly reached to his pocket as he met her gaze. "Are you sure?" he prodded.

"Fine," she huffed, reaching out to wave her fingers expectantly. "Cough it up, Parrish."

The smirk turned into a full-blown grin. "I don't have any cash."

"You are the *worst*." With a cross between a snort and a

laugh, she stacked her arms over her chest and shook her head.

"I can go to an ATM." He made a show of glancing around the café. "If they don't have one here, I saw one outside the place next door."

"I'll send you an invoice." She waved a dismissive hand. "But you're lucky today. I'm actually not busy, so I've got time for whatever the real reason you asked me to meet you here is."

Nope. He couldn't get anything across this woman.

"Honestly? I was curious what you were going to be doing now that you graduated. I heard Winter mention it, or at least mention that you had an interview with a private firm. I do have something I wanted to ask you about too."

"Efficiency," she surmised with a slight smirk. "I can respect that."

"Plus, it seemed like a good opportunity to double-check to see if you'd consider a career at the Federal Bureau of Investigation."

"Efficiency *and* persistence. I can see why you've made it so high up the FBI's food chain."

Though her wink was mostly sarcastic, there was another sentiment hidden behind the casual gesture. In that moment, he wished he had her uncanny knack for reading people. If he kept trying to puzzle over her motives, he would only drive himself insane.

"I'll take that as a compliment," he replied instead. "You're going to be doing a threat assessment, right?"

"Yeah." She nodded. "Workplace violence, recidivism, sexual assault, things like that. It's similar to what you do, I guess, but it's usually proactive versus reactive. And, hey," holding out both hands, she flashed a wide smile, "the partners at this firm said that they get contracted to do work for the government, and that includes the FBI. So, pretty soon, these Q-and-A sessions will be on the clock."

"I'm guessing my five bucks won't take me very far then, will it?"

"Nope," she said on a laugh. Her expression softened, and for a split-second, she almost looked vulnerable. "I know I've been giving you a lot of shit about it, but I actually like having someone to talk with about this kind of stuff. Someone other than another grad student or a professor, I mean. Someone with real-world experience in the field, someone who's actually had to interact with offenders on a regular basis."

He wasn't sure he could have kept the smile from his face if he tried. There had been an unfamiliar pang of guilt at the half-assed effort to coax her to a coffee shop under the guise of congratulations for her impressive academic feat. He was used to employing whatever tactics were necessary to get the answers he needed to clear a case, but whether it was due to the near disastrous exchange less than a week ago or the strange bond they'd formed, she was different.

"I'm glad. I'd hate for you to start billing me by the hour."

"If you saw the number that was on the job offer they gave me today, yeah, you really would." She hugged herself as she laughed this time, delight exuding from every pore. "Really, though, I'm happy to help." She turned serious again. "What's up?"

His smile faded as he turned his thoughts back to the Tyler Haldane case.

He could keep up the lighthearted dialogue with Autumn for longer than he could sustain a conversation with most people, but she was right.

"Based on that look, whatever it is, it isn't good." Her tone had sobered, and she propped her elbows on top of the wooden table as she fixed her attention on him.

"No," he replied. "No, it's not."

"Does it have anything to do with Tyler Haldane?"

"Yeah, kind of." In spite of the feeling of trust she invoked in him, he still had to be careful to keep the sensitive details of their case to himself. "In your knowledge, how common is it to run across something like, I don't know, like Frank Castle, The Punisher? An ex-military or ex-cop who just got fed up with everything and decided to take the law into their own hands, that sort of thing?"

She studied his face, frowned at whatever she read there. "Not all that common."

"It sounds like there's more to it than that," he pressed.

She sighed. "Maybe, but it's not usually something that cops like to hear."

"You ought to know by now that I'm not a usual cop," he advised, his stare unwavering.

"No, I suppose you're not."

"Let's hear it, then."

Shaking her head, she sighed again. "Based on everything I've studied, it's uncommon because most disgruntled cops tend to find a way to express their anger in their job. They bend rules, break rules, and just generally do shady shit, and a lot of the time that's enough of a release that they don't tend to go all Frank Castle."

"That makes sense," he replied.

"Well, like you said." A faint smile flitted across her face. "You're not a usual cop."

"Nope," he answered. "What about the people that do? The cops that go rogue, what's your take on that?"

As she drummed her fingertips against the table, she took a long drink from the paper cup. "I'm making sweeping generalizations here, and I feel kind of weird about it. I'm sorry, and this isn't a question of your integrity, but I really don't like answering stuff like this unless I know the context.

Do you think a cop went rogue and killed Tyler Haldane? Or what?"

He glanced around to ensure no one had settled nearby while they conversed. "It's not just Haldane. They killed another man outside Norfolk about six months ago, and today someone else turned up dead in Newport News. All three were killed with the same weapon, a military grade sniper rifle. Haldane was shot from almost a mile away, and the shooter hit him right between the eyes."

"Shit," Autumn breathed, pausing her fingers mid-tap.

"Whoever the killer is, they've got extensive marksmanship training. They're either ex-law enforcement or ex-military, or both. I wanted to know what you thought might drive a good cop to do something like that, or just a decent person, in the event we're dealing with someone who's got military training. And honestly, anything helps me at this point. We're working off little and less right now."

"Yikes," she muttered. "Okay, well, in the absence of a specific suspect, like I said, I've got to make sweeping generalizations, which I don't necessarily like to do. But I'll throw a few ideas out there for you."

"That's all I'm asking," he assured her, nodding to solidify the words.

"Okay, well, first." She leaned back in her chair and reached to fidget with the owl-shaped pendant of her gold necklace. "If it's someone younger, it could be the onset of paranoid schizophrenia. Or even someone older, but that's less common. In that case, you'd be looking for a genetic predisposition and a recent source of stress to bring on the symptoms. There isn't always a stressor that cues it, but there is one on enough occasions to make it more or less expected.

"Either way, in this case, if the person just recently snapped, there are going to be some signs. If they've become reclusive, if their attendance at work has dropped, or if they've been fired altogether. Changes in their personality too. They might've started making some dark comments or might've become more pessimistic. People don't usually snap like that without leaving a trail, I think is what I'm getting at."

"What kind of trail?"

She shrugged. "You look for the event first. Could be a diagnosis of a major, incurable illness like Multiple Sclerosis or cancer, loss of a loved one, a sexual assault, something like that. Then, after that, there would be a variation in their behavior. But..." She raised an index finger as her gaze met his.

"But?"

"And this is important, all right?" Her green eyes were fixed on his, and the intensity of her stare didn't diminish until he nodded his understanding.

"All right," he replied.

"All those 'signs' or 'symptoms' I just listed off, those are also indicative of posttraumatic stress disorder. And the likelihood that someone who experienced a traumatic event turning into a Frank Castle type vigilante is infinitely smaller than them developing a long-term stress reaction."

That was it, he thought.

All the oddities Cassidy Ramirez had mentioned about Sun's behavior over the past six months, everything she'd used to establish the potential for Sun to snap, it was post-traumatic stress disorder.

"Whoever killed Tyler Haldane had to plan for it," Aiden said. "They had to have monitored his routine for weeks or months to know exactly where they'd be able to get a clean shot at him."

Autumn nodded. "So, whoever this is, you're looking for someone who probably experienced a traumatic event a long time ago."

16

Golden sunlight streamed in through the wall-spanning window, and the rays glinted off the polished granite countertops, the stainless-steel appliances, and the syrupy splotch of drying blood and vaporized brain matter spattered along the tiled floor. But no matter how gruesome the scene of Ben Ormund's death, Winter had seen worse during their investigation of Douglas Kilroy.

Hell, she had seen worse before she was even in high school.

Ben Ormund hadn't been raped or mutilated, and whoever killed him hadn't painted the walls with his blood. Like Mitch Stockley and Tyler Haldane, Ormund's death had been painless. One shot that he likely didn't even see coming and Ormund's world had gone black.

"Agents," a brown and gold clad sheriff's deputy greeted.

He was young, likely no older than Noah, but his reaction to the gore was no more pronounced than Winter's. Based on the close-cropped military style of his dark blond hair, he had seen worse too.

"Morning, deputy," Noah greeted. "I'm Agent Dalton, and this is my partner, Agent Black."

"Morning." Winter's salutation was stiff, but she lacked the wherewithal to force herself to come across as amiable.

"I'm Deputy Eckley," he replied, extending a hand to Noah first, and then to Winter.

"Guess we're outside the city limits, huh?" Noah observed.

The deputy nodded. "Yeah, by a few miles. Along the coast here is a pretty wealthy area, and I'm sure you can imagine, there isn't a lot of this around here."

"Doesn't seem like it's bothering you all that much," Winter put in.

She made sure to keep her tone non-accusatory. In truth, after their unscheduled meeting with ADD Ramirez a couple hours earlier, she had started to wonder if they would have to resort to questioning every law enforcement agent in the Richmond and Norfolk areas.

They needed to narrow down their suspect pool, but so far, each crime scene had been immaculate.

With a smile that contained more than a hint of sarcasm, the deputy nodded again. "Two tours in Iraq, agent. A guy with his head blown off ain't nothing new to me, no disrespect to the dead. And this area might be pretty quiet, but Norfolk's a big city with a big Naval base. Plenty of folks up to no good wander outside the city limits and wind up dead in my jurisdiction."

Winter smiled, liking this man's forthrightness. "I'm sure."

"Now, this one here?" Eckley paused to gesture to the pool of coagulated blood. "I'm more'n happy to hand this off to the Feds. Guy shot in the head from a distance, not a shred of forensic evidence, no thank you. It's all yours, and for right now, I'm here to help *you*."

"Shot from a distance," Noah repeated before Winter

could respond. "Any idea where the shooter might've posted up?"

The deputy pointed at the bullet hole in the otherwise pristine glass. "See those rocks out there that sort of hug the edge of that cliff type thing?"

Winter followed his outstretched hand and nodded. "You think that's where he was?"

"More'n likely, yeah. We've got a couple people out there working on backtracking the trajectory right now."

"I'd say you're right." Noah glanced from Winter to the deputy and back. "I can see them out there, and it looks like there are only a couple of those boulders big enough to hide a full-grown man. Unless our guy was dressed up like a rock to blend in, or unless he was wearing a ghillie suit laying in the grass out there, I'd say he was hiding behind one of them."

"Well," the deputy chuckled, "I'd bet my right nut that our perp wasn't wearing a ghillie suit, but we'll let the pros determine that."

Noah offered the man one of his patented, disarming grins, and Winter fought against rolling her eyes. Even when he employed it on someone else, his charm was still so damn effective that it was aggravating.

"Shall we go see?" Winter asked, forcing the edge from her tone.

"After you then, agents," Eckley said. "Let's go see what we can see."

The two men shared the basic details of their respective military careers with one another as they walked through the lush grass of the yard and then to the more unruly vegetation beyond.

As the late morning sun gradually warmed the top of her head, she wished she had a hat. A giant, obnoxious floppy hat like Autumn had worn on the one occasion they'd driven out to the coast. Winter didn't know how the woman did it, but somehow, she made the hat look good.

Before the three of them had closed the distance to the rocky outcropping, a woman's voice cut through Winter's thoughts.

"Hey, deputy!" she called. When Winter glanced up from the tall grass, the woman waved an arm above her head. "We've got something. You...you need to see this."

Winter and Noah exchanged fervent looks and increased their gait to just below an outright jog. Deputy Eckley kept pace, and once they reached the crime scene tech, the sunlight glinted off a light sheen of sweat on his brow.

Beneath the standard, navy blue jacket emblazoned with the yellow block "FBI" letters, Winter was sure she had begun to roast. She could already feel her button-down blouse stick to her body, and she could only hope that the visible part of her shirt wouldn't be stained with sweat before they were finished.

"Amy." Eckley nodded to the woman. "These are the Feds, Agent Dalton and Agent Black."

"Agents," Amy replied. "You're going to want to see this too. I've been doing this for almost thirty years. I even worked in Miami for ten of that, and I've never seen anything like this."

Miami? The Florida metropolis was a hotbed for cartel activity, and almost every other organized crime group had set up shop in the last few decades.

Pablo Escobar's reign had only been the start of what was to become of Miami, and if Amy had spent *ten years* in the city, Winter wasn't even sure she wanted to know what she had seen.

But they'd already found their victim, so what in the hell was left that could cause the unabashed wariness behind Amy's dark eyes?

As they picked their way through the rocks and debris behind the shorter woman, the only sound was the distant rush of the Atlantic Ocean.

Winter's heart rate had picked up, but now, she knew the source wasn't physical exertion. Every step felt like it took a full minute, and by the time they arrived at the boulder beside which a second crime scene tech stood, Winter was sure an entire hour had elapsed.

She had imagined everything from a severed head on a pike to a Satanic altar, but when her eyes settled on the object of the tech's awe, she took in a sharp breath.

"Is that....?" Deputy Eckley began but didn't finish.

In response, Amy nodded as she brushed a piece of ebony hair from her face. "Yes, deputy. It is."

"Fuck me," Noah breathed.

WITH A SIGH, Winter wiped the beads of sweat from her brow. Over the past hour, her hopes that perspiration would not show through her pastel blue shirt had been dashed. She'd zipped up the lightweight FBI jacket to hide her sweaty shirt, and now she thought she knew what a pan felt like when it was covered in foil and stuffed in the oven.

As Noah and the sheriff's deputy conversed inside the air-conditioned house, she had slunk into a patch of shade to call Aiden Parrish to provide him with an update. He'd told her and Noah that he had a meeting scheduled for that morning, but by the time they returned to the house, it was close to one in the afternoon. After only one and a half rings, he picked up.

"Parrish."

"It's me." Even to her own ears, her voice sounded strained.

"How's it going out there?" There was a note of what she could only describe as a cross between curiosity and concern in his voice.

"It…it's going."

"Did you find anything?"

She couldn't help the dry chuckle that slipped from her lips at the question. "You could say that."

"Are we playing twenty questions?" Though pointed, the query wasn't hostile. Not yet, anyway.

"No, sorry. I'm just still trying to wrap my head around it."

"Jesus, what the hell happened out there? The victim was shot in the head, wasn't he? Wait, he didn't have family there, did he? No one said anything about that."

"No, no, nothing like that." Squeezing her eyes closed, Winter massaged her temple with her free hand. "You're not going to believe this. If I hadn't seen it for myself, I don't think I'd believe it, either."

When she paused, there was silence on the other end of the line. She pulled the phone away from her face to check if the call had been disconnected, but the sweat smeared screen told her the call was still live.

"Aiden?" she asked.

"I'm waiting on you. We've already established that I'm not playing twenty questions." His voice was as flat as she'd ever heard it, and she was reminded of their meeting with ADD Ramirez. Aiden had left the office before her or Noah, and she hadn't interacted with him since. Apparently, plenty of the irritability remained.

"Right," she sighed. "It was the weapon. The rifle used to kill Stockley and Haldane. We—"

"Wait," Aiden interjected. "Wait, you found the murder weapon? Where?"

"In the same spot where we believe the killer took the shot at Ormund."

"They left the *murder weapon* at the *crime scene?*" She could tell he still thought she was fucking with him. "Winter, I swear to god, you'd better not be—"

"I'm not," she replied quickly. "I told you it was crazy. But, yeah…a Barrett M98 Bravo was sitting behind a bolder that matches the trajectory our guys determined to be the sniper hide."

"A Barrett M98 Bravo was just sitting out there in the rocks when our shooter didn't even leave behind a shell casing at either of the other murders?"

"A *disassembled* Barrett M98 Bravo," she corrected. "And the shell casings were there."

"Casings, as in plural?"

"Yes. All three. And before you ask, we checked. No prints, no trace evidence. No footprints, absolutely *nothing*. As far as we can tell, we might be hunting a damn ghost. And, you know what else? You know what *one* piece of the rifle was missing? The firing pin. Our shooter kept the damn firing pin, or they tossed it off the cliff into the damn ocean."

Winter could almost hear Aiden shaking his head.

She lifted her braid from her sweat sticky neck. "That's not it, either."

"Christ, what else?"

"They left a note for us. It—"

For the second time, Aiden cut her off before she could elaborate. "A note? As in a BTK, Zodiac Killer, Ted Kaczynski *note?*"

"Not a manifesto." She was getting irritated now and knew it came across in her voice, but she was too sweaty and dehydrated to care. "A note. On a notecard. All three shell casings were lined up beside it. It was typed, so we won't be able to do any kind of handwriting comparison. It's on its way to forensics now to check for ink type, etc."

"What did the note say?" The sharpness had vanished from his voice, and he sounded as fed up with the day as she felt.

"It said, and this is verbatim: 'Stockley, Haldane, Ormund. This is just the beginning. Good luck, agents.'"

17

Noah glanced up as Winter made her way into the spacious kitchen. The click of a camera shutter was punctuated by the din of quiet voices as a pair of crime scene techs worked to wrap up their initial analysis of the area.

Strands of Winter's ebony hair had come loose from the neat braid, and he caught the glint of beaded sweat on her forehead as she pushed the matted pieces away from her face. He wondered how much of the flush on her cheeks was from the heat and how much was the start of a sunburn. After all the years spent at his grandparents' ranch, Noah had become accustomed to long-term exposure to the sun, and the occasions he suffered a burn were few and far between.

For the beginning six months of his first tour of Afghanistan, he'd been among the few Marines in his unit who had been able to withstand the bright sunlight without complaint. Between the ranch and the Middle East, he had sweated so much that he hardly paid any attention to the sensation these days.

"How are you not dying?" Winter asked as she approached.

With a grin he knew would make her at least a little crazy, he shrugged. "Good genetics, I guess. It's weird, you know. You're the one who's always cold too."

She crossed her arms over her dark jacket and huffed. "I guess that's bad genetics, then. What's going on here? What's our next step?"

"These guys are working on wrapping this up," he said, gesturing to where the techs milled around the breakfast bar. "There isn't much here, though. They're already pretty confident we aren't going to get much from in here. They'll do some more print dusting and picture taking, but that's about it."

"What do we know about Ben Ormund?" she asked. "So far, the killer's targeted other killers."

"That's our next step. We've got to figure out how Ormund fits the profile. He was a psychology professor at Christopher Newport University. I suppose we'll start there."

"If we're going to go talk to a bunch of college faculty members, then I need to change or take a shower or something." Gesturing to herself, she flashed him a flat look. "I'm pretty sure I smell like a week-old gym sock right now."

His sudden laughter drew the attention of the two techs, and he bit his tongue to stifle the sound. "That's graphic. You keep a change of clothes in the car, right?"

"Yeah."

"All right, then we'll stop by the cop shop, and you can do whatever you need to do there while I see what they've got on Ben Ormund. Two birds, one stone."

WHEN NOAH CAME across the report of a sexual assault Ben Ormund had been accused of some two decades earlier, he wasn't sure if he should be relieved or apprehensive. He consulted with a couple deputies while Winter donned fresh clothes, and they were all under the impression that the woman who had filed the report had moved to the other end of the country.

However, when Noah searched for her records in the federal database, there wasn't a thing. If she had moved to California or Washington, she lived completely off the grid. There were no utility records, no financial records, no housing records, or government welfare records. Nothing. According to his search, she had simply vanished.

Grating his teeth together, he closed the laptop as Winter emerged from a hallway at the other end of the room. A handful of sheriff's deputies sat at desks throughout the space, but no one paid any special attention to their FBI visitors.

The overhead light caught a droplet of water as it rolled from the end of her braid to streak down her blazer. Her cheeks were still tinged with pink, but the outright flush from earlier had lessened. Tucking the slim computer beneath one arm, he rose to stand.

"You took an entire shower?" he asked.

"As opposed to half a shower?" she replied, scrunching up her nose. "Or a quarter of a shower?"

"Well, you smell great now. Definitely not like a week-old gym sock."

"Uh, thanks, I guess?"

"Any time, it's what I'm here for. Moral support, compliments, you name it." He raised one arm to check the time. "Quarter after two. Plenty of time."

"I've never noticed that before." Winter's attention shifted to his wrist as she took hold of his arm and squinted at the watch. "Is it new?"

Even through the material of his suit jacket, he felt the unmistakable warmth of her grasp. As his pulse rushed in his ears, he fought to maintain his neutral expression.

How did this make any damn sense? How did an innocuous touch evoke so much nervousness *and* anticipation?

They were in the middle of a station full of sheriff's deputies, and all he could picture was wrapping his arms around her shoulders to kiss her, to taste her tongue on his, to get lost in the warmth of her closeness. The pervasive image was as frustrating as it was tantalizing.

But when her blue eyes flicked up to his, he was overcome by a realization that made his breath catch in his throat. The seemingly innocent physical contact had been made with purpose, and if they hadn't been surrounded by sheriff's deputies, he would have leaned in to press his lips to hers.

Clearing his throat, he ripped himself out of the space-time bubble in which he and Winter had just been suspended.

"Noticed what before?" he asked.

"Your watch. I don't know a ton about watches, but I learned a little bit growing up with Grampa Jack." The corner of her mouth turned up in a smile as she released her hold. "And, from what I can tell, that sure is a fancy watch."

"It is," he confirmed. "My granddad collects them. He gave me this one back when I got out of the military. It's been in the shop for a while now, just got it back a few days ago."

"How much is it worth?"

He shrugged. "A lot. I never bothered to check. It's old, vintage, I guess. Probably part of some limited collection from the '60s or '70s or something."

Her smile was more pronounced, but he didn't miss the mischievous glint in her eyes. "I didn't know that. That's pretty cool, though. Between that and your hair, it seems like you've got this sharp dressed thing down pretty well."

"I can't tell if you're teasing me or giving me a compliment."

"Might be a little bit of both." She gave him an uncharacteristic wink. "All right, enough fashion talk. Did you find anything about Ormund?"

Right. Ben fucking Ormund.

He barely suppressed a groan. "Yeah, I did. Got an address for the ex-wife, so I'll tell you the rest on our way to her."

She headed for the door. "Sounds like a plan."

On the short drive to Linda Cahill, formerly Ormund, he ran through all the information he'd unearthed on the sexual assault allegation from twenty years earlier.

The victim, a woman named Paula Detrick, had been a client at the counseling practice that employed Ormund. According to police records, during one of their sessions, Ormund had drugged and assaulted her and then tried to convince her the entire experience had not really occurred.

Like the case of Anne Timson, there hadn't been enough evidence for the police to pursue formal criminal charges against Ormund. However, there had been enough for the state to revoke his license to practice.

From there, the details became fuzzier, but in the long run, the black mark had been all but erased from Ormund's record. He went on to teach psychology at Christopher Newport University until he was shot and killed the night before.

By the time Noah rapped his knuckles against a wooden door, any semblance of amusement or flirtation had been thoroughly squashed. The portal opened a crack at first, and then wider after he and Winter flashed their badges at the teenage girl.

"I'm Agent Dalton, this is Agent Black. We're with the

Federal Bureau of Investigation. We're here to talk to Linda Cahill. Is she home?"

In response, the girl nodded.

"Can we talk to her?" Winter pressed.

"Hold on," the girl replied as she turned her head. "Mom," she called. "It's for you. It's the FBI."

"The *what?*" a woman exclaimed from the background. "Lucy, if you're screwing with me right now." The voice grew louder as the orator neared.

"No," Lucy chuckled. "Definitely not screwing with you, Mom."

"I'm Linda Cahill," the woman said, resting a protective hand on her daughter's shoulder. Her pale blue eyes flicked back and forth between him and Winter, but her expression was unreadable. "How can I help you, agents?"

"We've got some questions about your ex-husband," Winter said. "Do you mind if we come in? Honestly, I've been out in this hundred-degree nonsense all day, and I'd really appreciate a break."

Lips pursed, Linda nodded as she and her daughter stepped aside. "Come on in. We can chat in the living room. Can I get either of you anything to drink?"

"You should take her up on that," Lucy said from the foot of a stairwell. "Mom's lemonade is the *shit*. And she just made some."

"Thanks, Lucy," Linda returned. As she waved a dismissive hand, her daughter grinned and made her way up the steps. "But yes, agents. If you'd like some lemonade, I'd be happy to share. Why don't we just head to the kitchen and talk in there."

"Kitchen's my favorite room in the house," Noah replied with a grin.

"Smart man," Linda commented, waving an appreciative finger.

"This is a nice place," Winter said as they followed Linda into the sun-drenched kitchen. "Is it just you and your daughter here?"

"It sure is," their hostess replied. "Been that way for about ten years now. I guess marriage just isn't really my strong suit. Married and divorced three times." She set a couple glasses atop the granite counter and brushed a piece of golden hair from her face.

"So," she said as she pried open the stainless-steel refrigerator door. "What'd that shithead do now?"

"What?" Noah and Winter replied at the same time.

"I'm assuming that's why you're here," she answered, shrugging as she filled each glass from a plastic pitcher.

"You mean Ben Ormund, right?" Noah managed to ask.

"I do." Linda nodded. "What'd that prick do now?"

"No love lost there, huh?" Winter remarked as she took a sip from her glass. "Wow, your daughter wasn't kidding. This lemonade is amazing."

Mid-drink, Noah nodded his agreement. There was a balance between sweet and sour that he didn't realize could even be achieved with regular lemonade.

"Thanks. It's my mother's recipe. The trick is to make it with simple syrup instead of just sugar. You can put strawberries in the syrup, or raspberries, blueberries, whatever you feel like." Leaning against the counter, Linda crossed her arms. "And no, there's *definitely* no love lost between me and that asshole."

"Has he bothered you since you've been divorced?" Winter asked.

"Really?" Linda gawked. "You really don't know? Are you sure you're FBI?"

Noah drew his brows together. "Know what?"

"Three different times." She held up three fingers for emphasis. "Three damn times I tried to file a restraining order on that son of a bitch. Not for me, but for Lucy. That bastard is *convinced* that Lucy is his. He's got a Ph.D., but apparently, they didn't have any mathematic requirements for him to get that degree, because he can't figure out that there's no possible way she's his!"

Linda threw up her hands, a flush pinkening her pretty face.

"And considering it's my body, I'd say I'm the expert on the topic, right? But, oh, no." She laughed, a bitter sound. "Not to Ormund. He's been trying for the past two years to get a DNA test. And if I wasn't privileged enough to make the kind of money I do, the financial burden alone would've been enough to make me snap. I don't want my daughter to have to deal with that shit. I tried shielding her from it, but eventually, I had to tell her."

"Tell her what?" Winter asked.

"Tell her that some crazy dipshit thinks she's his!" Linda closed her eyes and raised both hands to massage her temples. "She knows all about it now, and her father's known since it started. Even he agrees with me that Ormund's a damn nutcase."

He and Winter exchanged looks of blatant confusion before either of them dared to speak again.

How in the *hell* had none of this shown up in the state or federal databases? How had *none* of the sheriff's deputies known about Ben Ormund's harassment of his ex-wife? Were they even at the right house? Was there a different Ben Ormund and Linda Cahill in Newport News?

"Ms. Cahill," Winter said, her tone as careful and measured as Noah had ever heard. "Where were you last night between eight and ten?"

"Last night? It's the last week before school starts, so I took a few days off to spend with Lucy. We went to a movie last night, and we didn't get home until around eleven. It was a long one, the new Tarantino movie."

If awards existed for "coolest mom," Noah thought that Linda Cahill would be a fierce competitor.

"Why? Wait, if you're not here because of all his court-ordered DNA test bullshit, and you're not here about the restraining orders I've tried and *failed* to get, then what's going on?"

"Ben Ormund is dead," Noah said, ripping the bandage off quickly. "He was shot and killed last night."

That seemed to take a little heat from Linda's sails, but only for a second. The moment the surprised had passed, Linda smiled. "Well, I'll be honest, agents. I didn't kill him, but I'm sure as hell not sad he's gone."

"Were you ever in the military, Ms. Cahill?" he pressed.

"No."

"Law enforcement?"

"No. I'm a real estate lawyer. So, unless that counts, then no."

"Are you familiar with a Barrett M98B?" He already knew the answer, but he felt obligated to ask.

"No. Look, do I need *my* lawyer?" She raised an eyebrow as her expression turned skeptical.

"No," he answered with a shake of his head. "But would you mind telling us what you know about Paula Detrick? If that name's familiar, I mean."

At the mention of the young woman, the sass on Linda's unlined face was abruptly overshadowed by a dark cloud. "What? Is someone *finally* going to actually investigate that poor girl's disappearance?"

"What do you mean, disappearance?" Winter prodded.

"Exactly what it sounds like. My shithead ex-husband assaulted that poor girl, and then she went missing. Everyone said she moved to the West Coast, but hell if I know where they got that idea from."

"You and Ben were married at the time, weren't you?" Winter asked. "Paula made the report twenty years ago, and you and Ben's divorce wasn't final until three years after that."

Whatever melancholy had come over her was pushed aside by the glint of malevolence in her pale eyes. "I'll tell you what I tell everyone else who says that same thing to me. Yeah, I was married to him for three years after it happened. And yeah, I was perfectly aware of what had happened. But you know what? At the time, I was trying to raise my son from my previous marriage, and I was trying to go to law school. I didn't have any money of my own. I didn't have any family, and all my friends were *his* friends. I was *completely* dependent on Ben. I didn't have job experience. I didn't have anything."

Noah was tempted to jump in and ask questions but decided to let the woman rant.

And rant she did. "But even if I'd had the means, I don't think either of you understand exactly how terrifying that situation is to a young woman. He'd raped and murdered a perfect stranger, so what in the hell would he do to me? Or my son? There's not a doubt in my mind that if I hadn't approached the end of that relationship exactly like I did, if I hadn't bided my time and waited until I had my JD, that I wouldn't be here right now."

"You were afraid."

Linda's snort was answer enough. She waved a hand. "And this, you coming here, investigating *Ben's* death, that's just great. You know, I thought about practicing criminal law, but I'm glad I stuck to the boring real estate. Because I don't think I'd be able to handle dealing with shit like this on a daily basis. Like I said, I didn't kill him. But if you find whoever did…" she pushed to her feet, "tell them I said thanks."

18

J ust as soon as Cassidy had taken a seat behind her desk, the retort of knuckles against the metal doorframe sounded out. She bit back a sigh and rubbed the bridge of her nose.

"It's unlocked. Come in," she announced.

As Max Osbourne stepped into the room, Cassidy could swear the temperature dropped by at least five degrees.

His slate gray eyes were alight with suspicion and ire, but as the door latched behind him, he still didn't speak. Cassidy had worked with the man for close to three decades, and she knew that look.

She had seen that glint of righteous indignation before. The storm that brewed behind that glint could sink ships and reduce entire cities to rubble. Tightening her grip on a ballpoint pen, Cassidy scooted forward in her seat to brace herself for the category five shitstorm coming in her direction.

Her decision to leave Max out of the initial discussion about the possibility of Agent Sun Ming as their prime suspect had been purposeful.

It would have made sense to include Ming's boss in the dialogue, but the group in the Violent Crimes Division was tight-knit. Max was protective of the agents under his command, and while the quality was admirable, Cassidy suspected his loyalty would only hinder a thorough review of Ming's activity in recent months.

To be sure, she hadn't intended to keep the news from him for long, and his presence in her office this afternoon was more or less expected.

"Have a seat, SAC Osbourne," she said after a prolonged silence.

Crossing both arms over his black suit jacket, the SAC shook his head. "I've been sitting all day. I'm fine."

Cassidy bit back a sigh as she nodded. "Understood. What can I help you with, Osbourne?"

He narrowed his eyes. "You're smart, Ramirez. I'm sure you already know why I'm here."

"You're here about Agent Ming." Cassidy twirled the pen between her fingers.

More than almost anyone else in the entire Richmond FBI office, she respected Max Osbourne. She knew he could have ascended to the Associate Deputy Director spot, but the position had never been his goal. He had a knack for bringing out the best in the agents under his tutelage, and that was where he had decided to stay.

But as shady as Cassidy felt for keeping such a volatile piece of information from him, she knew she had done what was best for the bureau, and for the victims.

The victims.

Two rapists and a mass murderer.

She pushed the thought to the back of her mind as she met SAC Osbourne's intense stare. No matter their crimes, the three men had all been murdered, and the FBI had a duty to investigate their deaths.

"I'm here about Agent Ming," Max said when she didn't elaborate. "And I'm curious why I'm just now learning about this when it seems like the inquiry into her has been ongoing for at least a couple days."

"No one other than an internal investigator and I knew about it until this morning. I needed to look over everything before I could make a decision to establish Agent Ming as a suspect. I've looked it over, and I've made my decision."

"Yeah? When did you plan to tell *her* about it?" Max shot back.

"Soon, but we need to finish gathering and processing evidence from the newest crime scene. Until then, I expect you'll keep this to yourself."

Cassidy's tone didn't so much as falter. High stress conversations weren't new territory for her, and she'd learned long ago that any display of weakness during a tense dialogue was like the scent of blood to a shark.

"You know I will. But I'd like to know, do you have any *hard* evidence, or is it just a pile of circumstantial bullshit?"

She clenched her jaw before she replied. "We're looking for someone with a very specific set of skills. Someone who's familiar enough with crime scene investigation to ensure nothing's left behind, and I mean *nothing*. And on top of that, we're looking for someone who can hit a target between the eyes from almost a mile away."

The muscles in Max's jaw popped, and she knew he knew what she was going to say next.

"Aside from the tactical team, all of whom have alibis for at least one of the murders, there are only four people in this entire office that are capable of making a shot like that. Three of them also have alibis. Agent Ming is the only one without an alibi for any of the deaths. She was in Norfolk yesterday, and the victim killed that night was in Newport News."

"She was there with Agent Brandt," Max returned. "And they left *together*."

"Only after they went to the local PD to talk to them about Anne Timson's case."

"That's what they *should* have done."

"You're right. But based on what I've heard from the Norfolk PD, Agent Ming took a particular interest in the case. She was overly critical, and one of the detectives said that her attitude bordered on outright hostile."

"She should have been," Max spat. "Have you seen the Timson case, Ramirez? Have you seen the detectives' notes from when they took her statement?"

He paused as if he expected her to respond, but he went on before she could speak.

"Anne Timson was sexually assaulted and escaped from a lunatic who went on to kill God only knows how many more women, and when she reported her assault to the Norfolk PD, they all but laughed her out of their office. Drunk college girl, probably hooked up with an older guy and regretted it later. I think that's almost verbatim what their notes said."

Cassidy nodded. He wasn't wrong.

"They didn't take any of what she said seriously until another girl disappeared a few months later. But by then, Anne was across the country in boot camp for the Navy. I know your values well enough to know you don't buy into that kind of victim blaming bullshit. Nobody in this office buys into that shit, especially not Agent Ming. I think that's pretty plain to see given her work so far to investigate the person who killed these three sorry excuses for human beings."

"That isn't our job to—"

The SAC held up a hand, his face growing redder. "Because if there are any *victims* that deserve to be blamed for what happened to them, they're Tyler Haldane, Ben Ormund, and Mitch Stockley. Agent Ming took a bullet for this office, and if she hadn't been there to make that shot and take out Kent Strickland, a hell of a lot more people would've died."

"I know what Agent Ming did," Cassidy said with a stiff nod. "And she was highly commended for it. But a traumatic event like that can bring out a different side to a person. I've seen it happen before, and I know you have too. Sun has gone off on her own before. During the Presley investigation, she kept a key piece of information to herself so she could be the one to close the case. We have to look at the context here, Max. We're not throwing her in a prison cell yet, all right? She's a suspect, not a defendant."

The seconds ticked away as Max kept his glare locked on hers, but Cassidy didn't balk. She had no idea how long they stared one another down, but she suspected close to a minute had passed by the time he finally spoke.

"Fine," he grated. "Keep me updated and let me know if there's anything I can do to help. And I *will* help because I know that Agent Ming didn't do any of this."

19

The recollection was so vivid that Sun could smell the faint aroma of fried food and cookies as it wafted over from the nearby food court. She'd never set foot into the Riverside Mall before that day, but whenever her sleeping brain took her back to that night, she felt like she had returned home.

Not the type of home that welcomed and provided shelter, but the type of home where a piece of her had been broken and left behind. The type of home that had changed everything. Almost like it was a monument or a shrine, a revered place where only a select few could set foot.

But it wasn't a privilege to go to this home. It was an obligation, a reminder, and a testament to her failure.

Sun knew she was in a dream, but no matter the effort she put into waking herself, she always witnessed the first part of the exchange.

The mannequins in the windows of the boutique clothing store were dressed in the newest spring styles, and on a normal day, Sun might have paused to consider the looks.

Tonight was far from normal, however, and her attention

was fixed on the line of people seated on the polished floor in front of the shop. Their hands had been bound behind their backs, and the same hallowed look darkened each of their faces.

Even from the distance where she'd crouched behind the ceramic pot of a decorative tree, she could see the malevolence in the eyes of the only two people who stood upright.

Each was clad in a Kevlar vest, a dated camouflage jacket, and matching cargo pants. But amidst the unremarkable shades of olive drab, a red armband stood out in stark contrast. In the center of the band was the SS insignia used by Nazi officers during World War II.

Bobby Weyrick was hunched down behind another tree on the opposite side of the wide hall, an M4 Carbine tucked tight against his shoulder.

When his eyes snapped up to hers, she knew they were out of time.

The corridor in which they hid sloped downward from the two gunmen and their hostages, but at any other angle, there hadn't been adequate cover to conceal their movements. If they had come in through the boutique, they would have been spotted almost immediately.

Maybe, if the damn mall had been two stories, Sun could have gone to the second floor with a couple members of the SWAT team to get a clean shot at one of the two men.

But she knew that Tyler Haldane and Kent Strickland had meticulously planned their offensive. They chose the front of the boutique because it bordered a security station that sported footage from each camera throughout the entire premises, and the store itself was open and had no alcoves or barriers behind which a law enforcement agent could hide.

They were at a tactical disadvantage in more than one way. Not only were they downhill from the hostages and the captors, but there was no way for them to advance for a clearer shot without making themselves an easy target. And as the two gunmen strode back and forth in front of the captives, they *needed* a clearer shot. If the angle was off, if they *missed*, the bullet was likely to hit a civilian.

But they were out of time.

The crack of a gunshot ripped through the uneasy quiet of the building like a machete through jungle foliage. A handful of terrified cries followed, and when Sun dared a glance past her cover, another shot rang out.

The newest victim had knelt, and the harsh fluorescence caught the crimson spatter that exploded from the side of her head.

Sun felt her stomach lurch at the sight of the blood, but the typical anxious reaction was overruled by the adrenaline that pumped through her body with every rapid beat of her heart.

It wasn't the sight of the blood that unnerved her when she looked out onto the scene. It was the woman's eyes.

Pale blue or gray, Sun couldn't tell from the distance. As her body slumped to the floor, Sun could see the life vanish from her features. The abject terror, the sadness, the apprehension, it all fell away, and what was left was…nothing.

"That was two!" one of the two gunmen called. "And if we go another sixty seconds without you giving us what we want, then two more are going to die! And two more after that!"

Now, Sun knew the voice belonged to Tyler Haldane, but at the time, she hadn't known which one of them had spoken.

Neither the local PD nor the FBI response teams had even entertained the idea of caving in to the shooters' demands.

They wanted to be broadcasted live by every major news network in the country, supposedly so they could rally like-minded men to their cause. Before the tech team had been able to loop all the security cameras, the shooters had rambled off a list of supposed justifications for their crusade against modern society.

Among the top of their list of grievances was technology, and Bobby Weyrick had made more than one comment about the Unabomber.

Sure enough, the two assailants had cited Ted Kaczynski as a source of inspiration. But then, what had taken Sun aback was the next man to whom they paid homage.

The Preacher.

Sun knew the man's real name, but neither of the shooters had. And none of them knew that Douglas Kilroy would die before the night was over.

"We're running out of time," a tinny voice in her earpiece advised. "It's pretty obvious that they weren't lying. With those two, the body count is up to five."

"If we go in there with our guns blazing, five is going to look like nothing," Bobby put in, his tone hushed. "We need precision."

"Which is why you two are in there," the voice, Max Osbourne's voice, replied.

Two more shots rang out after Max's statement, but in the dream, the sounds were always muffled.

"Okay," she said, fervently glancing over to Bobby. "Weyrick, can you lay down some covering fire for me? Aim high, but low enough that they'll realize they need to try to duck and cover."

He nodded. "The hostages are sitting, so that gives us a little bit of leeway, even if they've got the higher ground." She spotted a flicker of movement as the agent readjusted his rifle.

"I have to make a headshot," Sun advised. The volume

with which she spoke was barely a whisper. She was surprised Bobby could hear her at all.

"You're cleared for it, agents," Max put in. "Shoot to kill."

She'd never heard those words used during the line of duty until that night.

The minutes that followed were a blur, and until she awoke, she could never recall what exactly had transpired.

Next thing she knew, she was out from behind the potted tree as she lined up the sights of her handgun with Kent Strickland's head. The man was midway through raising his rifle when she squeezed the trigger, and as soon as his eyelids drooped, she thought for sure he was dead.

Only in the dream, the series of events never quite played out that way, and tonight was no exception.

Despite the care with which she'd targeted the center of Strickland's head, the projectile whipped harmlessly past the side of his face. Sometimes, even after crimson blossomed from beside his temple, he would continue to raise the military-grade rifle to take his shot.

Mercifully, every time he fired the high-powered weapon, she jerked awake.

As Sun sat bolt upright in her bed, her breathing came in short, labored gasps, and the night air was cool against the sheen of sweat on her forehead. Grasping at the site of the wound she'd sustained from Tyler Haldane's gun, she pulled her knees to her chest and took in as deep a breath as she could manage.

She had heard of soldiers, cops, or firefighters who had recurring nightmares, but every man or woman's recollection varied. Some relived the entire event in vivid detail, some only relived portions, and still others, like Sun, experienced a slightly different series of events each time.

The start was always the same: the scent of fried food and baking cookies from the food court, and then the execution of the woman Sun later learned was a high school chemistry teacher.

No matter what else occurred, even if the dream took a different turn entirely, she *always* saw the woman's face as the bullet from Tyler Haldane's weapon—the same weapon he had used to shoot Sun—blew through her head.

On some nights, she woke up as soon as the woman hit the ground, but on most, she lived through some bizarre rendition of the rest of the event.

Max hadn't been in Danville that night, but she so often heard him speak in the dream that she had to double-check to make sure she hadn't lost her grip on reality. On the other side of the hall, a couple black-clad SWAT members had been crouched.

Bobby Weyrick had been at her side, and when he raised his rifle to fire the first few rounds into the distance, a chunk of the ceramic pot had been ripped away by the abrupt return fire from Kent Strickland.

He had been forced to duck back down to cover, and as soon as he did, two more hostages were killed. Haldane and Strickland chided the attempt at a surprise offensive, but Bobby hadn't waited to hear the spiel before he'd raised his weapon and fired again.

Both gunmen had dropped to their knees to make themselves smaller targets and to put the line of hostages at their backs.

At the sight, Sun had been overcome with a cold resolve, the likes of which she wasn't sure she ever wanted to feel again. In that moment, she had been ready to die. If it meant the lives of the men and women at Haldane and Strickland's mercy would be spared, then she would die.

She had slung the more powerful M4 over her shoulder and retrieved her service weapon. As long as she didn't miss her target, the nine-mil had a far lower chance of piercing through to wound a civilian.

Sun never missed.

The row of medals in her house was proof of that.

As soon as Kent Strickland had slumped to the polished floor, a searing pain ripped through her shoulder. Weyrick had risen to his full height to fire two shots into the center of Haldane's vest. The Kevlar ensured the wounds were not fatal, but the force had been enough to knock Haldane off-balance.

In a blur of movement, a middle-aged man from the row of hostages had leapt up from the floor to tackle Haldane to the ground. Haldane's head bounced off the tile with a sickening crack, and just like that, the fight was over. Thirteen were dead, two critically injured, and seven more wounded.

It could have been worse.

It also could have been better.

Tightening her grip on her shoulder, Sun forced herself to focus on the feeling of the plush mattress, on the light scent of pineapple from the candle warmer on the nightstand, on the slats of moonlight that pierced through the blinds.

The technique was referred to as grounding, and she had learned it not from the FBI mandated counselor, but from Bobby Weyrick.

To this day, he was the only other person who knew about the lingering hardships she still faced. And even though the man had seen more than his share of combat during his tours of duty in the military, she knew the toll that night had taken on him as well.

But in the midst of the pervasive feelings of isolation, she and the agent from the night shift had formed a bond.

As she glanced to the glowing blue numbers of the alarm clock, she reached for her smartphone. At half-past two in the morning, Bobby would still be at the FBI office. He hated the night shift, but he stuck to the routine in a half-hearted attempt to keep his sinking marriage afloat.

For almost a year, he'd been convinced that his wife was having an affair, but he didn't have the heart to invade her privacy to confirm the suspicion.

Had another nightmare, she typed. *Doubt I'll be going back to sleep any time soon.*

His response was almost immediate. *I'm sorry. That sucks. I'm about to fall asleep at my desk—wish we could swap places.*

Me too. Want to take a break from work and stop over? I can make some coffee for you so you don't have to drink the poison from the breakroom.

Yes. Please. You are a lifesaver!!! The exclamation was followed by a heart emoji and a happy cat emoji.

In spite of herself, Sun chuckled.

For now, at least, their secret was safe.

20

W inter could sympathize with Noah's assessment that he felt more like an employee in a call center than a federal agent. Two days after Ben Ormund's murder, almost all she had done was call around to check alibis.

Their list of suspects wasn't so much a list of suspects as it was a list of people who matched the necessary skillset to shoot and kill Tyler Haldane from almost a mile away. Though casting a wide net was often useful to revitalize a case and keep it from becoming cold, a wide net also meant a hell of a lot of tedious work.

Twice, including earlier that morning, Winter and Noah had met with ADD Ramirez and Max Osbourne to answer a handful of questions about Sun Ming.

Has she been jumpy or especially irritable lately? No.

Has she taken a major interest in any one part of the case, like the murder weapon? No.

Have there been periods of time where her absence has seemed unnecessary or suspicious? No.

Even though she hadn't provided any incriminating

information about Sun's activities, Winter still felt like a narc.

And for what? To find whoever had killed Ben Ormund?

The crestfallen look in Linda Cahill's pale eyes as she explained the reason she hadn't reported Ormund to the police was still ingrained on Winter's mind.

As far as she could tell, Linda Cahill was a decent person, a good mother, and a tough woman. The fact that she hadn't been able to seek protection from the agency whose sole purpose was to *protect and serve* had struck a chord for Winter and, as best as she could tell, for Noah.

They had dug around in Ormund's records some more, and they learned he had been in the same fraternity as a state supreme court judge, as well as a couple of tenured criminal attorneys.

Just like that, the mystery of how Ormund managed to get away with so many despicable acts had been solved.

If the press hadn't been breathing down the bureau's neck, Winter would have dug in deeper to the histories of Ormund's judge and lawyer friends.

She would have dredged up anything and everything she could use to pin them with an obstruction charge for sweeping away Linda Cahill's requests for a restraining order. Even if she couldn't charge them, she would make the acts so well-known that the men's jobs would be jeopardized.

Instead, she jotted their names and pertinent information down in a notepad and stowed it away in her desk. Once the case was behind them, she would follow-up on the three men. The publicity from Ormund's murder and the speculation that the killer was a vigilante would be more than enough leverage to draw their transgressions out into the light.

Between the unease from her task to effectively spy on Sun Ming to the irritability that bubbled into her thoughts whenever she so much as glanced at Ben Ormund's name, the air in the Violent Crimes area of the building was all but suffocating.

It was a quarter after ten, but she felt like she'd been seated at her desk for at least twelve hours.

Whether due to the visit with Linda Cahill or another unknown reason, Noah's demeanor had returned to just a step away from brooding. Even outside the office, a little storm cloud had followed him around for the past couple days.

From the corner of her eye, she spotted a flash as the smartphone lit up to notify her of a new text message. She snatched up the device to unlock the screen as soon as she saw Autumn's name. At the hurried movement, she realized how desperate she was for a distraction.

All the paperwork went through! It's official. I get to start working tomorrow!

The announcement was a much-needed reprieve from the aggravating tedium of the day so far. Plus, now Winter had an excuse to leave the office for a long lunch.

That's great news! Let's get lunch to celebrate. I really need to get out of here right now. I feel like I'm in a fishbowl or something.

Yikes, Autumn replied. *Yeah, you definitely need to get out of there, then. Is Noah still being weird, or will he be there too?*

Winter couldn't help the sigh that slipped from her lips. *He's being weird, but he'll still be there. I'll drag him if necessary.*

Pocketing her phone, she pushed herself away from the cubicle and glanced up and down the short row. There was no one, and as she stood to peer over the partition that separated her row from the next over, Noah's desk was empty.

Yeah, I definitely feel like I work in a call center right now.

She had been employed by a small center for a few months during college, and the experience had been just short of soul crushing.

Before she could grab her phone to send Noah a text message to find out where in the hell he was, the first twinge of pain pulsed through her head.

Shit. It wasn't just a headache—the pain was too sharp for a regular headache.

Gritting her teeth, she spun around on her heel and set off for the bathroom at as rapid a pace as she could manage without drawing attention to herself.

Her vision swam, but she managed to lock the stall door before she dropped down to sit on the cold tile floor. After gathering a ball of tissue, she closed her eyes and gave in to the darkness.

THE CRACKLE of burning wood drew Winter's attention to the flames of a tall bonfire as they clawed their way up into the night sky. Pale moonlight glinted off a tarnished metal mug as a pair of women toasted one another.

Right away, Winter knew she was far from the modern world, and she was far from North America.

They were outside, and beyond the orange glow of the fire, she saw a shadowy line of trees. Near the blaze, a handful of people danced to the beat of a drum and the melodic sound of a woman's voice.

To avoid burning the lush grass, a circle of stones and earth had been erected around the bonfire. The barrier came up to Winter's waist, and she figured the pit was used regularly.

She was at a festival, and based on the attire of the men and women who milled about, she was in Ancient Greece. As she glanced over her shoulder, she spotted the gate of the community to which the festival's attendees belonged.

In the center of an arch above the open doors, a familiar

symbol was carved into the rich wood—the same symbol that adorned the pair of shields that rested on the stones around the fire.

The crescent-shaped bow and accompanying arrow were not only on the two shields and the arch, but it was featured prominently on rest of the décor, including the attendees' clothes.

"Artemis," she murmured to herself.

In lieu of an American history course, Winter had fulfilled her general education requirement with a class about Ancient Greece. She'd always enjoyed the stories of Greek deities on Mount Olympus, and she had fallen in love with the television show *Xena: Warrior Princess* when she was younger.

Artemis was the twin sister of Apollo, and she had sworn off marriage to be a hunter. Her weapon of choice was a crescent-shaped bow, and depictions of her often included the moon. In Ancient Greece, Artemis was the revered goddess of the hunt, and...

Winter took in a sharp breath.

Goddess of the hunt and...protector of girls and women.

WHEN HER EYES SNAPPED OPEN, there was no trace of the headache left, and only a slight splotch of red on the balled-up toilet paper. Blinking to clear her vision, she pushed to her feet.

She hadn't been unconscious for long, but as she washed her hands, she hoped enough time had passed for Noah to return to his desk.

Aside from the knowledge that the Ancient Greeks had dubbed Artemis the protector of women and girls, Winter had no idea how the goddess fit into their case.

Was the killer a deranged lunatic who thought they *were* Artemis? Or were they a worshipper of the Ancient Greek Pantheon? Or were they just Greek?

Ever since the death of Douglas Kilroy, her headaches and the visions that accompanied them had become less and less intense. And with the decrease in intensity came a decrease in specificity, at least this time.

Was this how they would be from here on out? Vague depictions with some hidden symbolism she wouldn't unearth until after it was too late?

Usually, a vision gave her peace of mind and a direction for a case, but now she was more fed up than she had been before.

Even her damn brain wouldn't cooperate with their investigation.

When she spotted Noah's empty chair, she almost groaned aloud. She needed to tell someone about what she had just seen, needed to throw out ideas that might point her the right way. Because if she had to make outbound calls for another workday, she thought she may well play hooky for the next month.

Then again, if she cracked and went insane, she wouldn't *need* to play hooky.

Rather than loaf around the VC cubicles, she started for the elevator. There was one other person in the building who knew about her sixth sense, and maybe *he* would actually be at his desk. For good measure, she typed a quick text message to advise Aiden she was headed in his direction.

His affirmative response came before the silver doors slid open, and she breathed a sigh of relief.

She still wasn't entirely sure how to act around Aiden anymore, but whether she wanted to delve into the subject or not, she was about to find out. The door to his office was open, and his pale eyes snapped away from the computer monitor as she stepped into the entryway.

"Hey."

"Morning." He waved her in. "Come in, have a seat."

For good measure, she flicked the lock into place after shutting the door. Within the walls of the FBI office, she took any and every precaution to ensure she wasn't overheard when she discussed her sixth sense. The last thing she needed was for someone like…well, someone like Sun Ming to overhear her. She'd already gone spastic enough around the other agent to give her some idea of how different Winter was.

"So."

When he spoke, she realized she had been silent since she entered.

She flipped her braid until it rested along her spine, then was angry at herself for fidgeting. "Sorry."

"It sounded like it was something important," he surmised. "Or did I read that message the wrong way?"

"No, well, maybe."

He lifted an eyebrow. "Want to be a little more specific?"

"I had a headache, or a 'vision,' whatever you want to call it," she explained, using air quotes because the term still embarrassed her.

A flicker of understanding softened his skeptical expression as he nodded. "You all right?"

"Yeah, fine. It wasn't a, a *big* one, I guess. I don't really know how to quantify these things. But it only lasted for maybe a minute or two. It was really short, and honestly, it didn't make a lot of sense. Or maybe it does. I'm not completely sure."

Straightening in his chair, he propped both elbows atop the polished wooden desk. "Let's hear it, then. Maybe I can help."

"Honestly," she said as she met his intent gaze. "I don't

even know if it has to do with the case. I mean, so far all my 'visions' have been about cases I've been working. Autumn said that might have something to do with my conscious thoughts being mostly focused on the case. So, if I was thinking really hard about something else, maybe I'd have visions about that too."

"Wait, *Autumn* said that?" he echoed, raising both eyebrows to fix her with a disbelieving stare. "You told her about it? What, when? And why?"

Winter's eye roll was all but involuntary. "A few days after we arrested Catherine Schmidt. And I told her because she's my friend, and I basically lied to her about snooping around in her past. Don't get me wrong, I'm glad she knows the truth now, but *I'm* not the one who screwed that up and then acted like a huge dick about it." She narrowed her eyes for emphasis.

Now, it was his turn to roll his eyes. "I told you, I talked to her about it. I apologized, and she accepted my apology. We're fine with one another now, at least as far as I know."

"Whatever," she muttered. "And just so we're clear, it's my brain, and I'll tell whoever in the hell I want about it, all right?"

"Yeah, I got it." He held up his hands in a surrendering gesture she didn't believe. "I didn't mean to sound like an ass. I was just surprised, that's all."

"All right, yeah." She blew out a breath, wanting to get back to the subject at hand. "Fair enough. But, anyway, this one just didn't make a lot of sense. It wasn't even anything from this century, even this *millennium*. It was like I was at this party in Ancient Greece. There was a bonfire, music, wine. There was a full moon, and everyone was wearing this crest around their necks."

Aiden's stare was intense.

She cleared her throat but didn't look away. "It was over

the front of the gate to their village, and on a couple of the shields that were sitting by the fire. It was a bow and arrow, but the bow was shaped like a crescent, like the moon. That symbol, that was the symbol for Artemis. The goddess of the hunt, *and...*" his eyes were already wide, but she paused for dramatic effect, "the protector of women and girls."

"Holy shit," he murmured.

Winter had expected a countenance of puzzlement, skepticism, or even outright frustration. After all, what in the hell did an ancient festival have to do with the murder of a mass shooter and two rapists? But she hadn't expected the unabashed awe on his face.

"What?" she asked. "Is there something I'm missing? Is there a cult I don't know about or something?"

He had already started to shake his head before she finished the questions. "No, at least not that I know of. But that, Artemis, I'm familiar with her too. Sun has a tattoo of Artemis on her back, between her shoulder blades."

Winter's mouth gaped open. "What?" she managed.

"She's got a twin brother." His face had paled just a little. "And he has a tattoo of Apollo on his arm. It's been representative of their dynamic since they were kids. She's had it for years."

"Oh my god," Winter breathed. "There's no way. It *can't* be Sun. I know she and I aren't going to be friends any time soon, but there's no way she's a murderer. There's got to be some other explanation."

"I don't know," he sighed. "I agree with you. I don't think it fits her at all. She might be a bitch a lot of the time, but she's not a killer. She's not even really a bad person, she's just introverted, and I think she masks her awkwardness with attitude."

"Like one of those fish that puffs itself up when there are predators around," Winter suggested. As soon as she spoke the words, she realized how stupid they sounded. "I'm sorry." She squeezed her eyes closed and pinched the bridge of her nose.

"No, don't be." There was a hint of amusement in his voice. "That's an accurate comparison. And those fish aren't predators, at least not for the most part. Puffing up is a defense mechanism."

"Right. But, shit, Aiden. How do we even *start* to prove it's not her?"

Pursing his lips, Aiden leaned back in his chair. "I've got an idea."

21

Autumn felt like she had been lagging behind schedule all day, and even though she was on time to lunch with Noah and Winter, she hustled across the parking lot to the entrance of the café like she was about to miss a flight.

Though the two cafés had distinct interiors, she still managed to confuse the place with the coffee house where she had met Aiden Parrish earlier in the week.

As soon as she spotted her two friends seated in a corner booth, she could tell they were stressed. Not long after her suggestion that they meet for lunch, Winter had sent a text message to ask if she and Noah could pick Autumn's brain for some insight on their current investigation.

Winter hadn't provided much in the way of detail, but Autumn suspected the questions involved the same case that Aiden had mentioned.

Licensed forensic psychologist or not, Autumn didn't care to speculate on a person's behavior when she was unaware of the context. If Winter and Noah wanted to discuss the same topic as Aiden, she would give them the same answers she gave him.

"Hey, guys," she greeted as she approached her friends.

Though they each offered a smile in response, Autumn could tell the gestures were strained, maybe even feigned altogether.

Her ability to tap into their emotional states with a touch might have been hindered by her familiarity with them, but she suspected that even an average Joe would have been able to tell they were stressed.

"Hey, congratulations." Winter scooted to the side to give Autumn room to sit. "You look good. Are those some of the new clothes you got with the gift card Shelby and Bree gave you?"

Glancing down to her teal semi-sheer blouse and accompanying gray slacks, Autumn nodded. "I had to go sign some paperwork earlier, licensing stuff. Figured I shouldn't show up in a band shirt and jeans, you know?"

"Good call," Winter chuckled.

As much as Autumn wanted to ask them what weighed so heavily on their minds, she bit back the inquiry and glanced over the laminated lunch menu.

Despite the medication prescribed by her doctor, her stomach had been a source of constant pain over the last few days. All she had managed to keep down in the last twenty-four hours was half a sleeve of saltines and some toast, and she realized that she was half-starved.

"So," she said, looking up to flash Noah a grin. "Are we going to have a scone eating contest? Winter said this place has pretty amazing scones."

His smile in response was only half-hearted, and her curiosity grew. If there was one thing on the planet that could cheer up Noah Dalton, it was food.

"Probably not right now." He shrugged, and she didn't miss the forlorn shadow behind his green eyes. "We've still got to go back to work, and if I'm all full of scones, I'm liable to fall asleep while I'm going through all these damn phone numbers."

At the mention of the calls, Winter groaned and rubbed her eyes. "He's not wrong," she muttered. "I was thinking about double fisting espressos on my way back to the office."

"That bad, huh?" Autumn chuckled. Her need to know what in the hell was going on had reached critical mass, and if she didn't ask a question to shift the dialogue, she thought her head might explode. "Well, what's on your minds, guys? You both seem, I don't know…*weird.*"

Heaving a sigh, Noah shifted his gaze to the window at her and Winter's backs as he shook his head.

"Well." Winter paused to look thoughtful. "I know you said that you're going to be doing threat assessment at your new job. Aiden told me a little bit of what he knows about it, and I was wondering if we could get an expert's opinion on something we're working right now?"

This time, it was Autumn's turn to heave a sigh. "I'm guessing this is the same thing I talked to Aiden about a couple days ago, isn't it?"

"Wait." Winter raised an eyebrow. "You already talked to him about this?"

With a shrug, Autumn leaned her back against the cushioned booth. "Sort of. It was all pretty vague. He just wanted to know more about what might motivate someone to become a vigilante. I told him that people turning into Frank Castle isn't all that common, and that most disgruntled law enforcement agents find ways to take out their anger in the job. Bending rules, breaking rules, or just generally doing shady stuff. They don't usually break away from everything and go rogue, though."

"So, what about your job, then?" Winter asked. "The threat assessment part. It's like a proactive version of profiling, isn't it?"

Autumn shrugged again and nodded. "That's a simplified way to put it, yeah."

"And what if we had someone we wanted you to, you know, *assess*?" Winter's expectant gaze was fixed on Autumn.

She bit down on her tongue to keep the wide-eyed stare off her face.

Now, *this* wasn't what she had expected. She'd expected more vague queries and hypothetical situations, not a job proposition.

"Well, yeah," Autumn said after a brief silence. "My new boss said that they have a history of working with the Richmond PD and the FBI. It's a case by case thing, for the most part. They get the requests from the cops or the Feds, and after they sign some paperwork to agree on payment and confidentiality, they help them with whatever they're asking for."

Some of the strain on Noah's face was replaced with curiosity as he glanced to Winter. "I think that might be what we need, actually."

Winter nodded her agreement. "Yeah, I think so too."

"For what?" Autumn managed, furrowing her brows. "Are you guys trying to hire me for something?"

For the first time since she had arrived, the typical good nature returned to Noah's grin as Winter chuckled.

"I think so, yeah," Winter answered. "We've got the budget approval from a SAC."

"Wait a second." Autumn held up her hands as she turned her incredulous stare from Noah to Winter and then back. "Wait, hold on. My first day of work isn't until *tomorrow*. And as far as I know, that's just like a getting-to-know-you day. They show me around the building, hook me up with an office, that sort of thing."

"Might as well hit the ground running, though, right?" Noah asked with a wide smile. "You've got friends that're

Feds, remember? You've got to get some kind of bonus for putting up with us."

"Oh my god," Autumn muttered. "I thought the 'all you can eat scones' were the bonus."

He lifted a lazy shoulder. "It's part of it."

"We could really use your help." When Winter looked at Noah, he nodded.

"Yeah, actually," he confirmed. "We really could."

"Look," Winter said. "Right now, we've got jack squat for suspects, and the only evidence we've got to work with is... it's just...it's basically nothing. Everything we're going off of so far is circumstantial, and right now, our boss is looking at one of the agents in our division as a possible suspect. So, we need someone to evaluate that person to tell us how likely it is that they're capable of committing these murders."

When they laid out the scenario so plainly, Autumn found it was difficult to argue with their logic. Plus, in a competitive field like forensic psychology, she would be silly not to make use of every possible advantage she had.

Like Noah said, her friendship with a handful of federal agents was a distinct advantage. For most in her field, a reliable connection to the bureau was only established after years of experience. Rare were the instances where a person fresh out of graduate school walked into the job with connections that took an entire career to develop.

Then again, what were the odds that her boss would be comfortable sending a brand-new hire to work a high profile case like the murder of Tyler Haldane?

Chances were good that if she relayed the offer to one of the partners of the firm, they would assign the task to a more tenured psychologist. They might let her tag along, but Autumn doubted she would be given full control over the job.

"All right," she finally conceded. "Let me call my boss."

As she fished the smartphone out of her black handbag, she could almost feel their relief.

"Thank you," Winter said as Autumn pushed to her feet.

With a quick nod, Autumn forced a smile to her lips. "There'd better be a platter of scones waiting for me when I get back." For emphasis, she jabbed a finger at the laminate tabletop.

Noah chuckled. "I think we can work something out."

As Autumn made her way back out into the sunny afternoon and toward her car, she wished she had a cigarette.

Ever since she had submitted the handful of applications to graduate school, she had been confident in her psychology-related knowledge. Her grades were always straight As, and her grade point average had been a perfect 4.0 since her undergrad.

Whenever an opportunity to learn outside the classroom had presented itself, Autumn had leapt at the chance. She was well-versed in clinical sessions and research, and she had plenty of hours racked up in both arenas.

Hell, her dissertation had been accepted without a request for revisions. She knew what she was doing, so why couldn't she seem to shake this ridiculous lack of confidence?

Earlier in the day, both partners at the firm had commended the work she'd done on her dissertation, and they had been impressed with the practicum work and internships she had under her belt.

So why in the hell did she want the man on the other end of the line to assign the request from the FBI to someone else?

"This is Doctor Shadley," a familiar voice answered after the second ring.

"Hello, Dr. Shadley," Autumn said once she was satisfied she had pushed the jitters out of her voice. "This is Autumn. Autumn Trent."

"Good afternoon, Dr. Trent," the man replied.

To Autumn, Dr. Mike Shadley came across like a cool uncle or a long-time family friend. Even through the phone, she could hear the smile in his words, and she felt at ease.

She was glad she had been able to get ahold of him instead of the other partner, Adam Latham. Dr. Latham smiled just as often as Dr. Shadley, but there was an undertone to the man's expression that made Autumn's skin crawl. As much as she wanted to convince herself that she was paranoid as a result of her upbringing, by now, she knew better than to question her intuition.

Pushing past the thoughts of Dr. Latham, she leaned against the passenger side of her car and rattled off all the details she had been given by Winter and Noah. Both Adam and Mike knew about her connection to the Federal Bureau of Investigation, and she figured it had been her competitive edge.

"All right," Dr. Shadley said once she finished her explanation.

"All right?" she echoed, her tone carefully neutral.

"Yeah, all right." He chuckled. "I'll send the paperwork over to the bureau. We've worked with SSA Parrish and the BAU before. What time is it right now? Little after noon? Everything should be sent over and signed before the end of the day. Congratulations on your first job, Dr. Trent."

There was no hesitation in his proclamation, no stipulation that she report each and every move of hers back to him and Adam, no suggestion that she be accompanied by a more tenured psychologist. Apparently, Dr. Shadley had the utmost confidence in Autumn's capabilities.

She was still in a state of dumbfounded shock as she swiped the screen to disconnect the call.

"What. The hell." Squeezing her eyes closed, she massaged her temples.

On the bright side, she would have a chance to rip off the figurative band-aid on her first day of work.

The "sink or swim" methodology had always been conducive to Autumn's learning style, and she had never been keen on hand-holding or micro-managing.

If her discussion with Dr. Shadley was any indication, she would fit in her new role at the firm just fine.

22

When Aiden saw Mike Shadley's name on the electronic form sent over on Autumn's behalf, his eyes widened.

He knew she had been hired by a private firm, but he hadn't known *which* firm.

Shadley and Latham was a nationally renowned organization, and though their staff wasn't numerous, those they employed commanded a certain level of prestige that was difficult to find elsewhere.

Shadley and Latham wasn't an entry-level employer for newly minted graduate students.

He had the utmost confidence in Autumn, but the fact that she'd been offered the job straight out of graduate school begged more than one question.

Intelligence and hard work weren't enough to land such a lofty career. Maybe they *should* have been enough, but in reality, positions like those at Shadley and Latham were only obtained via personal and professional networks.

In short, if a brand-new Ph.D. graduate wanted a job like the one Autumn had been given, they had to know someone.

Like Aiden, Autumn had come from nothing. She hadn't been born into the elite academic circles that comprised most of those employed at the elite firm.

Who in the hell did she know? It seemed clear to him now that, no matter the research they'd done into her past during the Schmidt investigation, there was much about Autumn Trent that he still hadn't learned.

Was her aunt well-connected? Her adopted parents? A college roommate?

A knock at his office door snapped him from the contemplation. He was tempted to send Autumn a text message to ask her about the curious nature of her employment, but he shot the idea down and cleared his throat.

"It's unlocked."

The door swung inward with a creak to reveal his unlikely visitor.

There was an unmistakable glint of irritability in Max Osbourne's gray eyes, but Aiden already knew the reason for the irascibility. And for the first time in recent memory, Aiden wasn't part of the cause of Max's sour mood.

In fact, when Aiden had proposed his idea to have a forensic psychologist evaluate Sun Ming, Max had grunted out his approval.

The tenured SAC had taken on the task of informing Sun of the interview they'd scheduled for the following day.

Aiden wasn't foolhardy enough to try to broach the subject of Ramirez's suspicion with Sun. Fortunately, she wasn't under his supervision.

"Parrish," Max said as he eased the door closed. "I talked to Agent Ming."

"How'd it go?"

"How do you think it went?" Max's response was flat.

Aiden drummed his fingers on his desk. "Yeah, fair enough."

"I didn't tell her everything. I figure Ramirez can do that herself if she wants to. But I told her that she's expected here for an evaluation tomorrow morning, and I sent her home for the night. You're sure this is going to help her, right?"

He nodded. "I'm sure. This'll prove to Ramirez that there's no motive. Even if it doesn't convince her outright, it'll take the heat off Sun. Ramirez won't be breathing down her neck anymore."

At least Aiden hoped so.

"Good. Because we need Agent Ming on this case."

"Agreed. We need just about any help we can get on this case." Aiden tapped his finger against the wooden desk as he gave Max a grave look. "It might not be Agent Ming, but whoever's doing this *does* have experience in law enforcement. Just because it's not her doesn't mean that it isn't someone just as competent as her. Someone competent enough to leave behind a murder weapon that's virtually useless as evidence."

"What're you thinking so far?" Max asked as he crossed his arms.

Aiden shook his head. "I don't know. Hopefully, the forensic psychologist tomorrow can be of some help there too. Obviously, whoever the killer is, they're familiar with crime scene investigation. The weapon we recovered didn't just have a serial number that was scratched out, it didn't *have* a serial number."

"So, it's someone who's familiar with the black market sale of firearms?"

"It'd go hand in hand with them having law enforcement experience. If they're a cop, they know where to go to buy weapons like that. That was a Barrett rifle, but I don't think it was made by Barrett."

Running a hand over his buzzcut, Max blew out a sigh. "Seems like the more we find out, the more damn questions we wind up with. There's no telling where that weapon came from. Could've been made in the Philippines, in Indonesia, in fucking Afghanistan. Shipped over here and sold by one of the cartels or the Russians. Either way, trying to trace it won't get us anywhere. It's just going to spiral into a bigger and bigger mess."

"Then hand the rifle over to the ATF," Aiden suggested. "They've got the databases for arms dealers. They'd probably have someone who knows where it came from, if nothing else. If we can establish a general geographic area where we think the weapon was sold from, or even just the organization that sold it, it might help once we have a suspect."

Max had started to nod before Aiden finished. "That's a good idea. I already told Amy I'd be here late tonight, so I'll head down to forensics and get it started."

Aiden relaxed a little. "All right."

The SAC paused just short of the door handle. "Real quick, Parrish." His gray eyes flicked back over to Aiden. "I appreciate you backing me up on this. I know you and Agent Ming don't like one another all that much, and it says something that you can set that aside."

Aiden was seldom at a loss for words, but at the unexpected compliment, all he could manage was a nod and a stiff, "Thank you."

Before her visitor could knock, Sun turned the deadbolt and pulled open the heavy door. He had sent her a text message to advise that he'd left work for the night, but she still had only half-expected to see him so soon.

Bobby Weyrick's amber eyes shifted up to meet hers as a slight smile crept to his unshaven face, the scruff just a shade darker than his dark blond hair.

For the past few months, that smile was one of the only bright spots in her life. She returned the expression as well as she could before she stepped aside to wave him into the dim apartment.

"You still not turning on your lights?" he asked, the words laden with his native Tennessee accent.

"I was just lying on the couch, watching the fish," she answered with a shrug. "Do you want anything to drink?"

"Got any of that beer left?" He propped one hand against the drywall as he stepped out of his shiny black dress shoes.

Sun wrinkled her nose. "That Black Star stuff? What, you think *I* drank that shit? I figured you'd know better than that by now, Bobby."

"I'll take that as a yes." His grin did something funny to her insides.

"Yes," she confirmed. At his lighthearted tone, her smile came a little easier.

"Then I'll take one of those off your hands."

"I almost drank one when I got home tonight." With a sigh, she made her way to the kitchen. Behind her, Bobby's footsteps were little more than a whisper of sound.

"Why?"

"I was out of vodka," she muttered, prying open the stainless-steel refrigerator door.

As she handed him a cold glass bottle, she didn't miss the flicker of concern in his gold-flecked eyes. It wasn't the same type of condescending concern to which she'd become accustomed in the last six months.

It was genuine, and she *knew* it was genuine.

Though Bobby Weyrick was only a month older than Sun, he was a self-proclaimed old soul. When he had first pointed out the quirk, her immediate response had been to ask him if he was the reincarnated avatar of an Ancient Egyptian deity.

She'd never been a fan of the term "old soul," and whenever a person used it in conversation, her first thought was of the sun god, Ra. Rather than huff and puff, however, Bobby had burst into laughter.

With a hiss and a light clink, he twisted off the top of the brew and dropped the cap on the granite counter. She pulled herself from the recollection to flash him a quick smirk.

"I didn't drink that gross ass beer because I went and got more vodka," she admitted as she pulled open a cabinet door to retrieve a clear bottle of mid-grade vodka.

The announcement might have sounded hum-drum to anyone else, but Bobby knew the challenges with which she'd been faced since the shooting at the Riverside Mall.

The corner of his mouth turned up into the start of a smile. "It's a little ironic, you know. You calling my beer gross while you're talking about going out to buy that nasty stuff."

Sun rolled her eyes in feigned exasperation. "That's why you mix it with something else. What kind of monster do you think I am, anyway?"

"The kind that drinks straight vodka, apparently," he chuckled, though the sound held a worried edge.

"Turns out it's easy to get over anxiety when you're pissed," she said as she plucked a clean glass from the dish drainer in one of the two stainless-steel sinks.

"I saw your message," he replied, nodding as he took a swig of the bitter IPA. "You said Max sent you home early. Why?"

Lips pursed, she dropped a handful of ice cubes into the pint glass before she returned her gaze to Bobby's gold-flecked eyes. She was surprised at her reluctance to mention the reason for her unexpected meeting with the Violent Crimes' SAC.

What would Bobby think of her if she said that the Associate Deputy Director had labeled her a suspect in the murders of Tyler Haldane and the two others? Would the pieces click together in his mind like they had in ADD Ramirez's?

No. She ought to know better by now.

Of all the discussions she and Bobby had over the last few months, he'd never once become judgmental. Arguably, he knew her better than anyone else in the Violent Crimes Division, and maybe anyone else in the entire Federal Bureau of Investigation.

If there was anyone who would side with her against the allegations, it would be Bobby Weyrick.

"Sun," he murmured. "Are you all right? What's going on?"

As he reached out to clasp her shoulder, she finally snapped her attention away from the glass of ice and vodka. The warmth of his touch elicited a long-forgotten flutter in her stomach, and she wasn't sure whether she should recoil from the sensation, or revel in it.

Resting one hand against the back of his hand, she nodded. "I'm fine. I was a little pissed, and I guess maybe I still am, but I'm all right."

"What happened?"

She heaved a sigh as she squeezed his hand. "They think that I might've had something to do with the Haldane murder."

As she twisted open a bottle of cranberry juice, he took in a sharp breath.

"Why?" he asked after a pause.

"Because...you know how Haldane was shot from almost a mile away, right?"

"Right."

"And the weapon that was used was a Barrett M98 Bravo. Not a weapon that most civilians have just lying around in their gun safes. Not really something you take out to the range."

"Not unless your range is at a military base," he put in. "Rangers use M98Bs."

"Were you a ranger?" she asked, glancing over to him as she topped off her drink.

She knew Bobby had spent more than six years in the army, but aside from some of his specific experiences, they'd never broached the subject of his job in the military. Each time she had tried, he changed the topic, and she respected his decision to keep that part of his life in the past.

Shaking his head, he took another long drink from the brown bottle of beer.

"Something like that," he answered. "That's why I didn't join straight out of high school. You've got to be twenty-one to be in Special Forces, unless you're some kind of hotshot, I guess. But I knew that's what I wanted to do, so I worked a bunch of bullshit jobs in restaurants until I was old enough."

"Why'd you leave?"

They had drifted away from the initial topic—from the damn Haldane investigation—but she wasn't in a hurry to circle back.

He shrugged as his eyes met hers. "Just got tired of the military life, I guess. Moving around all the damn time, taking orders from guys who didn't know what the hell they were doing. I was stationed in Fayetteville to start, and I liked that well enough. But then they moved me out to Fort Riley in Kansas, and Fort Hood after that. And I don't know what it is about it, but I can't handle that Midwest climate."

She smiled. He'd bitched enough about the temperature in Virginia too.

"My NCO was friends with an FBI recruiter at Quantico, so I started asking him what he knew about working at the bureau. The more he told me, the more I thought it was time to make a career change. Working for the bureau seemed like it'd be rewarding, you know?"

Sun forced the smile to stay in place. She remembered feeling that sense of altruism.

"Being able to help people and make a difference, feel good shit like that. My NCO said he could hook me up with a spot in Richmond, and that was that. I might be on the night shift, but it beats the hell out of living in Texas. Do me a solid and don't tell Dalton I said that."

Despite the stressful end to her day, Sun laughed at the request. "Don't worry. My lips are sealed."

In the ensuing silence, she sipped at her vodka cranberry. She could almost gauge how badly her day had gone by the strength of the drink she mixed when she returned home from work. Today, the beverage was potent enough to warm her throat as she drank.

"Is that why they think you've got something to do with Haldane?" he finally asked. "Because you've got experience making shots like that?"

Wordlessly, she nodded. "I don't have an alibi for the times when any of the three of them were killed, either."

"But when Haldane was killed, weren't you…" He paused to fix her with a knowing look. "You were here, and I was with you."

"I know," she managed, though her voice was hardly above a whisper.

How could she forget?

She had never done anything like that before, didn't even think she *could* do anything like that. No matter the reassurances Bobby offered her, the guilt still gnawed at the back of her mind.

Bobby and Kara Weyrick's marriage might have been over in all but a legal sense, but the fact remained that he was *married*.

It didn't matter that his wife's affair had started well over a year ago and that it still hadn't stopped. It didn't matter that he'd abandoned his wedding ring a few weeks earlier, or that whenever someone asked about it, he merely advised that the band had been damaged.

The man was married. Period. End of story.

Sun was almost thirty-one, and by now, she should have known better. After all, how many stories—how many damn Lifetime movies—had been made about the married man who led his mistress on for months or years with the promise that he planned to divorce his wife? And in all those stories, how many of the men actually followed through with their promise?

She grated her teeth at the thought and took an even longer pull from the potent cocktail.

For god's sake, she wasn't a starry-eyed twenty-some-thing who had her head stuck in a fantasy that would never come true. In a month and a half, she would be thirty-one. She wasn't a college student or a damn intern—she was a federal agent with an impressive record of arrests and case closures.

"Just tell them, Sun."

His soft statement jerked her out of the spiral of self-loathing as she flashed him a wide-eyed stare.

"What do you mean?" she managed.

Though intent, his expression had softened, and the wistful tinge was back in his amber eyes. "Max, ADD Ramirez, whoever you need to tell to get them off your back. Just tell them."

She was already shaking her head. "I don't want to drag you into this. What if I tell them, and then they label you as a suspect too? Or an accomplice?"

"I doubt it," he replied. "I was at the office when Ormund was killed, and I was out of town the entire week of Stock-ley's murder."

"But they might think we're partners in crime or something," she reasoned. "Plus, if I mention that, then your marriage is definitely doomed."

With a self-deprecating chuckle, he shook his head. "That ship's sailed, honey. Might as well rip off the band-aid, hammer the final nail in the coffin, break the camel's back, whatever saying you want to use. Might as well just make it official and get it the hell over with."

She pushed past the unexpected wave of hopefulness. Though he'd become increasingly more cynical about his marriage, this was the first time she had heard him dismiss the union altogether.

"I still don't want to drag you into it," she decided. "I'm not worried that I'll go to prison. I didn't have anything to do with any of those scumbags getting killed. At this point, all I'm worried about is what will happen at work until they figure out who *actually* killed those assholes.

"Don't get me wrong. I'm pissed. But," she paused to hold up a hand as he snickered, "I'm not worried. I know I'm innocent, and so do you. Max told me himself that he doesn't buy into any of it, either. He said they just have to find something to eliminate me, and he knows they will. He set me up with a meeting with a forensic psychologist tomorrow morning. An evaluation or something like that, something he hopes will get Ramirez off my back so they can figure out who their actual suspect might be."

"A forensic psychologist?" Bobby echoed, raising his eyebrows. "Huh, I know a forensic psychologist. She's the one who told me about this beer." For emphasis, he held up the bottle and took a long drink.

"I still can't really believe there are other people who drink that."

"*Lots* of people," he answered with a wink. Setting the bottle on the granite counter, he held her gaze as he stepped forward to close the distance.

As much as she wanted to bring up the litany of doubts and worries she had for the future of their friendship—or whatever in the hell it had become—she didn't want to break the spell.

Rather than ask what their future held, she followed his lead. She was mesmerized, even enthralled by his closeness, and she couldn't remember the last time she'd succumbed to such a hypnotic lull.

They had only slept together once, on the night of Tyler Haldane's death. But when he brushed his hand over her cheek, she felt like they had known one another their entire lives.

When he leaned in to kiss her, she didn't hesitate to circle her arms around his shoulders as she parted her lips. With the warmth of his body so close to hers, the worries of the outside world seemed distant and insignificant.

"I want you to know something," he murmured, his breath tickling the side of her face as he separated from the kiss. "This means more to me than just a fling. *You* mean more to me than that. I don't want you to think that this is some sort of distraction for me. I really care about you, Sun, and I don't want you to doubt that."

With a slight nod and a smile, she pulled away to meet his gaze. Like everything else about the man, his words were genuine.

23

Noah couldn't remember the last time Winter had been the one to show up at his door with food. More often than not, their dinner time was driven by his appetite. But tonight, their roles had been reversed.

The scent of garlic wafted past as she made her way into the galley kitchen of his apartment. Aside from the color of the wooden cabinets and the tile in the kitchen and bathroom, their places were almost identical.

He pried open the refrigerator door and picked out two glass bottles of the same craft beer they'd been stuck on since Autumn introduced them to it months earlier.

As he handed one of the brews to Winter, her expression was a cross between concern and curiosity. At the look, he realized he hadn't spoken since she arrived, not even to offer a greeting.

"Are you all right?" Her tone was gentle, but she kept her eyes on him as she sipped her beer.

He wasn't.

Even if Sun Ming wasn't responsible for the murders of Tyler Haldane, Ben Ormund, and Mitch Stockley, there was a real possibility that a fellow federal agent had been involved. If not a Fed, then an officer in another law enforcement agency or a veteran of the armed forces.

Since the start of the case, he had kept his thoughts on the injustice of the whole situation to himself, but now he was sure the musings had reached a breaking point. If he didn't talk to someone about them, he knew he would lose the sense of direction that had motivated him to pursue a career with the FBI in the first place.

"No," he finally replied. With a sigh, he raked his fingers through his hair. "No. Not really."

"Well," she said, leaning her hip against the counter. "It seems like it's been bothering you for a while. At least since we started this case. What's up? Is it anything I can help with?"

Squeezing his eyes closed, he rubbed his face with both hands. "I don't know."

"Might as well give it a shot then." When he dropped his arms back to his sides to look at her, she offered a reassuring smile.

"Yeah," he agreed. "We don't have to stand in here, though. Let's go sit on the couch."

"It's a sweet couch."

"Thanks," he replied as he scooped up the foil container of fettuccine alfredo. "Autumn helped me pick it out. It was on clearance."

She nodded her understanding and followed him into the living room.

Rather than parse through décor at a home furnishing store, he had dug out a few posters, framed them, and hung them on the walls. Though he didn't have a knack for interior design, he still hated bare walls. But at thirty-two, he figured the time to tape band and movie posters on the wall had passed. He was an adult now, and he could afford a damn frame.

"Your posters get me every time," Winter chuckled as they dropped down to sit.

"I've told you before," he said with an upraised hand. "I'm a man of many interests. Don't judge."

"Oh, no judgment. It's just weird to see Johnny Cash next to Kurt Cobain, and *Scarface* next to John Wayne next to *The Wire*. It never gets old."

"I'm eclectic." He twirled a huge bite of his pasta onto his fork. "I've got a *Deadwood* poster somewhere, but I still need to buy a frame for it. That one might go in the kitchen."

"The one with Calamity Jane?" Winter asked before she shoveled a bite of ravioli covered with tomato sauce into her mouth.

"Yeah, that one. She's my favorite character in that show."

"I can see that. If she was around today, I feel like you guys would be friends."

"I think so too," he agreed.

The room lapsed into silence as they ate their Italian take-out, only the soft drone of the television in the background. Though Noah had never been keen on paying an absurd monthly fee for the ability to tune into the three channels he'd actually watch, cable had come free with the apartment. Before Winter showed up with dinner, he had stared absent-mindedly at a rerun of a competitive cooking show.

Try as he might, by the time they'd each finished most of their food, he had been unable to come up with a way to approach the subject of the bizarre guilt that had wracked his mind over the last week.

"It's this case," he blurted.

"That's what's been bothering you?"

He was glad he hadn't needed to elaborate. "Yeah."

"How so?" Her query was gentle, and he could see the concern in her blue eyes.

Heaving a weary sigh, he flopped back in his seat and shook his head. "It's the whole damn thing, honestly. All of it. Everything from how shitty Anne Timson and Linda Cahill were treated by the police, the people who were supposed to *protect them,* all the way down to Ramirez asking us to narc on Sun."

"Not to change the subject," Winter said, a glimmer of determination on her fair face. "But once we wrap this case up and get the press off our backs, I'm going to look into the people who helped Ormund push all his dirty secrets under the rug. Linda and her daughter deserve some kind of justice."

He made a sound that was close to a growl. "They got it, though, didn't they? Not from the cops. I mean, those guys didn't do a damn thing, but whoever shot Ormund in his perverted head was looking out for them more than the damn sheriff's department."

Winter sighed. "You're not wrong."

"And that's part of it. Part of what's wrong with this whole thing."

"What do you mean?"

"We're trying to track down someone who's looking out for real victims. I don't think it's Sun, and I know you don't either, but what if it's someone *like* Sun? What if it's a federal agent or a sheriff's deputy who just got sick of watching all this shit happen and decided to do something about it? How does it make any damn sense that we're trying to lock them up for life or execute them?"

Winter lifted an eyebrow. "Because it's illegal?"

He grunted. "I know it's illegal, and I know that even if they *are* in law enforcement, it doesn't give them free rein to go rogue and start shooting suspects in the head. The

Constitution is there for a reason, and we adhere to it. I get all that, but how is what they're doing any different from what I've done, you know? Scott Kennedy and Douglas Kilroy. I shot them both, killed them. I don't feel bad about it. I don't think I'll ever feel bad about it. You know I did two tours when I was in the military, right?"

She nodded and swallowed a bite of pasta before she answered. "Afghanistan and Iraq, right?"

"Yeah. Afghanistan was the second one, and Iraq was the first. Then I was in the Dallas PD for four years after I got back to the States. I've seen people like Ben Ormund and Tyler Haldane. I responded to two different active shooter situations while I was in Dallas. One was downtown, and the other one was on a college campus. The one downtown, no one died except the shooter. A couple people got hurt, but they made it through. The gunman blew his own head off before we could get to him."

Winter reached for his hand, gave it a quick squeeze. He wanted to link their fingers together, take comfort from the contact, but he didn't. He just dealt with the sense of loss when she moved her hand away.

"The one on the campus, though, that one was different. I got a bead on the guy, and I didn't even give it a second thought. I just pulled the trigger. And if I hadn't, I don't know how many people would've died. But I didn't get arrested or sent to prison or even reprimanded. The brass gave me a damn medal and a recommendation when I applied to the bureau. How's that any different? How many women do you think this person saved by taking out Ormund and Stockley?"

"Yeah, I get it." Winter shrugged as she reached out to clasp his shoulder. As she kneaded her fingers against the fabric of his shirt, the warmth of her touch seemed to radiate through his tired muscles.

He scrubbed his hands over his face. "It just feels like we're hunting the good guy."

"I think it's all right for us to feel like that," she said. "I don't think feeling that way and wanting to find them are mutually exclusive, you know? We can acknowledge that they might not be a bad person, but we still have to do our jobs. Even if they're decent, we can't let vigilantes run around killing people. But just because we know we have to put them away doesn't mean we can't sympathize with what they're doing, at least a little bit."

"I hate it," he muttered.

She squeezed him again. "I do too, but we've got to play by the rules, and so do they. Kennedy and Kilroy were both guilty, and they were both killed to save someone's life. *My* life, actually. Society doesn't work if we all just go off and do our own thing. I mean, maybe we agree with this person's morals, but who's to say some other asshole out there won't start killing people based on some messed up set of ideals like Tyler Haldane and Kent Strickland? And I hate what Linda and Anne had to deal with, but we don't fix that by letting people get away with murder."

"We won't," he rushed to assure her. "We fix that by doing *our* jobs and holding the people who fucked up accountable."

She nodded. "We fix that by doing our best, not by letting someone make up their own rules. And, honestly, we both know there's no way this guy or gal is going to be executed, right? There are mitigating circumstances out the wazoo, and I doubt any judge in their right mind will give the death penalty to someone who's only killed murderers and rapists. My best guess? I doubt it even goes to trial. I bet the US Attorney pleads it down to life in prison without parole, and that's that."

As she released her grip on his shoulder, she leaned forward to pick up the dinner roll that had come with her meal. She tore off a piece and used it to mop up some of the leftover sauce.

Each movement was fluid and nonchalant, like she hadn't just made one of the most profound observations he'd ever heard in his law enforcement career.

"You're really going to do that?" he finally asked. "Follow-up on Ormund, I mean."

"Yeah." She nodded as she swallowed the first bite from the roll. "And if Max won't let me work it, then I'll hand it to someone who can. Everyone and their brother will know about this case by the time we're done working it, and I intend to make sure that everything those scumbags did gets dragged out into the light. Even if I've got to do it on my own time."

A crumb was glued to her lower lip, and Noah had to look away in order to fight the temptation to not lean in and lick it off.

She didn't seem to notice his predicament. "Like I said, just because I'm trying to find the person who killed them doesn't mean I have to like or even tolerate Ormund or Stockley. They were pieces of shit, and they deserved to be put in prison a long time ago. Same with anyone who helped them get away with what they did. I might not be able to put Ormund and Stockley away now, but I can make sure their buddies pay for letting them get away with it."

"Yeah." He took a drink of his beer. "You know I'll help you, right?"

She turned her head and flashed him a warm smile. "Of course. And you know I wouldn't exclude you, right?"

He laughed. "Right."

An impossible burden—a burden that had called into question the same set of ideals around which he'd based his entire life—had been lifted, but he couldn't think of anything to say that would convey the depth of his gratitude.

"Thank you, Winter." He thought the statement sounded silly after what she had just said to him, but she smiled back at him just the same.

"Any time."

"I told you," he said with a grin. "Remember that day you felt bad, like you'd been hogging all our conversations?"

She smiled, a gentle curving of her lips. "Yeah, I remember."

"I told you that, someday, I'd be the one who needed help."

Her eyes grew shiny. "And today is that day?"

He reached out and squeezed her hand. "Yeah. Today is that day."

24

When Winter made her way to the main entrance of the FBI office, she could tell right away that Autumn was antsy. Once Autumn had been provided a visitor's badge, Winter gave her a quick tour of the building or at least the part of the building used by the Violent Crimes Division.

Though some of the nervousness left Autumn's demeanor after Winter introduced her to Max Osbourne, she was still on edge.

"Your boss is a good dude," Autumn observed as they made their way to a breakroom. "He really looks out for you guys, doesn't he?"

The first memory that came to Winter's mind was Max's refusal to let her in on the Douglas Kilroy investigation, but she bit back the knee-jerk irritability.

No matter her personal stake in the case, she knew Max had made the right decision. He knew the danger that Douglas Kilroy had posed, and he had only kept her off the case to ensure the cleanest possible investigation.

"He does," she replied.

"Oh, this must be the fabled breakroom coffee I've heard so much about." Autumn gestured to a half-full pot of dark liquid that resembled tar more than coffee.

Wrinkling her nose, Winter nodded. "Yeah, that's it. If you've got any furniture you need to strip paint from, I think that stuff'll do the trick. And it's free, so that's a bonus."

"Sure, I'll just go grab my paint bucket real quick, if that's all right with you?" Arching an eyebrow, Autumn jerked a thumb over her shoulder.

"If it'll save you a trip to the hardware store, then sure." Winter laughed. "You've got a little while before your interview, right?"

"Technically, I can do it whenever I want as long as the person's here," she replied with a shrug.

"Okay, then let's skip the paint bucket." Winter waved a hand at the coffee maker. "There's a place in walking distance that Noah and I always go to. Let's go grab some coffee and a scone. It's still really nice outside too. It's a good time for a walk, so we can take the long way back. Noah calls it the scenic route."

"Where is he, anyway?"

Winter flicked off the overhead light as they stepped back into the hall. "I think he had some calls to make, something to follow-up on. We've basically been telemarketers for the last week."

"Yikes," Autumn replied. "I worked a telemarketing job when I was in my undergrad. It was probably the most soul-sucking experience I've ever had. But every day when I'd go home from work, I'd be super motivated to do my homework."

"You did, really?"

"Yep. For a whole four months. Worst four months of my adult life, and that's not just because I was taking calculus at the time."

"Calculus was rough." Winter wrinkled her nose. "I worked at a call center too. We did inbound customer service, and it was still terrible. I'd always be extra motivated to do my homework too. It's like that job reminded me how terrible everything would be if I didn't put some effort into school."

"Exactly," Autumn snickered.

As they walked through the Violent Crimes department and out into the cloudy morning, they exchanged call center horror stories. From their coworkers to the customers to their bosses, there hadn't been a single aspect of the job they had enjoyed.

At the early morning hour, the inside of the coffee shop was sparsely populated. Most patrons were stopping by to pick up a caffeinated drink on their way to work, so not many had seated themselves throughout the space.

Winter and Autumn accepted their drinks and their scones, a chocolate chip scone for Winter and a blueberry scone for Autumn, and made their way to a table near the corner.

After the first bite, Autumn nodded her approval and complimented Winter for her breakfast decision.

"I should make scones more often," she mused. "They can be kind of a pain, though. You have to cut the butter into the flour and stuff, and when you've got the start of carpal tunnel like I do, it hurts your hand."

"You really need to meet my grandmother," Winter replied. "She would love you. I was interested in cooking for a little while when I was in high school, but I think that's because I was more interested in eating, honestly."

"Why do you think I like cooking so much?" Autumn asked with a grin. "It makes it a lot easier and a lot cheaper to stuff my face."

"I bet that's why Noah taught himself how to cook earlier this year."

"No doubt about that." Autumn nodded and sipped at her latte.

"So," Winter said after a short silence. "How are you feeling about your first job?"

"I don't know. All right, I suppose. It's not like I've never interviewed someone in a clinical setting before, you know. But, it's just a little weird since it's one of your coworkers. Not that it's a conflict of interest, I double-checked that. Since I don't know her and you guys aren't necessarily friends with her, that part's fine."

"That's good." Winter offered her friend a warm smile. "You've got this, then."

Her green eyes darted back and forth as she tapped the side of her paper cup. "Can I tell you something? Ask you something, I guess. About, you know, your sixth sense, or whatever you want to call it."

Once she glanced around to make sure no one could overhear them, Winter nodded. "Of course."

"Okay, this is going to sound really weird, so I'm just going to say it. That thing with your senses, that same thing happened to me."

Winter's mouth drooped open, and she didn't bother to conceal the awe from her dumbfounded stare. Before she could ask for an elaboration, Autumn went on.

"There was that, and then this other thing. Kind of like your headaches, I guess, but it's different. And no matter how many classes I've taken about cognition and brain function, I've never been able to find anything detailed about something like this happening. It's not uncommon for people to come out of serious head injuries with a different personality or something like that, but not, you know. *Abilities.*"

Winter made a soft snorting sound. "That makes us sound like the X-Men."

Autumn laughed and seemed to relax. "It kind of does. Sorry, I talk a lot when I'm nervous, and I guess I'm a little nervous. I've never really told anyone this before. I kind of told my ex, but I didn't tell him the extent of it. But, well, you said that sometimes you'll see something and it'll kind of jump out at you, right?"

Winter had managed to swallow most of her shock, and she nodded. "Right. It's like it'll almost glow red. It does glow, but it's not like a normal glow, you know what I mean? Because I don't see it lighting up anything around it, it'll just be that one thing that's lit up."

"That makes sense. Well, as much as it can make sense anyway." Autumn paused to take a drink of her latte and shrug. "For me, it's different. When I touch someone, like shake their hand or something, it's almost like I can feel what they're feeling. Their motivation, their emotions, whether or not they're lying. It's all really vague, but it's hard to explain."

"Wait a second," Winter said. "You can tell if someone's lying just by shaking their hand?"

"I can usually tell more than that." Autumn twisted her fingers together. "And sometimes, it's stronger than others. That probably has something to do with how strong the emotion is for the person, though."

"So, you could tell me what's going through my head right now if you shook my hand?" Winter asked, eyebrow arched.

"No." Autumn shook her head. "Not after I've gotten to know someone, or after I've spent a lot of time around them. I think that might be because by then I've got my own perception of them, and it messes with what I can pick up on. Jesus, I sound like I'm a damn weather balloon or something."

Winter snapped one hand up to cover her mouth as she

swallowed the drink of mocha before she had a chance to spit it all over the table. "A weather balloon?" she managed to say without snorting coffee through her nose.

"Hey, that's what it sounded like to me, all right? Talking about interference and whatever." Waving a dismissive hand, Autumn took another sip of coffee.

"Wow, though, that's a pretty useful ability, isn't it?"

"Yeah," she sighed. "I suppose. Sometimes I'd rather not know what people are thinking when I shake their hand, though. It makes you keenly aware of how many creeps are out there."

Winter wrinkled her nose. "I guess that's a downside."

"I'm just wondering, though. How do you do it? Obviously, it helps you with your work, right? So, how do you balance it? Or keep other people from finding out about it?"

"It's not always easy," Winter admitted. "Especially with the headaches. They got really intense while we were looking for, well, while we were trying to find who killed my parents. But the other part, for me, it's just a matter of making sure I've got a reason for why I found something that I probably wouldn't have if I didn't have this sixth sense. Usually, I just call it a hunch or say it's instinct. Because I guess, in a way, that's what it is."

With a thoughtful look, Autumn leaned back in her chair and nodded. "That makes sense. Yeah, I think I see it. For me, I'd just have to almost tailor my questions to what I already know."

"Exactly."

Winter smiled. For the second time in the past twenty-four hours, one of her close friends had sought her out to ask for her advice. And for the second time, she had been able to deliver.

25

Autumn took in a steadying breath and brushed off the front of her button-down blouse before she pushed down on the metal lever and shoved open the door.

She had been told by the special agent in charge of Violent Crimes that the woman she was scheduled to interview would meet her in the cramped conference room. There were plenty of free interrogation rooms, but Autumn had been clear that she didn't want their discussion to feel like an interrogation.

She wasn't a cop; she was a psychologist. And she wasn't here to interrogate a federal agent. She was here to collect information.

As Autumn stepped into the dim space, a pair of dark eyes snapped up from the polished tabletop to scrutinize her.

She didn't have to touch the woman to know that mistrust and flat-out paranoia brewed beneath her otherwise calm veneer.

Pocketing her phone, the shorter woman pushed to her feet. The overhead light caught the shine of her shoulder-length ebony hair. Each movement stiff, almost reluctant, she stuck out a hand and nodded at Autumn.

Here it was. The moment of truth.

Autumn forced a smile to her face as she accepted the handshake.

The suspicion alight in the woman's eyes had been expected, but what she hadn't anticipated was the feeling of anxiety that lurked beneath the irritability. Right away, Autumn knew she had a secret, but at the same time, she knew the secret wasn't on the level of first-degree murder.

No, this woman's secret had to do with a romantic inter-est. She had hidden her conflicted thoughts about a man, not a crime.

"Special Agent Ming," Autumn said as she took a seat on the opposite side of the circular table, "I'm Dr. Autumn Trent. You have some idea why we're here today, don't you?"

The agent nodded. "I do. This is about the Haldane case. Specifically, about whether or not *I* killed the little shit."

"Right," Autumn replied once she had pushed down her chortle. "And you know that your Fifth Amendment right to silence still applies here, right? This isn't a clinical session, and anything you tell me can be used in a court of law."

For the second time, Sun nodded.

She already knew Sun Ming had not killed Tyler Haldane, and by proxy that she had not killed Ben Ormund or Mitch Stockley. Now, like Winter had suggested, she had to back-track to obtain evidence to prove what she had already discovered.

Sun's thoughts were wrapped up in a romantic conflict, so maybe all Autumn had to do was reveal the office romance to clear the woman from the list of suspects? That felt like the right direction.

"I'll start simple, then. Agent Ming, did you kill Tyler

Haldane?" Autumn clicked the end of her pen as she met the woman's intense gaze.

"No," Sun answered. "I didn't."

Autumn couldn't help but wonder what the agent's expression would look like if she gathered up her notepad and pen, thanked her for her time, and left.

Instead, she continued on through a series of questions, the answers to which had been proven to yield valuable insight in threat assessment. Unsurprisingly, all Agent Ming's responses—combined with what Autumn had learned of her temperament and her history at the bureau—were consistent with low risk.

"All right, Agent Ming," she said, flashing the other woman a quick smile. "I'd like to ask a couple personal questions, if you don't mind. Are you in a romantic relationship?"

Though the gesture was slow, Sun shook her head. "No." Either Sun had lied, or she was unsure of her standing with her romantic interest.

Until she spotted the fib, Autumn had not intended to pry into Ming's interpersonal relationships, but now, she wanted to know why the woman had lied.

Autumn clicked her pen and set the utensil atop the notepad. She kept each motion measured and slow as she folded her hands atop the table and glanced up to Sun. So far, Autumn had been relaxed and agreeable, but now, the sudden shift to stern and disciplined was designed to throw Sun off-balance. And as far as Autumn could tell, the tactic had worked.

"Have you ever dated someone from work? From the FBI office?" Fingers interlocked, Autumn didn't let her stare waver.

Maybe she *should* have used an interrogation room.

When Sun started to shake her head, Autumn raised her eyebrows.

"Who the hell are you?" the agent managed as she narrowed her eyes. "And what do these questions have to do with *anything?*"

"Relationship status has been associated with predictors for violent behavior. Whether or not you've dated a coworker establishes the type of environment where you work. Hostility toward coworkers, grudges, things of that nature." The statement was sweeping and broad, but technically, it *was* true. There was a reason car insurance rates declined when a person got married. "Of course, you're still entitled to your Fifth Amendment protections, Agent Ming."

The shadows shifted along Agent Ming's face as she clenched and unclenched her jaw. "I'm not dating anyone right now, but..." She paused to sigh. "There is someone. It's just, it's complicated."

"Complicated how?"

"Complicated as in he's at the tail end of a failing marriage, and I feel like I'm just some kind of fucking reprieve!" she snapped. Wide-eyed, she raised a hand to cover her mouth.

"It's all right," Autumn replied, spreading her hands. "Look, no notes, see? This isn't being recorded, and unless there's something I don't know about, no one's listening in. Off the record, I know the feeling."

This time, she had not exaggerated or otherwise stretched the truth. Not long after she moved to Virginia, she had been in the same situation that clearly weighed so heavily on Sun's mind.

Now, almost a year after their split, Autumn attributed the entire debacle to her youth and the naivety that came with it. He was twelve years her senior, and at the time, she thought the idea of dating such a smart, savvy man was thrilling. And maybe it still was, but she was no longer the starry-eyed graduate student who had just moved from the Midwest to the coast.

"Well, thanks," Sun muttered. "To answer your question, yes, I've dated a coworker. That relationship ended a while ago, and we weren't ever in the same division. He's in the BAU, and I've always been in VC."

"He was in the BAU?" Autumn echoed, raising an eyebrow.

"Still is," she confirmed.

So, maybe the work environment at the Richmond FBI office wasn't conducive to an agent's violent tendencies, but there were plenty of unorthodox dynamics that lurked beneath the polished surface.

As AUTUMN FLIPPED to the second page of her notepad, her expression was thoughtful but calm. Aiden couldn't remember the last federal agent who had been as relaxed in the presence of the SAC and the Associate Deputy Director, much less a brand-new Ph.D. graduate.

But try as he might, he could not spot so much as a hint of unease in her demeanor.

"You said Agent Ming has been acting bizarre, isn't that right?" Autumn asked, glancing up to Cassidy Ramirez.

Ramirez nodded. "She's always been standoffish, but lately, it seems like she isolates herself more. Like she's been more cut off from her coworkers. You had a chance to speak to Agent Vasquez and Agent Camp, didn't you, Dr. Trent?"

"I did," Autumn replied with a quick smile. "And it does seem like she's been markedly less sociable since the Riverside Mall, but..." Before Max could interject, Autumn held up a hand. "I don't think it's because she's snapped and become a vigilante. Everything Agents Camp and Vasquez told me, plus what I heard from Agent Ming herself points to posttraumatic stress."

"Are you—"

Autumn powered on. "How tall is Agent Ming?" When her emerald eyes settled on him, he didn't miss the knowing glint. "A few inches over five foot? She's petite, and a Barrett M98 Bravo isn't a small weapon. It's not as dramatic as some others, but considering Agent Ming's recent shoulder injury, I don't think it's all that likely that she lugged a weapon of that size around with her up six flights of stairs."

"But—"

Autumn wasn't finished. "And Mitch Stockley was killed *before* the shooting at the Riverside Mall, correct?"

The question was rhetorical, but Ramirez nodded. "Yes. A week before."

"But the working theory here is that the Riverside Mall was Agent Ming's breaking point, isn't that right?"

Aiden could almost hear Cassidy's teeth grind together as she nodded for the second time, and he struggled to keep the expression of awe off his face.

The smirk that tugged at the corner of Max's mouth was unmistakable. He was right, and he now had the word of a psychologist from an elite firm to back his assertion.

"Then if Agent Ming is still a suspect, the Riverside Mall doesn't explain Mitch Stockley. In addition, Agent Ming is almost thirty-one. That's past the usual age for the onset of disorders like paranoid schizophrenia, so the likelihood that she suffered a psychotic break is slim. There's no history of schizophrenia in her family, either, and schizophrenia is usually precluded by some sort of genetic predisposition."

The ADD raised a brow. "People snap."

"With all due respect, ADD Ramirez, people don't snap and decide to go on a killing spree without leaving a trail that spans months, even years. There's nothing else in Agent

Ming's history to suggest that she was nearing a breakdown before the Riverside Mall. She was raised in a middle-class, two-parent household with a twin brother, pets, and a close extended family.

"She's well-established at this office, and despite the recent reports of social isolation, she has a strong connection to what she does at the bureau. It's my professional opinion that Agent Ming poses a low risk of violent behavior, and it's my professional opinion that she's not responsible for the murder of Tyler Haldane, Mitch Stockley, or Ben Ormund. I'll have a written synopsis sent to you by the end of the day, but those are the highlights."

"Thank you, Dr. Trent," Ramirez replied as she rose from her seat to extend a hand to Autumn. Autumn's smile wobbled a bit as they touched, then brightened through what looked like some effort.

What was that all about?

When Autumn stepped to the side to shake Max's hand, Aiden half-expected the man to offer her a high-five instead.

With a kindly smile, the likes of which Aiden seldom saw the tenured SAC wear, Max defied Aiden's expectations and merely shook her hand. Her expression was unreadable as she bade Aiden farewell, but the blank look only invited more questions.

He excused himself before he could bear witness to Max's victory stretch—the same exaggerated, casual motion he made whenever his point was proven.

As he hurried around the corner, he caught the glint of the overhead lights on the polished silver doors of the elevator as they started to ease shut. Attention fixed on her phone, Autumn leaned against a metal handrail.

"Hey," he called, waving an arm for emphasis.

Her bright eyes snapped up from the screen, and for a split-second, he thought she intended to let the elevator shut before he could close the distance. At the last possible instant, she stepped forward and stretched out one hand to halt the motion of the doors.

"Do you have a minute?" he asked as he moved to stand at her side.

She shrugged and pocketed her phone. "That depends."

"It depends on what?"

"On what you want to talk to me about," she replied with a sweet smile.

"What do you *think* I want to talk to you about?"

Another shrug.

"Seriously? Did I miss something?" He furrowed his brows and turned to flash her an exasperated look. "Well, did I?"

"Isn't this a conflict of interest?" she asked once the doors had closed.

"What? What the hell are you talking about?"

"You, right now." She turned to face him full-on. "Asking me about a forensic risk assessment I just did for your ex-girlfriend. Isn't that a conflict of interest, or do you guys operate under different rules here at the bureau? Should you have even *been* in that meeting?"

"For the love of…" Snapping his mouth shut, he squeezed his eyes closed, searching for calm. After a second deep breath, he said, "That relationship ended two years ago. So, no, Autumn. It's not a damned conflict of interest." He should have known she would figure out his and Sun's history. There was no way to keep a secret from the woman, was there?

"So, then it's just unprofessional?"

"What?" He came very close to sputtering, then managed to calm himself. "Why do you care?"

"I'm just trying to make sure you aren't prying into her personal life. Two years or not, an ex-girlfriend's an ex-girlfriend. Honestly, if someone did a forensic interview with my ex, I think I'd still be a little curious. Granted, that only ended one year ago, and not two." There was a hint of petulance as she offered him a sarcastic smile.

He decided to turn the tables. "How did you get a job at Shadley and Latham?"

When she narrowed her eyes, he knew he'd hit a nerve. "What the hell does *that* mean?"

"Take it at face value," he shot back. The number beside the control panel changed from a three to a two, and he doubted she would stick around for long once they had reached the main floor. "You're accusing me of being unethical, so it only seemed fair. Doesn't feel great, does it?"

"Oh my god," she muttered. "Point taken. Really, though, you could have mentioned it before I went to talk to her. Could have saved me a whole series of questions."

"Maybe. I'll keep that in mind next time. You know, just in case you wind up interviewing another murder suspect I used to date."

Her laugh sounded more like a snort as she glanced back to him. "Do you have a type, Aiden? Or do you just make a habit of picking up chicks from the FBI office?"

"Yes, I do, but it's not murder suspects. And no, I don't. Now, could I ask you a real question?"

She made a show of appearing thoughtful. "I guess so. What's up, chief?"

"Chief? No, can we not do that? Please?"

Feigning an exasperated sigh, she planted her hands on her hips. "Fine. What's your question?"

"Now that you've got all the details of this investigation, and now that I don't have to talk to you in hypotheticals, could I get your opinion on what we have so far? We, meaning the BAU."

"Sure." She leaned against the wall. "I've got a little time."

"I appreciate it." Even as he spoke, he was unsure of his motivation. He wanted to know who had recommended her for the position at Shadley and Latham, but at the same time, he valued her input.

And then, of course, there was the inexorable draw he felt to her.

He was well and truly on the way to being fucked.

26

As I watched a man push open his car door to step beneath the neon glow of a vacancy sign of the Greendale Motel, I dropped my finished cigarette into the ashtray in the cupholder.

After six years in forensic science, I knew better than to leave behind any piece of evidence, even if it was as innocuous as a cigarette butt. The pock-marked parking lot of the shabby hotel might have been littered with cigarette butts, but I wasn't about to take the chance.

It was a nasty habit I had picked up during basic training for the army. Once my daughter was born, I finally found the motivation to quit.

My wife had given up smoking during her pregnancy, but since I had been overseas for half of it, I hadn't followed suit right away. That had been a stressful time, and I doubted I would have been able to quit even if I'd tried.

Tina had said as much when she called me to tell me the news. She had suggested I wait until I was back in the States, but that was just the type of person Tina was. She was always more understanding than I deserved, and there wasn't a day that went by where I didn't miss her and my little girl with every fiber of my being.

Life had been good. Hell, it had been better than I ever thought it could be.

But then, a man like James Bauman—the sleaze I had tailed for the last couple days—had taken it all away from me.

Once Tina and Evie were gone, I didn't see any reason to stay away from the nasty nicotine habit. In those dark days, I had wanted to die right along with them, and with every drag, I got a little bit closer.

But as long as I was here, I'd make good use of the skills the army had given me.

Before I lost Tina and Evie, I had been sure I would make my career in the Army Rangers. I was a lieutenant before I turned thirty, and a captain before I turned forty. The military taught me to work as a part of a team, but it had also taught me to be a leader.

More than anything, it taught me how to kill.

There were few groups in the world more skilled at the art of death than the elite factions of the United States military.

While I was in the army, I'd never focused on how good I was at killing. What was more important to me was ensuring all the soldiers under my command made it home to see their families again.

It was ironic, but I never gave much consideration to my unorthodox skill set until after I left the military. Over in the desert, we all knew how to kill, but over here, well...

That was a different story.

Men like Mitch Stockley, Tyler Haldane, and Ben Ormund might have dabbled in death, but I *was* death.

Those three men thought they held the balance of life and

death in the palm of their hands, but they didn't know anything.

Haldane knew how to fire a gun, Stockley knew how to strangle someone to death, and Ormund knew how to smother someone while they were unconscious. Maybe if they had familiarized themselves more with the innumerable methods to snuff out a human being's life, they wouldn't have died so easily.

Sometimes, I wondered if a day would come where I would learn that one of the men on my list met my level of physical prowess, but I doubted it.

Those with a firm handle on the ability to kill weren't the same types who stooped to the level of Ben Ormund. To be as effective as I was required discipline, and men like Tyler Haldane were far from disciplined. Plus, if they wanted to face me and live to tell the tale, they needed a physique that far surpassed that of Mitch Stockley.

I knew that today would not be the day I met my match, and James Bauman would not be that person.

Despite his six-foot-two, broad-shouldered frame, Bauman was a peon. He was a pitiable excuse for a human being, and he took out his insecurities on some of the most vulnerable, the part of society for whom the media held little sympathy. The part that had been thrown to the wayside by the decent folks of the surface world.

To me, that made James Bauman the worst of the worst, and tonight, I intended to make that perfectly clear to him.

Bauman was a drop in the bucket, and I knew none of what I did would start a revolution in the streets. More than likely, it wouldn't make an average person look twice.

Not until I made my way through a few more of the names on my list, at least.

Once Bauman obtained his room key from the clerk, he made his way back to the door numbered eight and let himself into the room. When he reemerged, he cast a quick glance up and down the parking lot, but I was slumped down too far in my seat for him to see me.

After the thud of a car door, the quiet drone of an engine came to life. I waited until the sound grew faint and eventually faded away altogether. As I straightened myself, I saw the vacant spot where Bauman's car had been.

Clenching and unclenching my gloved hands, I patted the sheathed hunting knife inside my zip-up hoodie and double-checked to make sure the lockpick was still in my pocket.

It was showtime.

I kept my hood up and my head down as I strode across the parking lot. The place was a shithole, but there were still a handful of security cameras set up around the perimeter. I didn't know if they were for show or if they were active, but like I'd decided with my cigarette, there was no need to take the chance.

To any passersby—though there were none, not at this hour—I didn't look like someone picking a lock. I had picked more locks than I could count, and it took the same amount of time it would have taken if I had a key.

In the relative cover of the dingy room, I pushed the hood away from my face. As I retrieved a matte black nine-mil from beneath my sweatshirt, I stepped back into the shadowy bathroom. There, I waited.

When the metallic click from the door told me that Bauman had returned, I reflexively tightened the sound suppressor I had attached to the barrel of my weapon. I didn't intend to shoot James Bauman, not unless he made the act necessary.

From where I stood just inside the doorway to the bathroom, I could see Bauman's tall form block out the lamplight as he led his female companion into the space.

Her green eyes flicked back and forth, her posture stiff,

movements rigid. Her denim miniskirt ended at mid-thigh, and her halter top was so low-cut that the red lace of her bra peeked out from the neckline.

By my best estimate, she was barely legal.

That was Bauman's preference. He liked girls—and they *were* girls, not women—that were far too young for him. Bauman had turned forty-seven earlier in the year, and he and his wife had been married for sixteen years.

What a miserable union that must have been.

From the way the working girls around the area told it, Bauman had a penchant for luring prostitutes to his hotel room where he inflicted all manner of horror on them. None of the women ever went to the police, and that was precisely why the asshole continued to target them.

At least two, both under seventeen years old, had disappeared after they had been tortured and raped by the lunatic.

Though most of the prostitutes in this part of the city knew to avoid Bauman, there were still plenty of newcomers who weren't aware of the man's reputation. He knew it, and he counted on their unfamiliarity. He counted on their desperation.

In one fluid motion, I stepped out into the light and leveled the nine-mil at Bauman's head. He had been speaking, but I didn't especially give a shit what he had to say.

"Whoa!" he exclaimed as he threw his hands into the air.

At his side, the girl's mouth gaped open as she glanced from me to Bauman and back.

"Who the hell are you?" he asked. His voice was high-pitched and panicky, and the tone brought the start of a scowl to my face.

I didn't answer. I preferred to let him stew.

"What do you want?"

"Take out your wallet. Keep the movements nice and slow, James. Or do you prefer Jim?"

"Money?" His question sounded more like a squeak, and I almost laughed aloud. When he produced his wallet, he shot me a pleading look.

"I don't want your fucking money. Give all your cash to her." I inclined my chin in the girl's direction.

"Wh-what?" he stammered.

"Did I stutter?" I kept my voice level. Calm. Dangerous. "Give her your money, or I'll blow your fucking head off, James."

His hands shook as he opened the leather wallet and pulled out a wad of twenties. The girl's wide-eyed stare hardly wavered from me as she accepted the cash.

"All right, kid," I said. "Get out of here."

She didn't pause to question my motive before she pocketed the money, pulled open the door, and sprinted out into the night.

Now, it was just Bauman and me.

James Bauman owed me, and it was time to collect.

27

Noah and Winter hadn't made it halfway to the office before Max Osbourne called to redirect them to a shabby hotel close to the edge of town. According to what Noah could hear of Max's dialogue, the Greendale Motel was a shithole just off the exit ramp for the interstate. Drifters and vagrants frequented the area, and murders weren't uncommon.

This murder, however, was different.

"The guy was killed some time in the middle of the night. There's another index card," Winter advised after she returned the phone to the pocket of her blazer. "Osbourne wants us to swing by and talk to Dan Nguyen after we leave the scene. He said Dan got called in in the middle of the night, so he might be a little grouchy."

Noah was feeling a little grouchy himself. "Should we stop and get him a coffee?"

"Not a bad idea," Winter replied with a yawn. "And a scone. It's physically impossible to be angry while you're eating a scone."

Noah nodded. "That's a scientific fact."

If an outside observer had witnessed their conversation about scones and baked goods on the drive to a gruesome crime scene, they would have thought Winter and Noah were insane.

But as soon as they flashed their badges to the crime scene tech at the door of room number eight, their focus returned, and they walked through the crime scene with keen eyes and clear heads.

"What does it say this time?" Noah asked as Winter retrieved the evidence bag that contained the index card.

"There are a couple of names on it," Winter replied, holding the card up to the light. "And dates. It's typed, just like the last one. Same font and everything."

Noah leaned in to squint at the writing. "Alicia Perez, June twentieth, 2015. Melody Harrison, October thirtieth, 2017."

"We've already sent the names over to have someone take a look at them," one of the crime scene techs, a woman with a platinum blonde pixie cut, advised. "That was just a little bit ago, but chances are good they'll have something for you soon. That's pretty specific information."

"Victims." Winter's tone was grave as she shifted her blue eyes back to Noah. "They're James Bauman's victims, I guarantee it."

"It fits," Noah agreed. "Is the person who worked the front desk still here?"

The tech nodded. "She is. She's out in the lobby."

Winter headed for the door. "Let's go talk to her."

They ducked under the yellow crime scene tape and made their way to the end of the row of hotel rooms. The silvery tinkle of a bell sounded out as he pushed open the glass and metal door, and a gray-haired woman and the Richmond police officer at her side both snapped their attention over to the entrance.

Reaching into his suit jacket for his badge, Noah offered them both a smile and a nod.

Though faint, the woman returned the expression.

"Good morning," he said. "I'm Agent Dalton with the FBI, and this is Agent Black. I know you've probably been answering questions all morning, but if you don't mind, we've got a few quick ones for you before we head out."

"Of course," the woman replied, straightening in her office chair.

"What can you tell us about the victim? Is he someone you've seen around here before? Anyone you're familiar with?" Noah asked.

She shrugged her bony shoulders. "I've seen him around a few times, I think. Always pays in cash up-front, always leaves well before checkout the next day. I've been doing this job a while, agents, and I can tell when folks who come through here don't quite fit in. Mostly business types, you know? Guys with a tan line on their left ring finger come to dip into the slums for a little fun."

Winter smiled at the woman. "I know their type."

The woman's smile warmed a few degrees. "Don't we all, honey. They don't give a shit about anyone around these parts. They just come to get what they want, use us up, and then forget we exist until the next time they need their fix. They might walk and talk like they're better'n me and mine, but they ain't no different."

"And that's what this guy was?" Noah asked. "James Bauman, that was his name. He was one of those?"

Crossing both arms over her chest, she nodded. "He was. A wolf in sheep's clothing, that's what he was. Like I said, agents. I've been doing this job a long time, and I know the dangerous ones when I see 'em."

"Was there anyone with him?" Winter asked.

"Not when he checked in, no. That's the only time I saw

him, and he was alone. They usually are when they pay for the room."

"Do you have any security cameras around here?" Noah gestured to the doorway. "I saw some on the parking lot lights. Do they work?"

"They do," she answered with a stiff nod.

"We've already got all the footage sent over to the bureau," the officer put in. "We know this is your jurisdiction, but we're here to help."

"Appreciate it," Noah replied. "All right, ma'am. That's all the questions we've got for you for now. I'll give you my card, and you just give me a call if you remember anything else, all right?"

Jaw clenched, the woman accepted the business card from his outstretched hand. "Yeah, all right, agent, but I have to say…the world is a better place with the likes of him no longer in it."

NOAH FELT strange bringing food to the medical examiner's office, but he and Winter had stopped at a café to purchase a peace offering for Dan Nguyen.

In all his interactions with Dan, Noah had never seen the man in a sour mood, but he suspected that was a bridge he didn't want to cross. Even if Dan wasn't grouchy, the scone and caramel latte would keep the potential for grouchiness at bay.

"Agents." Dan's dark eyes flicked away from the computer monitor as he turned in his chair to face them.

The man's office was impeccable, but then again, the space was minimally decorated. Aside from the computer monitor and a wireless keyboard, a notepad, and a cup of pens, his desk was unadorned. There were a couple succulent plants on the windowsill at his back, and his medical degree and various certifications decorated one wall. Other than the two chairs that faced the desk, the space was unadorned.

"You should get a potted plant or something in here," Noah said as he held out the paper cup of coffee.

"I put up a tree for Christmas," Dan replied with a shrug. "I usually put it up at the beginning of September and hang little ghosts and stuff on it. Then I switch them out for turkeys, and then actual Christmas ornaments after that. My ex suggested I keep it up year-round and just decorate it for each season, but I'm not sure if that'd be tacky."

Winter laughed. "Tacky, but awesome."

The suggestion sounded familiar, but Noah couldn't place where he had heard it before. They had a long day of sifting through security camera footage and criminal records ahead of them, and he decided to drop the topic altogether.

"We're here with peace offerings," he said instead. "A caramel latte and a chocolate chip scone."

"You guys spoil me." Dan chuckled as he accepted the brown paper bag from Winter. "My guess is you want to see James Bauman, though, don't you?"

With a grin, Noah nodded. "You guessed right, my friend."

"Right." Dan pressed both palms against the polished wooden surface and pushed to his feet. "You can leave your coffees in here if you want." He made his way around the desk and beckoned them to follow.

"It looked like there was a lot of blood on the carpet in that room," Winter observed.

Dan sighed. "Yeah. If there hadn't been an index card with this guy, I wouldn't have guessed it was the same killer. This one was up close and personal, not like the last two."

"Serial killers vary," Winter said. "They vary in how strict their ritual is, and how many details they include in it. Same with the way they pick victims. Some serial killers will fixate on a certain appearance and age, others fixate on a profession. And while a lot of them kill their victims the same way each time, there are some that just kill their victims without a real ritual. They're still serial killers since they're targeting a specific type of person, and the thought process is probably the same for each time they kill someone."

Dan was nodding. "Sounds about right."

"Like our killer, here," Winter went on. "He shot the first three, and even though those three were pretty distinct from one another, they shared one common thread. For our guy, that's what he really fixates on. It's not about the way he kills them or what they look like, or their lifestyle, at least not for the most part. Even though Ben Ormund and Mitch Stockley were a lot alike, Tyler Haldane didn't really fit with them, at least not at first glance."

"Damn," Noah breathed, glancing over to her as they descended a set of steps. "Did you get that from Parrish?"

She shook her head. "No. From Autumn. We talked about it last night after you went home and went to bed."

"Shit, remind me not to do that anymore."

"She's right," Dan put in. "Some serial killers are opportunistic, and some are really methodical. They've all got rituals, they just vary in where they apply that ritual. For this guy, the only ritual is that he kills them. It's quick and clean. He doesn't kick their ass or torture them, doesn't sit down to have a long conversation, doesn't do anything sexual. He just kills them."

"He executes them," Noah surmised.

Dan nodded as he pushed open a set of double doors. "Exactly."

Snatching a pair of latex gloves from a box on a stainless-steel counter, they were bathed in a harsh fluorescent glow as Dan flicked on the remaining overhead lights.

"How did this guy die?" Winter asked. They followed Dan to the silver exam table.

As Dan pulled down the white sheet, his mouth was set in a straight line. For the first time, Noah thought he might have caught a glimpse of the man's irritability.

Good thing we brought those scones, he thought.

"There aren't any other wounds, just the stab wound that killed him." Dan glanced up to them as he clamped one hand down on the dead man's shoulder to roll him to his side. With one gloved hand, he gestured to a single red slash. "One incision, right here. Blade entered between the middle two ribs, sliced through the lung, and then nicked the bottom of his heart."

Noah leaned in for a closer look. "That's a little different than a bullet to the head."

"Yes and no," Dan replied, shrugging. "There's one distinct similarity between this wound and the shots that killed Haldane and Ormund."

Winter studied the ME. "Which is?"

"They're both indicative of elite military experience." Dan eased Bauman's shoulder back to the silver table before he pulled the sheet back up to cover his lifeless face.

"How so?" Winter asked. "And what do you mean by *elite* military?"

"Special Forces," Noah answered. "Navy SEALs, Rangers, groups like that."

With a snap, Dan removed the latex gloves and tossed them into a biohazard bin. "Exactly. I wasn't a SEAL, but I was around enough of them while I was in the Navy that I picked up a few things. This stab wound, this was one of them. It's a technique that the special warfare factions of the military would use when they needed stealth. The knife cuts through the person's lung, so they can't shout or scream, and as soon as it nicks their heart, they die. Usually, they'd hold one hand down over the person's mouth just to make sure they couldn't make a sound, just in case."

"Shit," Winter managed. "That's hardcore."

Dan nodded. "Whoever you're looking for is hardcore too. Look, I know I'm not part of the BAU, but I spent enough time around the military life to say with some certainty that whoever you're looking for, they've got elite military training. They can handle a Barrett rifle well enough to hit someone between the eyes from almost a mile away, and now this."

He paused to wave a hand at Bauman. "I know Parrish has been looking at this from the pissed off cop angle, but I think you need to add 'elite military' to that descriptor. But, like I said." He held up both hands as if to show them he was unarmed. "I'm just the ME."

"Great." Noah shoved his hands into his pockets. "It's one thing to have a disgruntled cop running around, but a disgruntled cop that's a Navy SEAL too?" He sighed and shook his head.

Winter shrugged. "It makes sense. It fits with everything else we've got so far, and it narrows down our suspects."

"You're looking for a combat veteran, without a doubt," Dan advised, his expression flat as he crossed his arms over his chest. Let me know once you find out why James Bauman was in this guy's crosshairs. Based on where his body was found, he's got some skeletons in his closet."

28

A twinge of guilt followed the wave of relief that rolled over Sun when she received the announcement about James Bauman's murder.

Bauman had been killed at approximately three in the morning. Sun hadn't been able to sleep, and she had asked Bobby if he needed help with anything at the office. That had been at two, and she hadn't left the office again until she went to get coffee at six.

There weren't many alibis better than the FBI office.

Ever since her interview with the redhead psychologist, she had felt the scrutiny on her actions lessen, but until now, she hadn't allowed herself to breathe a sigh of relief.

And as soon as she was relieved of the stress and frustration, the energy that had kept her from sleep that night dissipated like a cloud of smoke on a temperate breeze. It was only nine in the morning, but she needed a damn nap if she wanted to be useful for the rest of the day.

Stifling a yawn with one hand, she ignored her better judgment and typed a text message to Bobby. She knew he was still in the building, but she hadn't spoken to him in a couple hours.

I'm going to head home and take a nap, she wrote. *How much longer are you going to be here?*

Any time she sent him a message that had to do with more than just an aspect of their job, she felt like a naïve kid again.

Sure, his wife had been cheating on him for more than a year, and sure, his marriage was over in all but name, but what in the *hell* was Sun doing? She was in uncharted territory, and she had lost her compass sometime after their first kiss.

I was going to leave in the next half-hour, he answered. *Do you think I could get in on that nap?*

Something curled deep and low in her belly as she composed her succinct response. *Of course.*

Good. I've got something I want to tell you too. Good news.

Good news? She could use some of that.

Her thumbs flew over the screen. *Hurry.*

FOR THE NEXT HOUR, Sun had to fight to keep herself from biting her freshly painted fingernails. She knew Bobby well enough that she was confident his text message had not been sarcastic or misleading, but her imagination had started to run rampant before she even left the FBI building.

Was he going to propose to her? No, that was ridiculous.

Had he been promoted? Transferred? Offered a job as a private investigator for some ritzy firm? Or had he found a kitten on his way home the day before?

By the time he followed her into the living room, she thought an explosion in her head was imminent.

"What's this good news you told me about?" she blurted before they had a chance to sit.

His amber eyes flicked away from the blue glow of the fish tank and over to her, the start of a wistful smile on his lips. Even when his dark blond hair was messy and tired shadows darkened his eyes, he still looked like he had just walked off a Hollywood set.

Blowing out a sigh, he combed a hand through his hair and dropped to the couch. "I've never been real great at shit like this," he admitted. "Telling people stuff like this, at least unless it's part of the job."

"Stuff like what?" she prodded. Her steps toward the sectional couch were slow and tentative, but she closed the distance when he smiled up at her.

"I don't know if this is supposed to be a happy announcement or not, but I didn't want to say anything until it was official. The day before yesterday, I talked to Kara."

Sun felt the moisture vanish from her mouth as she took a seat at his side.

Why couldn't he have just found a kitten?

Her family had taken in a handful of stray cats over her lifetime, but since Sun's fifteen-year-old cat, Noodle, had passed, she hadn't been able to bring herself to adopt another.

"Yesterday," Bobby went on, jerking her attention back to the present. "I had her served."

"Served?" Sun echoed. As the realization dawned on her tired brain, her mouth drooped open. "Served? As in?"

"As in a sheriff's deputy went to her boyfriend's house and handed her divorce paperwork," he answered. "I've known the deputy since I moved to Virginia, so I gave him the guy's address, and he went with it. I told her about it the day before, but I don't think she believed me. She didn't try to lie about any of it, I'll give her that."

"What about you?" Sun asked, her voice hushed. "What did you tell her? You know, about *this*." She gestured to him and then to herself for emphasis.

Shrugging, he leaned back against the plush couch. "I told her I'd moved on. No hard feelings."

"You did," she managed to say with what little breath remained in her lungs. "Oh my god, you did?"

He flashed her a wide smile as he nodded. "Yep. We bought a house at the beginning of the year. Both our names are on it, but I told her I don't want the damn thing. The whole reason we got it was so she could get a dog. Speaking of which, my cats are going to need somewhere to stay sometime soon. Do you think you could—"

Before he could elaborate, she reached out to touch the sides of his scruffy face, leaned in, and pressed her lips to his. There was a tickle against her lower back as she felt the warmth of his touch against her skin.

"Yes," she murmured once they separated. The corner of her mouth turned up in the start of a smile as she met his eyes and nodded.

"Thank you," he whispered. "For everything. For dealing with this bullshit, all of it. I'm sorry I dragged you into the end of my stupid marriage. I wish I'd at least figured out what in the hell I was doing before any of this happened. But thank you for sticking with me while I did."

"Of course." The breathless response was all she could manage. She had hoped he felt the same way about their unorthodox relationship as she, but until now, all she had was hope.

"Now," he said, brushing a piece of hair from her eyes. "How about that nap?"

"A nap?" She leaned in and kissed him until they were both out of breath. "I don't really think I'm tired anymore."

29

As Noah taped the final picture to the whiteboard, Winter stepped back to admire their handiwork. All the printouts had been taken from the security footage they had been provided by the hotel where James Bauman's body was found. Hands on her hips, Winter scanned over the still shots and sighed.

Noah glanced to her and then back to the last of six printouts.

"That's him," he said, rapping a knuckle against the whiteboard. "Can't see a damn thing, but this is the best shot we got of him."

The man's shadowy figure had stalked across the worn parking lot to James Bauman's hotel room, but the man had not glanced up from where he had fixed his gaze on the asphalt. When he made the return trip to his car, the story was the same.

Whoever he was, he knew how to avoid security cameras, and he knew how to avoid leaving any trace forensic evidence. They'd managed to see the very front corner of his car, but other than that...nothing but shadows.

"What about her?" a voice asked from one of the tables at their backs.

Winter spun around to face the newcomer to the briefing room. His pale eyes flitted over the series of photos before he met her gaze.

"Her?" Noah asked, tapping the photo of a woman's panicked face. Where their killer had been savvy enough to avoid the cameras, the young woman's face had been in plain view. The local vice squad hadn't taken longer than a minute to identify her as a prostitute who worked a nearby corner.

Aiden nodded. "Any idea who she is?"

"She's a working girl," Bree put in. She sat atop the table closest to the whiteboard as she leafed through a manila envelope.

Bree pulled out a paper. "I looked through the files on the two girls named on our killer's notecard, Alicia Perez and Melody Harrison. We got a lucky break, because it turns out our girl up there got busted for prostitution in the same sting as Melody back in summer 2017. Her name's Gina Traeger, and she was only sixteen when she got popped with her first solicitation charge. She wound up going to a juvenile detention facility, but as soon as she turned eighteen, she was back out on the streets."

"As much as I hate to say it, her story's pretty typical for working girls as young as she is," Aiden said.

Bree nodded. "She dropped out of high school after her sophomore year when she ran away from home. Her father had been molesting her since she was eleven, and her mother was in and out of rehab. For her and a lot of the girls like her, the street is a better alternative than what they have to deal with at home. Minus a couple of the details, Alicia and Melody's stories are just about the same."

Winter's mind was abruptly drawn to her vision of

Autumn's childhood, and she wondered how close her friend had come to a fate like Gina's.

"What about the dates on the notecard, what did those mean?" Aiden asked after a short silence.

Bree flipped to another page. "Those are the dates the girls were reported missing. From what I can tell, they were reported missing by some of the other women around that area. The cops couldn't do much about it. They said Melody and Alicia had probably moved to another part of town or left Virginia altogether. Which isn't unheard of. It makes it hard to find and identify working girls when they go missing. That's why people like James Bauman go after them."

"Do we have anything to tie Bauman to their disappearances other than this notecard?" Noah asked. "Not saying I don't believe it, it's just nice to have evidence that didn't come from a serial killer, you know?"

Bree pressed her fingertips to her temple, a sarcastic smirk of agreement playing on her lips. "Bauman has a few priors. One for solicitation, and one for a domestic disturbance. That was back about twenty years ago, and he was in Charlotte at the time. The victim dropped the charges, and that was the end of that."

Noah's eyes were on the whiteboard. "If he targeted working girls, there won't be nice, neat case files about it. That's why Ted Bundy got away with killing women for so long. He targeted prostitutes. Same with guys like the Cleveland Strangler. It takes a while for law enforcement to catch on."

"So, we should go talk to the girls?" Winter proposed.

"Sounds like it," Noah replied with a nod.

"You two?" Bree snorted, shaking her head. "Have either of you ever tried to interview a working girl before? Dalton? Did you deal with any of that while you were in Dallas?"

"Not really." He sighed. "I wasn't involved with Vice."

"Then one of you take either Agent Stafford or Agent Brandt with you," Aiden decided. "Someone who speaks the language."

THROUGH THE LIGHT CLOUD COVER, Winter could see the faint glow of the sun as it hovered near the horizon. Finally, after more than three hours and four different women, she and Levi Brandt had been able to start a dialogue with a young woman who went by the pseudonym, Alice. As they'd approached each wary prostitute, Winter had been glad to have the victim services agent by her side. The man oozed assurance and calm.

Alice was petite, and her blue eyes seemed almost too big for her face. She had accompanied Winter and Levi out of the neighborhood after they had settled on a deal: they would give her fifty bucks, buy her dinner and a coffee, and she would tell them what she knew about James Bauman as well as his victims, Alicia Perez, Melody Harrison, and Gina Traeger.

"Wow," Alice managed, glancing around the space with a slight smile on her lips. "It's been years since I've been in a place like this. It's pretty retro."

"My wife told me about it," Levi put in. "She and a couple of her girlfriends meet up here every month for lunch."

"It's a nice place," Winter said, smiling warmly at the girl. "Smells good, and it's got that homey feel you don't get from a lot of the chain places."

Levi nodded his agreement. "From what my wife says, their triple berry pie is killer."

Winter made a mental note to bring a piece back to Noah. A week or two earlier, he and Bree had engaged in a heated debate about pie versus cake, and Noah had been staunchly pro-pie.

They gave their drink order to a young man who couldn't have been more than eighteen years old, and once he disappeared, Alice's expression turned grave.

"You guys probably don't just want to talk about pie though, do you?" she murmured.

"Personally," Winter said, spreading her hands, "I'd be fine with just talking about pie, but you're right. We're technically here to ask you some questions, and they're not about any type of dessert."

"Right." Alice's smile was strained, but she nodded her understanding. "And you're sure this won't get any of the other girls in trouble, right?"

"That's right," Levi replied. "Agent Black and I are with the FBI, Alice. We aren't looking to get any of you or the other ladies in any kind of a bind. You won't have to give us an official statement unless you witnessed something. We just want to know more about this guy, James Bauman."

The girl licked her lips, clearly nervous. "Okay."

Winter watched as the girl swallowed her uncertainty and replaced the worry with a look of determination. What kind of past had Alice run from? Had she been assaulted by a family member like Gina had? Or had she been tossed around like a ragdoll like Autumn?

Biting back the twinge of rage, Winter forced herself to maintain an amiable visage.

"He went by Jim," Alice said after their server had dropped off their drinks and taken their orders. "Jim the brute, that's what some of the girls called him."

"You guys knew about him, then?" Levi asked.

"Yeah." Alice paused to sip at her soda. "Big guy, burly, bearded, the whole thing. I only ever ran into him once, and I was lucky that one of the more experienced girls was there with me. He always offered a whole lot of cash, but Toni said that's how he tricked them. They'd see that wad of twenties and get tunnel vision."

"Tricked them?" Levi echoed. "What did he do to them?"

With a shaky sigh, Alice took another drink. "Beat them up. Cut them."

"Raped them?" Winter asked when the girl paused.

Alice looked confused. "Isn't that what we're paid for?"

Compassion made Winter's sinuses burn. "No, honey. There's a difference."

Alice just shrugged. "Anyway, it all depended on what kind of mood he was in, I guess. Some of the girls said he didn't do anything like that to them, but they still said he gave them the creeps."

"Why didn't you go to the cops?" Winter blurted out the question and immediately wished she could take it back. "I'm sorry," she said before Levi or Alice could speak. "I didn't mean it like that, didn't mean to sound like I was accusing you of anything. I'm not. Promise. I guess I just want to know a little more about everything, if you don't mind."

"There are some cops that come around," Alice said. "A couple women and a guy. They're good people. They'll drop off food and blankets when it's cold, and they'll ask around to see if anyone's been bothering us. They do their best, you know. But they can't be everywhere, and there's only so much that three Richmond police officers can do."

Levi unlocked the screen of his phone and slid the device across the table for Alice to see. "Do you recognize her?"

Pursing her lips, Alice shifted her blue eyes from the picture of Alicia Perez and back up to Levi before she shook her head. "No."

With a finger, Levi swiped to the next photo—a high school picture of Melody Harrison. "How about her?"

Alice stiffened in her side of the booth. "That's Mel," she

breathed. "She…she went missing a while back. The cops, the ones who come around to help us out sometimes, they couldn't find anything out about where she went. They filed a missing person's report for her, but eventually, we stopped asking them for updates."

"Is she the first girl to go missing?" Levi pressed a button on the side of his phone, and the screen went dark.

"No." Alice still looked shocked. "Girls come and go a lot. They'll move to different parts of town, or they'll just leave the life altogether. That doesn't happen very often, though, and when it does, they usually come back. But, I don't know how to explain it, but it was just *different* with Melody. Usually, you can tell when someone's about to pack up and hit the road, you know?"

"What about the last time you saw her?" Winter asked.

Alice stared at the wall to Winter's back, clearly searching her memory banks. "Mel just acted like she always did, like I'd be seeing her the next day or something. And when she was gone, she was just *gone*. None of her stuff was gone, it was just her. I mean, for shit's sake, she was only seventeen, you know. We never want to see girls like that out there, but when we do, we do what we can to help them."

"We?" Levi asked, sliding a glance to Winter. "Meaning you and the other women who've been out there for a while?"

"Yeah, exactly. We tell them what we know, who to avoid, what types of places are more dangerous, stuff like that."

"Was James Bauman part of that? Part of what you warned other girls about?"

The shadows shifted along her throat as she swallowed. "Yeah. He was."

For the rest of their time at the diner, Winter and Levi tried to shift the discussion to a more lighthearted topic. Alice had taken a few classes at a community college when she was younger, and she had planned to transfer to VCU to study psychology.

Winter tried to offer encouragement, tried to lift Alice's spirits and point her in a direction that would lead away from the dangerous line of work into which she'd fallen.

But regardless of Alice's smiles and nods, Winter knew the effort was futile. There was more at play in Alice's background than just financial trouble, and a few feel-good words from an FBI agent wouldn't be enough to make that turbulence disappear.

As promised, Winter and Levi bought Alice a bus ticket to take her back to the area where she and the other girls worked and lived. Winter gave her a business card, along with the usual spiel to either call or email if she remembered any other details that might help their investigation.

As they waved goodbye to the young woman, Winter wasn't hopeful.

Her heart ached for Alice and all the other young women and girls like her, but more than that, her heart ached because she knew she couldn't help them.

She hadn't expected the sudden dejected feeling, but as she plodded toward the black sedan, she wanted nothing more than to go home and pour herself a stiff drink.

Winter had taken on the task of driving them back to the office, and she had half a mind to drive them to a bar instead. As she pulled to a stop at a red light, she spotted a flicker of movement at her side.

The red glow flashed on the screen of Levi's smartphone as he raised the device to his ear. "Agent Brandt."

A tinny voice replied to the curt greeting, but Winter couldn't make out their words.

"Yeah, that's her," he said.

The caller rattled off another response, and Levi's eyes widened. "You *what?*" he snapped. "You've got to be kidding me! She's a federal witness, detective! And you *booked* her? What the hell is *wrong* with you?"

"Whoa," Winter mouthed. She didn't envy the person on the other end of the line.

"I'll be there in ten. Why don't you use that time to pull your head out of your ass!"

She half-expected Levi to toss the phone out the open window, but he clenched his teeth and swiped a thumb across the screen instead.

"Where are we going?"

"Downtown," Levi grated. "The Richmond PD just arrested the only witness who's ever seen our killer's face and lived."

As it turned out, Levi and the detective who booked Gina Traeger had a history of disagreements.

Detective Olson was the polar opposite of Levi Brandt: the man was short, rotund, and bald. Though Olson wore a navy-blue suit and tie, he might as well have been dressed in a tracksuit when he stood beside Levi.

Agent Brandt might not have been as perpetually well-dressed as Aiden Parrish, but the man had a sharp sense of style.

Winter stood on the sidelines as Levi pointedly explained to the precinct captain the reason for the bureau's interest in Gina.

"What did you guys even pop her for?" Though calm, Levi's tone was laden with condescension. "Prostitution? A little bit of weed?"

The middle-aged man behind the polished wooden desk clenched his jaw, but he didn't respond.

"Do you know what she witnessed, Captain?" Agent Brandt hissed.

"My detectives didn't know she was a federal witness until after they booked her. We'll release her to your custody, and we're sorry for the misunderstanding," the captain replied.

"Didn't know?" Levi sputtered, waving his hand at the notices tacked to the bulletin boards. He knew they'd also gone out to every computer, every phone. "Does your detective live in a hole? That would be the only way he didn't know."

The captain reddened and opened his mouth to speak.

"Oh, it's too late for that." Levi waved a dismissive hand and took a deep breath. "You think she's going to say a damn thing to us now? She saw the man who shot Tyler Haldane, Captain. The serial killer who's been all over the local news lately, that's who she saw. And if you think she's going to cooperate with us now that you hauled her in here and charged her, then I'd like to know what planet you live on."

The older man grumbled out another apology before he escorted them to the interrogation room with Gina Traeger. He advised them where they could find the necessary paperwork to take with them back to the bureau to have her transferred to their custody once she could be officially released, and then he bade them a stiff farewell.

"So, wait," Winter said before Levi could reach for the doorknob. "We can't even take her back to the office?"

"Nope," Levi grated. "We might have jurisdiction in this case, but we can't release someone after the local cops have charged them for a crime. The cops or the DA have to drop the charges, and that takes hours at best. Our hands are tied."

"Wow," Winter sighed. "What a day."

"That's no kidding," he muttered. "I doubt we'll get much

from her, but we ought to at least give it a shot before they throw her in holding for the rest of the night."

Winter nodded her understanding. The heavy door creaked as Levi pulled it open, and the woman seated at the rickety table took in a sharp breath at the sudden disturbance.

"Sorry," Levi said, "we didn't mean to scare you. You're Gina Traeger, right?"

As the door latched closed, Winter and Levi pulled out a couple of metal chairs to sit across from the redhead.

"Who the hell are you?" Her eyes darted back and forth between Winter and Levi.

"We're with the Federal Bureau of Investigation," Winter replied. For what felt like the hundredth time that day, she flashed her badge. "I'm Special Agent Black, and this is Special Agent Brandt. We're just here to ask you a few questions."

"You're not in any trouble with the FBI," Levi added. "But we're following up something." He paused to slide a picture of James Bauman over to Gina.

Narrowing her eyes at the picture and then at them, she pursed her lips. "What do you want?"

"Do you know this man?" Winter asked.

Though the gesture was stiff, Gina nodded. "I've seen him. Why? What'd he do?"

"He's dead." Levi's voice was flat. "We know you didn't kill him."

There was a touch of cautious relief on Gina's face, but she made no move to speak.

"We want to hear what happened when you went with him to the Greendale Motel," Levi said. "And we know you were there, Gina. We have you on camera. We know you walked into room eight for about thirty seconds, and then you ran back out."

"Yeah," Gina returned, crossing her arms as she leaned back in her chair. "The guy was a creep. Soon as we got in that room, he said some weird shit about how he wanted to cut me, so I got the hell out of there. He was alive when I left."

"Who was the other man in the room with you and James Bauman?" Winter pressed. She propped her elbows atop the metal table and leaned forward. "We know there was someone else there. He's on camera too."

Gina's expression was blank as she shrugged. "I don't know what you're talking about."

"Ms. Traeger…" The warning was clear in Levi's voice.

"Just Gina," she shot back.

"Gina," he corrected. "The man you saw, whoever was in that room with you. He *killed* James Bauman. And we've got reason to believe he's killed other people too."

"What, you mean like some kind of serial killer or something?" she huffed.

"Exactly like that. He's killed three other people that we know of," Winter replied.

Levi nodded. "Which makes him a serial killer."

The seconds felt like they stretched into minutes as Winter watched Gina's facial expression. Though Gina was only a little over eighteen, her arrest tonight was far from her first brush with the law. But even more than that, she had dealt with her abusive father for close to six years before she finally ran away from home. To someone who had been through a hell Winter couldn't even imagine, the sight of two federal agents must have seemed like a cake walk.

Levi had been right in his admonishment of the precinct captain. The arrest had shaken her, but not in a way that was conducive to a cooperative witness. Instead, her brush with the Richmond PD had the opposite effect.

If Winter and Levi had reached Gina before she was

slapped with a pair of cuffs and read her Miranda rights, they could have made a deal with her. The US Attorney would have been more than happy to provide witness protection or any other means of security for an eyewitness to provide a description of the man who had killed James Bauman and three other people.

But now, even if they obtained a meeting with Gina and the US Attorney, Winter doubted the girl would cooperate. If there was anything Winter had learned today, it was that the balance between law enforcement and the groups of people who survived on the periphery of society—people like Gina Traeger and Alice—was precarious at best. One wrong move and that relationship could be shattered like a piece of cheap glass.

"I didn't see anyone," Gina said, crossing her arms over her chest. "I was drunk, so maybe I'm remembering it wrong. Either way, I hate to break it to you, agents. But I didn't see a damn thing."

30

A iden crossed his arms over his chest as he watched Bree Stafford tape a new photograph to the whiteboard.

Over the last two weeks, they had added four more pictures. There had been a break of a few days between James Bauman's murder and the next victim, but after that, the deaths of the other three had occurred every other day.

Tom Cotman, the newest addition to the whiteboard, had been killed last night. If the current pattern held, tonight would be quiet.

Each of the four subsequent victims—if that was what they could even be called—had shared the same traits as the first four. They were wolves hidden in sheep's clothing.

Under the guise of an electrician, a customer service manager, a long-haul truck driver, and even a sous chef, each man had painted a picture of normalcy. But when Aiden leaned in to scrutinize the picture, the image changed.

Though formal charges had never been pressed against any of the four, each had left a trail of victims in their wake.

Like James Bauman, two of the men had targeted prosti-tutes. One had been in Norfolk, and the other had been in Lynchburg. The other two relied more on opportunity than a set ritual, but they were predators just the same.

Extensive searches into the backgrounds of the four men's victims had yielded a couple promising leads, but neither had panned out. They had run into one dead end right after another, and Aiden could only assume they would see more of the same as they delved into Tom Cotman's case.

"Agent Brandt and Agent Ming are at the scene." Bree's announcement interrupted Aiden's pessimistic speculation.

"Did he leave another notecard?" Winter asked, leaning back to sit atop the table closest to the whiteboard.

To her side, white light glinted off Noah Dalton's eyes as he scrolled through his smartphone.

"He did," Bree confirmed. "Same thing as the others. Names and dates, all typed, no prints. Standard index card with no special markings. Ever since the press found out a few days ago, they've been writing articles about how he's 'taunting' the bureau. But, personally, I wouldn't call this taunting. I'd call it something more like 'being informative,' or 'leaving an explanation.'" She ended the statement with a shrug.

Aiden swept his gaze over the photographs of the note-cards that were left with the bodies of the six most recent victims. "Every time he tells us what one of these guys did, he's telling the press by proxy. He wants everyone to know why he's doing what he's doing."

"They're calling him The Norfolk Executioner," Noah put in as he glanced up from his phone. "And let me tell you, the comment sections for these articles are something else. The only other time I see people at each other's throats like this anymore are in political debates. But these aren't really political. I mean, there's people from both sides who think the FBI ought to pin a medal to this dude's chest when we find him, and then there's people on both sides who think he ought to be locked up just like any other serial killer."

Winter rubbed her face with both hands. "Might be the first time you get people from opposite sides of the political spectrum to agree on something."

"With elections coming up, you'd better believe we're going to hear about it from whoever's running for whatever office." Noah sighed and pocketed his phone. "Sooner we find this guy, the sooner we get the press off our backs. I'm getting sick of going to press briefings every other damn day."

"Well," Bree said, "when we finally do catch him, there's going to be a pretty long line of people who want to shake his hand. Or her hand."

"There'll be more than a few federal agents in that line. Plus, the medical examiner," Aiden advised. "If it weren't for the press on our backs, I doubt the bureau would even allocate the funding to catch this person."

Bree stepped away from the whiteboard to observe her handiwork. "You're not kidding. He's doing half of our job for us, and he's saving the state of Virginia a lot in trial costs. How much do you suppose he's saved us all in tax dollars, anyway? That's eight cases that never have to go to trial. It's got to be in the millions by now, right?"

"A killer's still a killer." Winter's voice was as flat as her unimpressed stare. She was clearly tired of this same old argument.

"At least this one's doing us a favor," Aiden shot back.

"By making us look bad?" There was a glint of petulance in Winter's blue eyes as she shifted her attention to him. "There are just as many people talking shit about the FBI and the cops as anything. He's pointing out what these guys have done, and it makes law enforcement look like they don't know what they're doing. I mean, if one guy can figure out all these cases, then why the hell didn't the cops?"

"That's not on the bureau," Aiden reminded her. "None of these would've been federal jurisdiction, at least not at first."

"And besides," Bree said. "If the local PD, or even if the *Bureau* was missing all these cases, cases that are apparently so obvious even a civilian can find them, then maybe we deserve for them to be dragged out from under the rug. Seems like LEOs dropped the ball more than once, and that deserves to be pointed out, especially since it cost these young women their lives. It just goes to show that even when we pat ourselves on the back for doing a good job, there's still room for improvement."

Bree's stony expression took him aback. Even in the midst of a case as stressful as the hunt for Douglas Kilroy, Bree's mood had been amiable and even upbeat. She was quick with a smile, and he had yet to witness her humor falter.

Until now, that was.

Though Winter's countenance softened in understanding, the spark of determination didn't so much as waver. "Maybe, but I don't think a vigilante serial killer is the best way to shine a light on what needs to be fixed."

"Seems to me that the only thing everyone's willing to stop and take note of is a vigilante serial killer," Bree replied as she straightened a stack of papers. "Because God knows they didn't pay attention when all those girls went missing."

"Yeah," Aiden answered the unspoken question when the argument appeared to be over. "That's everything. You're all free to go. I'll update Agent Brandt and Agent Ming when they get back. By then, Agent Weyrick should be in the office too."

"Looks like we're right on time for me to make another

phone call," Noah Dalton muttered as he rose to stand. Noah followed Bree into the hall, but Aiden stopped Winter before she could step out of the conference room.

"Hey."

One eyebrow arched, she turned to meet Aiden's gaze. "Yeah? What's up?"

"You really think we should treat this guy like any other killer?" he asked before he could think to refine the question.

She crossed her arms over her black blazer. "What's that supposed to mean? You don't think we should work this like a normal case?"

"It's not a normal case." His response was so dry it might have crumbled if it was touched. "It's a case where the perpetrator probably has experience in law enforcement, and where the perp is more than likely a decorated combat veteran. All the victims are, for lack of a better term, pieces of shit. So, no, Winter. I don't think this is a normal case."

"We can't hold back or work something differently just because we don't like the victims," she returned, her eyes narrowed. "What we do isn't always black and white. I'm pretty sure you're the one who told me that when I got out of Quantico, aren't you? It's hardly ever black and white. We're almost *always* in the gray area. That was you, right?"

Aiden narrowed his eyes. "How is what he's doing any different from what you were gunning for during the Kilroy investigation? Hell, if Kilroy had been identified while this guy was around, we would have found his body next to a notecard too."

If there was one surefire way to grate on Winter Black's nerves, it was by mentioning Douglas Kilroy.

"But the difference is that I didn't do that," she bit back. "I didn't go all cowboy and start murdering people. I pulled my head out of my ass and played by the damn rules, Aiden.

Besides, if I remember right, I wasn't the only one who acted like a jackass during the Kilroy investigation, was I?"

He clenched his jaw at the candid observation. She wasn't wrong.

"And if I can control myself and keep myself from going rogue on the guy who killed my family, who raped and mutilated my *mother*, then I don't think it's too much to ask that someone else restrain their anger too. I know what you're going to say, Aiden. I've seen the profile, and I know you think that the killer went through something like that as well. And that's exactly what I'm saying. There's a right way and a wrong way to deal with all that pent-up aggression, and murdering people isn't the right way."

Before he could offer another rebuttal, she turned on her heel and stalked out into the hall.

He hadn't expected such a convicted stance from the same woman who had thrown morality to the wind to sniff out even a tentative lead on Douglas Kilroy.

Apparently, he had misjudged her ideals. He had assumed she would fall in line with his assertion.

After all, hadn't he been one of the main sources of her inspiration to join the Federal Bureau of Investigation in the first place?

So much of her life had been modeled after her idolization of *him* that he assumed she would defer to his stance in a moral gray area. And until now, he had not even realized the bias through which he viewed Special Agent Winter Black.

Six months ago, he might have been disheartened by her break away from his expectation, but today he could find no such holdup.

Today, the smirk that crept to his lips was borne of pride.

The emotion was alien to him, and he could only assume the sentiment was akin to what a parent might feel when their kid graduated with a perfect grade point average.

He and Winter may not have shared the same view of The Norfolk Executioner, but they still shared one major trait: they didn't waver in their commitment to a given principle.

He had taught her well.

31

I didn't like to think of myself as a serial killer, but that was exactly what the media had labeled me.

The term "serial killer" evoked images of a man who had lost touch with reality, a man who killed for no better reason than the dirty thrill.

Even though I was sure my actions wouldn't lead to a revolution, I picked my targets for a damn good reason. After I collected the debt they owed me and the rest of humanity, the world was a little less dark.

Maybe I was technically a serial killer, but I preferred the term "vigilante."

At the least, the writers of all these damn articles could add "vigilante" in front of "serial killer" to differentiate me from scum like Ted Bundy, Richard Ramirez, or more recently, like Douglas Kilroy. It was a good thing the Feds had put down Kilroy. Otherwise, I would have had to find a way into prison to kill him myself.

I hadn't been to mass in an age, but I had been raised in a religious household. Until the day she died, my mother had been a devout Catholic, and her faith had gotten her through some hardships that most people could only imagine.

She didn't gain her citizenship until I was already in the military, and there were more times than I cared to count where we were shielded from deportation by my mother's friends from church.

Even though I might not have been devout like my mother, I knew the good that could come from religious communities. Every breath drawn by men like Douglas Kilroy—men who used their so-called faith to justify rape and murder—was a slap in the face to those communities.

I glanced down to the crescent-shaped bow and arrow tattooed on the inside of my forearm to pry myself from the unsavory thoughts.

Raking one hand through my hair, I unlocked my smartphone with the other. The photo that lit up the screen was old—there wasn't any silver sprinkled throughout my hair like there was now. Tina's dark, wavy locks had been pulled away from her face in a ponytail, but Evie's fell over her shoulders like it always did.

The day we took that picture was still etched clearly in my mind, almost like it had happened yesterday and not more than a decade ago.

If Evie was still alive, she would be in college by now. Maybe she would have turned her obsession with Greek mythology into a degree in history. By now, she could have even been a graduate student.

Evie was the reason for the tattoo on my arm. She had been in seventh grade, and their history class spent an entire semester on Ancient Greece and Rome. Evie was already a Greek mythology buff, so it was no surprise that she hadn't learned much new material from the course.

I could still remember the day she came home and huffed

about how the teacher had glossed over the story of the goddess Artemis.

"I'm sorry, girls," I murmured to the photo as I sat in the empty living room, dropping my face into my hands.

Even I wasn't sure why I made the apology. I knew it wasn't my fault that Tina's brother, Brian, had crept into Evie's room that summer, but I don't think Tina ever realized that it wasn't *her* fault, either.

For some fucked up reason, Tina's parents blamed me, but Tina only ever blamed herself.

We thought we were such a great family when we offered that prick a room to stay for a few months so he could get back on his feet financially. We thought we had done a good deed, thought we had stepped in to help someone who needed it, but all we had done was lead a predator to his prey.

He was down on his luck at the time—his wife of five years had filed for divorce, and they had been in the midst of a vicious custody battle over their two children. A custody battle that, thankfully, the children's mother won.

I came back on leave over the Fourth of July that year, and the atmosphere in the house felt *off*.

I wrote it off as change, but I should have trusted my gut. I should have dug deeper, should have asked the right questions, should have made it clear to my little girl that, even though I would be across the Atlantic for the next few months, I was still just a phone call away.

Then again, if I could travel back in time, I knew exactly what I would do.

I wouldn't hesitate, wouldn't second-guess myself, wouldn't wait until after that scum had killed my little girl. Before he could lay another finger on Evie, I'd slit Brian's throat from ear to ear. I would still dismember his body and bury the parts in five different Texas fields, but I would do it sooner.

That was why I did this.

I killed men like Ben Ormund, Tom Cotman, and Mitch Stockley so that another mother and father wouldn't have to face the same pain. I killed those men so they couldn't hurt anyone else, though they had done their share of damage by the time I got to them.

Like the saying went, it was better late than never.

Tonight, I had another debt to collect.

32

"Matt Lewin, age forty-three, was murdered in his home late last night."

Noah hardly suppressed a groan as Bobby Weyrick recited an early morning news article.

"Authorities believe Lewin was allegedly killed by the same person who has been involved in eight other murders over the past six months," Bobby went on as he leaned back in his chair. "Hold on, y'all. We haven't even gotten to the good part yet."

Noah linked his fingers behind his head. "The good part?"

"That's right, Agent Dalton." Bobby chuckled. For emphasis, he waved his phone at the small gathering before he began to read, "The killer, also known as The Norfolk Executioner, has amassed a cult-like following in his short tenure as a serial killer. Sources indicate that Matt Lewin was targeted due to reports of his alleged attraction to underage girls."

"Wait," Winter interjected, her blue eyes wide. "What? How the hell do they know that and we don't? I didn't see anything like that in Lewin's file."

"Because none of it's official," Sun Ming answered before Bobby could speak.

The Tennessee native nodded. "Exactly. They don't need probable cause to put something in an article. They get it on decent authority, and if they slap the word 'alleged' on it, they can publish it wherever the hell they want. Only thing at risk for them is their credibility, and if they're really unlucky, maybe a libel lawsuit."

As Noah glanced back to the front of the room, Max Osbourne cleared his throat. "Agent Weyrick's right. That's how our killer has known about all these guys' crimes even when we didn't. He can snoop around and break the law, and he doesn't need probable cause. But what I'm more interested in is why he hit someone last night. Parrish? Any ideas?"

From where he sat in the corner of the dim room, Aiden Parrish looked like he had just been roused from sleep. His attire and his hair were as neat as always, but there was a weariness in his pale eyes with which Noah had become well acquainted.

Truth be told, he suspected they had all been hit with the same level of fatigue. Once the case was over, Noah planned to sleep for sixteen hours straight.

"It means he's getting close to the end of his list," Aiden replied after he stifled a yawn. "We know he's had a list. There's no other way he could've been prepared with the names and the dates of these men's victims. But his list is finite, and it has an end. The murders have all been spaced out, but now that they aren't, it could mean he's getting close to the end of the list."

A silence descended on the space as he and Winter exchanged paranoid glances.

"What happens when he gets to the end of the list?" Winter asked. "Does he move to another state? Like he did after finishing his ten in Texas?"

Aiden adjusted the silver band of his watch as he shrugged. "It depends. Based on what we know about it, and based on the profile we've put together, there's a possibility he'll just stop. He might start looking for more rapists and pedophiles so he can make a new list, but there's no telling if he'll stay in Virginia. A lot of serial killers are transient."

"Shit," Noah spat. "Then our window to find him is about to close, isn't it?"

In response, Aiden Parrish merely nodded.

"Crime scene was clean," Bobby Weyrick put in. "Just as clean as all the other ones. No security cameras, no witnesses. ME estimated the vic's time of death was somewhere around four in the morning."

Winter stretched her neck to one side, trying to work out a knot. "Explains why there weren't any witnesses."

"What about the index card?" Sun asked, her dark eyes flicking to the man at her side.

"It was there. Two names and two dates, same as the last ones."

"All right, then," Max said as he uncrossed his arms. "You know the drill, agents. Same drill we've done four other times in the past two weeks. Research the victims, look through friends and family members, so on and so forth."

By now, the fact that the killings were impersonal had been well established, but the lack of forensic evidence meant there were no alternative leads to pursue.

None of the men who had been killed shared any social or professional connections, and virtually, the only common thread among them was their penchant for abusing women and girls.

So far, each name typed on the index cards had led them to a woman or a girl who had been forgotten, whose file had been dropped into the "cold case" catalog. But that was only if the police had investigated their disappearance or assault in the first place.

Though almost all the so-called victims had killed at least once, there were only a couple who could be classified as serial killers: Ben Ormund and Mitch Stockley.

James Bauman had killed two underage prostitutes, but his motive had been the desire to avoid the potential for a statutory rape charge. The concept of irony must have eluded the asshole.

The remainder were run of the mill predators, if there was such a thing.

Noah had learned over the past two weeks that the majority of sexual assaults were perpetrated by a small number of repeat offenders. Statistically speaking, chances were good that once a person committed a rape, they would offend again, especially if they hadn't ever been caught.

And until now, none of The Norfolk Executioner's victims had been caught.

As Noah stepped into the hall, the light sensation of a hand on his shoulder jerked him out of the musings and back to the present. He barely suppressed a surprised jump as he snapped his head to the side.

"Hey," Winter said, a faint smile on her lips. "Sorry, didn't mean to scare you."

"It's all right." He waved a dismissive hand before he was forced to stifle a yawn. "At this time of day, it's pretty easy to do."

"I hear that." She leaned against the doorframe. "You want to go take a coffee break before we get started with our tele-marketing for the day?"

With a groan, he scratched his scruffy cheek. "I think that's pretty much a requirement anymore, darlin'."

"Do you think we could write this off on our taxes?" she

asked. "As a work-related expense, you know. Seems to me like coffee is pretty critical to us doing our jobs."

When he laughed, some of the strain lifted from his shoulders.

AFTER CLOSE TO four hours on the phone with law enforcement agents and relatives of Matt Lewin's victims, Noah confirmed what he had suspected in the briefing that morning. All the roads for a normal investigation led to nowhere.

By the time he dropped the smartphone atop the laminate surface of his desk, he was ready for a drink. Today, he fully understood why the bureau had adopted a mandatory retirement age of fifty-seven.

Like each of the four prior to Matt Lewin, the notecard left by the killer had been accurate.

Levi Brandt was assigned the unenviable task of reaching out to Lewin's victims, only one of whom was still alive. The other victim, Maria Hernandez, had disappeared shortly before her fifteenth birthday.

The investigation into her absence had been half-assed at best. Relatives and friends reported that Maria had fallen in with a bad crowd, and her father was too strung out to notice.

When Maria was only eleven, her mother and her younger brother had been killed in a car accident.

Before the loss of her mother, Maria had been a good student and a loving daughter and sister. Her parents were divorced, and her father was uninvolved in her and her brother's life, but by all accounts, Maria's mother had more than picked up the man's slack.

The little family wasn't wealthy, but they had been happy.

That all changed when Yolanda Hernandez's little Honda

sedan had been hit by a drunk driver in a Lincoln sports utility vehicle. The man in the expensive SUV had survived, but Yolanda and her son were pronounced dead at the scene.

Almost all Yolanda's family still lived in their native El Salvador, so custody of Maria had been granted to her drug-addicted father. For a short time, the man cleaned up his act, but the charade didn't last.

Little more than a month before she had gone missing, Maria had been caught in possession of marijuana at a house party. Based on Levi's writeup, the tone of which exuded only a fraction of the irascibility Noah knew must have been present in the man's eyes, there was a good chance Maria had met Lewin at the party.

At the time, Lewin had been twenty-nine, and his younger cousin—a senior at Maria's high school—had hosted the party. There were a number of other drugs passed around that night, including methamphetamine and cocaine.

Five weeks later, Maria Hernandez dropped off the face of the planet.

Classmates had expressed concern about her attendance at school, and some of her friends indicated that Maria and a few other freshmen had started to use harder substances like meth and coke.

When Maria was reported missing by her father, police assumed she must have run away. They made a half-assed effort to find her, but ultimately, the disappearance of a lower-class teenager whose father was a drug addict didn't appeal to the mainstream press.

Over the past couple weeks, Noah had worked with and learned more about Levi Brandt, including his motivation for obtaining a position in the Victim Services Division of the FBI. Levi's background was similar to Autumn Trent's, and he worked in Victim Services to make sure that people like Maria Hernandez didn't fall through the cracks.

Levi was a good man and a damn fine agent, but if Noah was honest with himself, the man was scary as hell when he was mad.

Winter told him about the incident with Gina Traeger and the Richmond PD, but Noah had been convinced that her description was exaggerated.

Some people swore a lot when they were angry, and some had difficulty focusing themselves enough to form comprehensive statements, but not Levi. Agent Brandt was as articulate when he was pissed as he was when he was calm. According to Bree, Levi would have made a good mob boss.

When the screen of Noah's phone lit up, he blinked a couple times to ensure he had not fallen asleep.

No, he was still awake.

With a quiet groan, he grabbed the device to squint at the number. Though he assumed the caller was a follow-up on one of the six-thousand outbound calls he had made that month, the area code didn't belong to Virginia.

"A Texas area code," he muttered to himself. Maybe his mom or his sister had gotten a new phone number, he thought. Either way, his curiosity was piqued, and he swiped the green key at the last second.

"This is Agent Dalton."

"Agent Dalton," a man drawled in response. His tone was upbeat, almost excited, but Noah couldn't place his voice.

"Who is this?" Noah asked.

"Mark Quesada, SAC from the Violent Crimes Division of the Dallas office. One of our friends in the Dallas PD, Detective Jake Nielson, put me in touch with you. You used to be in the Dallas PD, right?"

"That's right." Noah rubbed his eyes with his free hand. "I was in the Dallas PD for four years. Tactical response for most of it. Detective Nielson was in narcotics, so we ran into one another whenever he'd be doing a raid on some cartel facility. What can I do for you, SAC Quesada?"

The SAC chuckled. "That's exactly what Detective Nielson said, and you're right. I'm not just calling to shoot the shit with you. Like I said, I'm with Violent Crimes. That's your division too, isn't it?"

"It is," Noah confirmed, but he guessed the SAC already knew every detail of his life, down to his shoe size.

"Great. We've been looking into what you guys are working on out there in Virginia, The Norfolk Executioner. He's been killing rapists and pedophiles, is that right?"

"Yeah. Murderers too."

"Right, right," Quesada replied. "That's what we saw out here too."

Noah sat up straighter, grabbing his pen to take notes. "Go on."

"It's about five years old now, at least the most recent one is," the SAC explained. "But, yeah. We popped open some old case files out of curiosity, and it seems like we might be looking for the same guy. About five or six years ago, we had a series of murders just like you're looking at in Richmond and Norfolk."

"How many victims total?" Noah asked.

"Ten that we know of. One about six months before the rest. The weird part about it all was that he shot the first ones. The first four, actually. All with the same weapon, but when we found the fourth body, the weapon was there. A Heckler and Koch G36 automatic rifle. No serial number, no nothing. Far as we could tell, he made the damn thing himself."

The hair on the back of Noah's neck stood up. "We found a Barrett Model 98 Bravo sniper rifle at the scene of the third murder. He killed the first three with the same weapon, and after he got rid of it, he's been—"

"Killing them with a hunting knife," Quesada finished for him. "Yeah, Agent Dalton, that's exactly what happened here too. About half the bodies were around Killeen, and the other half were closer to Dallas. They weren't all necessarily in an urban area, though. Some were in rural areas outside the city."

"There's no pattern to the location, at least not as far as we can tell," Noah replied.

"Bingo. The only pattern is the victims' pasts. And the notes that are left behind. Believe it or not, they were like those ransom notes you used to see in movies. Letters cut out of a magazine or newspaper."

"Notecards this time, and the words are typed."

"Guess our vigilante has gotten more efficient over the years," Quesada mused. "Sure seems like we're looking at the same killer, don't you think, Agent Dalton?"

Noah leaned back in his chair. "I'd say so, yeah."

"We'll send you everything we've got from those murders, including our BAU people's profile and all the suspects we ruled out. I'll also have one of my agents fly out to Richmond this evening to help you and your people go through it. She worked on the Killeen Executioner case right after she got out of Quantico. She's Special Agent Chloe Villaruz, and she'll be there a little after supper time."

33

There were more people in the briefing room than Winter had ever seen at one time. Considering the amount of news coverage devoted to The Norfolk Executioner case, however, the manpower was warranted.

After her evaluation of Sun Ming, Autumn had been called back for a consultation on the new information about the killer's activity around Killeen. Her green eyes flicked back and forth as Winter eased the glass door closed behind herself.

Even as she felt a pang of sympathy for her friend, she was glad for her presence at the early morning o'clock meeting. Like Aiden, Autumn had a keen eye for details that a normal person might overlook.

As Winter took a seat beside Noah, she didn't miss the scrutinizing glance Sun cast to her friend. If Sun flashed any more of the venomous looks at Autumn, Winter would make a mental note to ask the tenured agent what in the hell her problem was.

Chances were good Sun's issue had to do with the slight tilt of Aiden's head as he leaned in to say something to

Autumn, or with the way Autumn's lips curled into a faint smirk at the softly spoken comment.

Over the drone of the handful of conversations in the room, Winter couldn't make out what Aiden said, but apparently, the fact that he had uttered a private word to another woman was enough to set Sun on edge.

Winter fought against an eye roll as she lifted her paper mug of coffee to her lips.

Well, at least Sun's anxiety from her brush with the business end of their investigation had worn away. The woman seemed to be back to her usual prickly self.

The chatter died down as Max cleared his throat, and within moments, all eyes were fixed on the front of the room. The SAC stood beside a tall, willowy woman whose green and amber eyes seemed to sparkle beneath the light overhead. She had pinned her ebony hair back in a neat ponytail, and she held a black leather jacket in one arm.

When Winter glanced over to Noah, she felt as if a hand might have constricted around her throat. The corner of his mouth had turned up into the start of a smile, and there was an unmistakable glint in his eyes.

Brushing a stray piece of hair from her face, Winter swallowed against the tightness in her throat and forced her focus back to Special Agent Chloe Villaruz.

She hardly heard a word the woman said.

A chasm had opened up in Winter's mind, and the pit of darkness threatened to swallow her whole.

Stomach in knots, the burn of bile in the back of her throat, Winter went through the perfunctory motion of note-taking as Max talked them through the murders that had occurred five years earlier around Dallas, Texas.

When she looked down to read over what she had written, all the material felt new. She could hardly recall hearing the words she had scrawled, much less writing them.

She was in one of the most important briefings so far in her career, and her thoughts would not stay put.

Her gaze was fixed on Max, but all she could see was that damn look on Noah's face. As she paused to consider her visceral reaction, she wasn't so sure she could label the sentiment as jealousy.

That's what she *should* have felt, wasn't it? Was that what a normal woman would have felt if they watched their friend —a friend who they had begun to view in an entirely different light—gawk at an attractive woman?

Had Noah even gawked?

The more thought she gave his fleeting expression, the more unsure she became.

Despite the new light in which she had started to view her friend, the fact remained that Winter and Noah were not together.

In fact, until recently, she had done a damn fine job of making sure he knew they weren't together. Just because something in her head had shifted didn't mean that same thing had shifted in Noah's mind.

As far as he knew, they were still friends with a couple of awkward kisses under their belt.

Winter knew they weren't the only pair of friends who had shared an awkward kiss—she could still picture Autumn's sarcastic grin when she first told her the story.

During her undergraduate, Autumn had been friends with a grad student who studied Industrial Organizational Psychology. Though their relationship was platonic, there had been at least one misunderstanding between them that had resulted in a kiss.

They laughed off the misstep, and now, they still communicated regularly through text messages and emails.

Autumn's friend was married now, and he and his wife

expected the arrival of their first child in January or February.

Was that how Winter and Noah's friendship would go?

A year from now, two years from now, would they be connected only through a series of electronic messages? An occasional video chat? Would Noah send her an invitation to his wedding through email, or would she receive a physical copy?

She didn't want that. She didn't want any of it. She didn't want to type out a periodic update to send to him after he had moved back home to Texas, didn't want to add him on Skype just so she could see his bright smile, and she sure as hell didn't want to watch him marry a veritable stranger.

But whenever she looked to Chloe Villaruz, all she could see was his inevitable absence in her life.

No one stayed single forever, especially not someone like Noah. And when he found the woman of his dreams, what would that mean for Winter?

The thought was selfish, she knew. She should want what was best for her friend, and if that was another woman, then so be it.

She wanted him to be happy, but for the first time, she realized she wanted the cause of that happiness to be her. Not Chloe Villaruz, not a woman he had yet to meet, but Winter.

She didn't want to lose him, but she reminded herself what had happened the last time she was overcome with the same type of anxiety. In a panic brought on by the thought that he might vanish from her life, she had initiated their second awkward kiss.

At the time, she had stepped away, horrified that she might have ruined the only real friendship she'd had since grade school. Now, if they were back in the galley kitchen of her apartment, she would have wrapped her arms around his shoulders and held on like it was the last chance she would ever get to be so close to him.

Because, as far as she knew, the evening in her kitchen might have *been* the last opportunity.

"Agent Black."

Max's gravelly voice jerked her out of the darkening pit of anxiety like a flare brought to life in the dead of night.

Rather than vocalize a response, she met his steely gaze and nodded.

"You and Agent Villaruz head to the ME's office and see what you can find out about our newest victim, Alex Rolaz. Dr. Nguyen should've had enough time to look over the body by now."

Without a glance to Chloe Villaruz, Winter nodded again. She felt like an alien who had just stepped off their spacecraft for the first time.

As Max delegated tasks to the remainder of the room— aside from Autumn, at least—Winter brushed a finger along the adhesive at the top of her notepad. She paid special attention to each indentation and scratch, and at the same time, she focused on the faint strawberry and vanilla of her body spray.

It was a scent Noah often complimented, but she forced the thought from her head as soon as it surfaced.

The entire purpose of grounding was to avoid a panic attack, not instigate one. Maybe tomorrow she would use the lime and coconut fragrance Autumn had given her for Best Friend's Day. Autumn had gifted Noah with a candle from the same store, and ever since, he went back to buy a replacement each time the wax was gone.

Damn it.

She barely prevented herself from uttering the words aloud. Grounding didn't work when every damn thought led her back to the person she was trying to forget.

"Thanks again for coming by, Dr. Trent," she heard Max say when she managed to focus her hearing.

"No problem," Autumn replied. With a smile, she extended a hand to the tenured SAC. As Max accepted the handshake, Autumn's pleasant expression didn't waver.

There, she told herself. *Think about Autumn, or Max, or even Aiden. They're all over there smiling at one another, and you're here with your head stuck in the clouds like some kind of high schooler with a crush on the homecoming king.*

No, Noah had never been crowned homecoming king, nor prom king, nor any other type of teenage royalty. He had hated high school, and he'd spent the majority of his time on his grandparents' ranch as they helped set his uncle up to take over the property.

Then, as soon as he graduated, he joined the military to follow in the footsteps of his stepfather, Chris.

Damn it, she thought. *You're doing it again. Stop it.*

"Agent Black?" a woman's voice asked.

Winter snapped her attention away from Autumn, Aiden, and Max as she and Noah looked over to the speaker.

"Hi, that's me," Winter said. Good lord, she sounded like a bumbling idiot. "Sorry, it's early, and I haven't had very much caffeine yet today. It's nice to meet you." With a practiced smile, Winter shoved to her feet and offered her hand to the woman.

"I can sympathize," Chloe laughed. The sound was pleasant, almost melodic. "I'm a caffeine junkie, so you're in good company. We can swing by a Starbucks on our way to the ME's office."

"Just stay away from the coffee in the breakroom," Noah advised.

Winter wanted to put a hand over his mouth to keep his usual charm at bay, but she forced herself to maintain a smile instead. "Yeah, it's pretty disgusting."

"Thanks for the tip," the agent replied with a grin. "We all pitched in and bought a coffee maker to put on one of our desks. Our SAC has one in his office that he lets us use too. When some of the higher-ups were there a couple years back, they asked us why in the hell we needed a coffee maker when there was one in the breakroom. We told them to try that sludge, and after that, they didn't give us any grief for keeping a coffee maker on hand. I think each shift even has its own by now."

"We've got one." Winter almost jumped at Bobby Weyrick's voice. "Sorry, wasn't eavesdropping. Or at least I didn't think I was, anyway. It's past my bedtime, that's about all I know for sure." For emphasis, he stifled a yawn.

"Wait," Noah said, narrowing his eyes at the agent from the night shift. "Y'all have a coffee maker that you've never told us about?"

"Hey, you heard the woman." A smirk tugged at the corner of Bobby's mouth as he spread his hands. "Each shift gets its own. Y'all want one, y'all go get one. Or, you know, come to the night shift."

"No, thank you." Noah looked appalled at the thought. "I'm good. I did that for two years while I was in Dallas."

When Chloe flashed a smile at Bobby, Winter was almost relieved.

She learned a couple days earlier that Bobby and his wife had decided to divorce, but as far as she knew, the man didn't have a new love interest.

Weyrick was a year younger than Noah, and for the first time, she let herself take stock of his appearance.

If it hadn't been styled, the ends of his dark blond hair would have hung just past his earlobes. His black suit was tailored, though she doubted the price of Bobby's attire surpassed that of Aiden Parrish's.

Winter wondered if part of the men's training at Quantico had involved suit selection.

Without a doubt, Bobby Weyrick was a good-looking guy. Autumn had mentioned as much from the weeks she had been under Bobby's protection, but until now, Winter had merely taken Autumn at her word.

A quick glance to Noah confirmed that he had noticed her inspection of Bobby, but the disheartened shadow behind his eyes hadn't been the reaction for which she had hoped.

Why couldn't he just roll his eyes or huff at her like a normal guy?

Rather than elicit any form of reassurance, her stupid stunt only made the knot in her stomach tighten. She wished she could hug him, or at least offer him a comforting smile. But they were in a briefing room in the heart of the FBI building, and she had to maintain some semblance of professionalism.

Fortunately, neither Bobby nor Chloe noticed the exchange as they struck up a discussion about their preferred coffee beverages.

The dialogue had rolled around to coffee flavored ice cream when Winter excused herself to the bathroom. She half-expected Noah to follow her to ask what in the hell her problem was, but when she glanced over her shoulder, the hall was empty.

She had announced that she was headed to the bathroom. No matter Noah's curiosity or his stake in the outcome of their exchange, he wouldn't follow her to the ladies' room.

And if he did, who knew what might happen.

To her relief, she was the only occupant of the bathroom as the sudden flush enveloped her cheeks. What in the hell was wrong with her this morning? Her thoughts oscillated between despondent and dirty so quickly that she didn't have time to consider how her mind had gotten there in the first place.

As she turned on the faucet, she wondered if she should splash water on her face, or if she should *slap* herself in the face instead.

A WIDE, dark red gash ran from beneath one of the man's ears to the other, and the cut was so deep that Winter could see the severed cartilage and ligaments of his throat. Despite the corpse on the exam table, Dan Nguyen was as hospitable as he always was.

If Winter closed her eyes to listen to Dan's greeting, she could have tricked herself into thinking she had walked into a bakery and not a morgue.

"Same cause of death as the others," Dan advised as he waved a hand at Alex Rolaz's lifeless body. "Aside from James Bauman, that is."

Chloe nodded as she shifted her green flecked eyes up to Dan. "That's the same way the men in Killeen and Dallas were killed. Throat slit. As far as we could tell, they were all taken by surprise. Are there any defensive wounds or anything else that might've indicated a struggle?"

"No, I didn't find anything. Based on that, and based on what we know about him, I'd say you're right. He's taking them all by surprise."

"What about Bauman?" Winter asked. "You said he was stabbed in the back, right?"

"Right. That's true. Were any of the victims from Texas stabbed in the back?"

"No," Chloe answered. "The first four were shot, and the final six were just like Rolaz here. Throat slit, the cut so deep that it almost decapitated them."

"So, why was Bauman different?" Winter asked, glancing from Dan to Chloe and back.

"Maybe Bauman put up a fight," the agent from Dallas suggested. "Dr. Nguyen, do you remember if you found any defensive wounds on James Bauman's body?"

"A bruise on the bridge of his nose." Dan looked thoughtful as he shrugged. "Could have been from being shoved against a wall."

"And instead of slitting his throat, the killer stabbed him before he could do anything to try to fight back any more than he already had," Chloe said with the lift of both shoulders.

"It was a precise wound," Dan reminded them. "Right between the middle two ribs, up through the lung to nick the bottom of the heart. It's the same technique the Navy teaches to SEALs, which means there's a good chance the person you're looking for has elite military training."

This time, it was Chloe's turn to draw her brows together. "How do you know that?"

"I was Navy Intelligence for six years," Dan answered. "Spent a lot of time around SEALs and Special Forces people, picked up a few things. I've got an alibi, by the way. It's already been vetted."

As Agent Villaruz opened her mouth to protest, Winter couldn't help her burst of laughter.

"I'm sorry, Villaruz," she said, "I'm not laughing at you. I'm laughing at Dan. He's got a weird sense of humor."

Dan looked pleased. "You would too, if you dug around in dead people's bodies all day."

Chloe joined in the mirth as they said their farewells. Though they had learned more about the case, they hadn't gleaned any *useful* information from their visit to the medical examiner's office.

Business as usual.

"The ME we usually wind up with is a stuffy old guy," Chloe said. The unexpected comment drew Winter's attention over to the passenger seat.

"That must suck," Winter replied. Even though she thought her voice sounded stiff, she hoped Chloe didn't notice.

"We're all pretty used to it by now, so it only really sucks when we realize that not all the medical examiners out there are stuffy old guys. Especially not the ME here in Richmond." Though Chloe's words were devoid of the same prominent twang with which Noah spoke, there was enough of an accent to give homage to her Southern heritage.

"Dan's pretty cool." Winter's response was absentminded as she flicked on the blinker.

"If I met him in a bar or somewhere, I'd never guess he was a medical examiner."

Winter frowned. She was beginning to like the tall, willowy, beautiful agent. Dammit. "Yeah, me neither."

Before Chloe could reply, the first few guitar riffs of a familiar song sounded out on the car's radio. As the woman snapped one hand out to the radio dial, Winter gritted her teeth in preparation for a marked increase in volume.

To her relief, the song fizzled out of existence as Chloe changed the station.

"Sorry," she blurted, patting the air with her hands. "No offense or anything, I just can't stand '80s hair bands."

"Really?" Winter laughed. "Me either."

"Thank god," Chloe sighed. "I don't know what it is, maybe it's something in the water, but all the guys in the Dallas office just *love* hair bands. It drives me absolutely batshit. I'm always the one who offers to drive because I want to be in charge of the radio. I don't give a damn if we listen to AM talk radio, but we sure as hell ain't going to listen to that hellacious screeching. Not if I'm driving, hell no."

"NPR." Winter glanced to the other woman and shrugged. "That's what I'll throw on sometimes. Usually, the local rock station doesn't play a lot of hair bands, but for some reason, they sure love Motley Crüe."

With a groan, Chloe leaned back in her seat as she shook her head. "I'm so glad that Nirvana and grunge music killed the hair band era. I don't think I'd be able to function in a place pre-1991."

"That's what killed hair bands?" Winter flashed Chloe a puzzled look. "I had no idea."

"Oh, yeah," Chloe answered with a vehement nod. "When Nirvana got big, everyone started thinking about what songs actually meant, and it turned out that folks like tunes that have a little more meaning than some strip club jam. Vince Neil, the lead dude in Motley Crüe, he *hates* grunge music. Which, honestly, is part of why I love it so much. It did us all a huge favor."

"Holy shit," Winter laughed. "I didn't know that. I might have to go out and buy a Nirvana shirt now. I mean, I like 'Smells Like Teen Spirit,' but I wouldn't say I'm a Nirvana expert. That's Noah, Agent Dalton." As she trailed off, she felt her smile fade.

"You guys are cute together," Chloe observed after a spell of silence. "Relationship goals, isn't that what all the kids are saying?"

"Oh." Winter felt her eyes widen. "No, we, we aren't together. We're just good friends."

"Really?"

Winter bristled in preparation for the agent to ask if Noah was single, but the remark never came.

"That's too bad," Chloe replied instead. "What about your ME? Is he single?"

"Dan?" Winter coughed as she strangled on the name. "I'm not sure. I've never seen him wearing a ring, but I've never heard him mention anything about a girlfriend. Just an ex."

Chloe picked a piece of lint off her pants. "He seems like a pretty cool guy."

"Yeah." Winter slid the other agent a look. Was she attracted to the man? "Dan's pretty funny."

Winter smiled and considered what else she could say to build Dan up in Chloe's mind. After all, if Chloe's attention was fixed on Dan, then it wasn't fixed on Noah.

For the love of...

What sort of childish nonsense had wriggled into Winter's head, anyway? Better yet, how in the hell was she supposed to get *rid of* the childish nonsense? Another awkward kiss in the kitchen?

Her fingers gripped the steering wheel so hard they began to hurt.

She was seriously driving herself crazy. Was it because she no longer had The Preacher to focus on? Was it because she was doing her damnedest not to think of her lost baby brother?

For someone with enhanced intuition, she didn't have a clue when it came to herself.

Maybe...

Maybe she didn't have to do this by herself. It was a strange thought.

She had become so accustomed to facing all life's challenges on her own, she had all but forgotten that Noah wasn't her only friend.

If anyone would be able to shed light on Winter's predicament, it was Autumn Trent.

34

S chool had only been back in session for a few weeks, and Emma Olmsted had already decided to stay late after volleyball practice.

Her friends on the team laughed and shook their heads, but Emma reminded them that she was a junior this year. College was right around the corner, and if Emma wanted to make it through Virginia Tech with a degree and *without* a lifetime of student debt, she had to be at the top of her game.

The girls' volleyball coach, Irene Spring, was out on maternity leave for the next few months, but she had still put Emma in touch with a recruiter from Virginia Tech. If Emma kept up her performance, she was all but guaranteed a full-ride scholarship and a spot on the Virginia Tech volleyball team.

As much as Emma enjoyed volleyball, her dedication was for practical reasons more than any real desire to play the game at a high level.

Her parents had divorced when she was young, and they both maintained blue-collar jobs to support their families. Emma's mother had recently explained the concept of "paycheck to paycheck," and the realization that it was how her parents survived was a dose of reality.

Now, Emma was determined not to strain her parents' finances, and that meant she had to make her own way into college. Coach Spring was a feisty woman with a sharp sense of humor and the uncanny ability to laugh at herself. Emma and almost all the other players loved her, and their affinity for their coach was no small part of what made them such a cohesive team.

But with Irene on leave to look after her first child, they were stuck with the assistant coach, Marco Yarr.

Mr. Yarr was the tenth-grade biology teacher, but even the pirate jokes hadn't taken long to wear thin when Emma was in his class.

The guy was a creep.

Brushing the wayward strands of curly hair from her face, Emma glanced around the spacious gymnasium as she thought of Mr. Yarr.

She half-expected to see him in a corner, his beady little eyes trained on her every move. When she didn't spot the balding creep, she trotted across the polished floor to scoop up a volleyball.

Though she had intended to stay until seven to practice her serve, the glowing screen of her smartphone advised her it wasn't even quarter 'til seven.

Goose bumps raised on her arms. It was time to go.

She had a volleyball at home, and she would drag her little sister to the park with her to practice if she had to. Her mom worked the night shift as the manager at a diner not far from their house, and the responsibility to look after her twelve-year-old sister fell on Emma six days out of the week.

At first, she had hated the babysitting duty, even though Jenny was asleep for almost the entire time their mom was gone. Ever since Jenny hit her growth spurt, however, she and Emma had found games and activities they both enjoyed. Of course, volleyball was one of their shared interests.

Was that really why Emma had chosen to stay after school? Had she really decided to subject herself to the perpetually creepy Marco Yarr just because she didn't want to hang out with her little sister?

At the thought, she snorted aloud.

She was used to Coach Spring, not Mr. Yarr. When Coach Spring was around, Emma could stay late to ask for advice and pointers. With Yarr, on the other hand, Emma was loath to ask just about anything.

When she first told her mom about the weird feeling she got around Mr. Yarr, her mom had dismissed the vibe as some type of hormone-driven paranoia. Emma had been a freshman at the time, and their family was brand new to the school district.

By the end of that school year, Emma had heard more than her fair share of stories about the creepy coach.

Like her mom, she had dismissed the accounts as outlandish at first, but there were too many of the rumors for them all to be false.

Marco Yarr was new to the district as well, and word in the rumor mill was that a girl at his previous school had gone missing right before he moved to Richmond. Then, there was the way he looked at Emma's teammates when he didn't think anyone was watching him.

Despite her parents' divorce, Emma's life had been good, but she knew the predatory glint in the man's eyes the second she saw it.

A handful of Emma's classmates had quit the team, and whenever they were asked for the reason for their departure, they would get nervous and change the subject.

But as sure as Emma was that Marco Yarr was a rapist and a predator, she didn't reveal the breadth of the situation to her mom. If she did, Mom would pull her off the team, but only after she went for Yarr's throat—figuratively or literally. Each was a distinct possibility with Amber Olmsted.

Emma didn't hide the ugly truth from her mom because she was worried that her ire would be a source of embarrassment. She hid the secrets about Marco Yarr because she couldn't get a scholarship for volleyball if she wasn't on the damn team.

With one hand clamped down on her phone, Emma dropped the ball into a plastic container. As she picked her way past the bleachers and to the hall, she felt like she was walking in the midst of a minefield. At any second, the shadows might explode into motion to carry her off into the bowels of the school.

Once she was past the rickety wooden bleachers, she trotted down the hall to the girls' locker room. Now, she felt like the idiot in a horror movie who made the mistake of going back for their stuff when it was obvious they were about to be killed. Her palms were damp, and she heard the rush of her pulse as her heart hammered in her chest.

She couldn't leave her backpack in the locker room—her house key was in the outside pocket. Mom and Jenny were both home, but she would never hear the end of it if her mom found out she had left the key to their damn house in a locker.

Emma glanced to every corner, every crevasse, every inch of space in the dim room. Before she reached her locker, she was sure she had cast a paranoid glance over her shoulder at least fifty times. Aside from the drone of the fluorescent lights overhead, the air was quiet. No, it wasn't just quiet, it was *silent*.

She was definitely in a horror movie. In the background somewhere, a person was shouting at her to get the hell out of there while another leaned over to their friend to ask why that stupid girl had gone back for her bookbag in the first place.

Shit, shit, *shit*.

Why hadn't she used the buddy system? Since second grade, her teachers had preached the gospel of the buddy system, but Emma either hadn't cared or hadn't listened.

Though Emma's mom permitted her to carry pepper spray during the summer months, a can of mace would be enough to expel her during the school year. As she shouldered her backpack and crept away from the short row of lockers, she wished she had taken the chance. Instead, she would have to make do with her smartphone.

She dared a glance down to the screen only long enough to type in the PIN. Then another to tap the phone icon. And finally, a third to type the numbers 9-1-1. She moved her thumb to hover over the call button.

There. Now, if any creepy assistant coach leapt at her, the cops would show up to knock down the doors in less than ten minutes.

Each step Emma took was measured, and even her footfalls were soundless as she pushed open the metal door. She glanced up and down the hall before she willed herself to ease the door wide enough to let herself out of the locker room.

The set of double doors at the end of the corridor were automatically locked after five, and she mentally berated herself for the oversight. Since she couldn't use the main exit —the doorway that led straight out into the parking lot—she had to walk the other direction. The alternate route would take her past the boys' locker room, the entrance to the gym, and then the faculty offices. Any student who stuck around later than five had to checkout with the security guard in the principal's office.

After a quick swipe to make sure the touchscreen didn't

go dark, she started on her painstaking journey. Another set of heavy double doors separated the hall from the main portion of the school, and Emma could only assume they would muffle any shouts or cries for help.

Swallowing against the sudden dryness in her mouth, Emma forced one foot in front of the other. A slat of golden light fell across the drab concrete floor, a slat of light that hadn't been there before.

An hour earlier, the overhead lights had dimmed to a faint glow, and the brighter illumination stood out in stark contrast. The office was shared by a couple different assistant coaches, but this time of year, there was only one likely occupant.

She snapped her head around to take stock of the corridor, but nothing stirred. If Emma didn't get out of that hallway soon, she was liable to lose her damn mind. *Someone* was here —she could hear them as they shuffled around the office.

"Mr. Yarr?" she called, her eyes flicking from her phone to the doorway and then back.

The crack between the door and the frame didn't yield Emma a wide glimpse to the interior of the office, but her attention was drawn right away to the splotch of vivid crimson.

At first, she thought the red pool must have been a decoration or a prop.

Maybe one of the assistant coaches had taken it upon themselves to put out an early Halloween decoration.

If it was a prop, what in the hell was it supposed to be? A zombie? A dead person seated behind the coach's desk?

As the door creaked inward, she heard herself take in a sharp breath.

The figure that blocked out the light from the doorway wasn't Marco Yarr.

This man wore a black hoodie and dark wash jeans, not the polo and khakis that comprised the entirety of Yarr's wardrobe. His eyes were dark, not the pale shade of blue she so often saw linger on the other volleyball players. From beneath the hood, she could see his ebony hair, could see that he hadn't been stricken with the same receding hairline as Mr. Yarr.

But the cause of her gasp wasn't the stranger, it was the way the white light glinted off the bald patch on the top of Marco's head as he lay facedown in a growing pool of his own blood.

Every nerve ending in Emma's body told her to run, to push open the heavy doors and sprint out past the principal's office and into the parking lot.

She had saved money diligently over the past few years to buy her own car, and she wanted to find out how fast she could drive it away from this damn building.

Beneath the icy stranglehold of adrenaline, she struggled to breathe, much less manage an escape.

"I won't hurt you." Though the man's tone was hushed, the bass in his voice gave the words a commanding edge.

"Y-you won't?" she stammered.

He shook his head. "Nope."

He was playing her. Again, she could hear the imagined movie watchers screaming at her to run. Instead, she found herself stammering, "B-but, I-I mean, I s-saw you, d-didn't I?"

The slightest smile played across his clean-shaven face. "You did. And I'm sure you'll do what you think is right once I leave."

"What do you mean? Y-you, you killed…" Her eyes flitted past the man, and she had to swallow back bile. "Who are you?"

He chuckled softly as he held up both gloved hands. "Me? I'm no one. I got who I came for, and it wasn't you."

"You mean Mr. Yarr?"

Why was she conversing with a killer? She could hear the movie audience moaning at her stupidity.

As he nodded, the corner of his mouth turned down in a scowl. "That's right. Marco Yarr was a predator. He preyed on the weak and the vulnerable, and he exploited his position of authority to keep his victims quiet. But Marco didn't know that there are deadlier predators out there."

"Holy shit," Emma breathed. "Y-you killed him because he...because of what he did to those girls? That was all *real*?"

"It was," the stranger confirmed.

She was curious now. Although she was still afraid, she wasn't as afraid as she probably should have been. Was this man a hero? Saving her and others from the creep who could never ever hurt any girl again?

"But why?" she asked, her voice steadier now. "Did you know one of them? Are you one of the girls' fathers?"

"No. You've heard the story of Artemis, right? The goddess of the hunt?"

She didn't have to stray back far in her memory banks. She loved history. It was one of her favorite subjects. "Yeah. I have."

"Artemis wasn't just the goddess of the hunt," he said, showing her the tattoo of Artemis on his forearm. "She was a protector for girls and women, for those who the scum of society might have preyed on otherwise. There's no one like that in our society anymore. No one to catch the victims who fall through the cracks. The police do the best they can, but they can't be everywhere, can't know everything. So, that's what I do. I take out the trash."

"Oh my god," she managed.

Though Emma didn't pay much attention to the news,

she'd spent enough time online to familiarize herself with The Norfolk Executioner. The last time he had been mentioned on television, Emma's mom had muttered a comment about how the police should give him a job once they caught him.

The smirk was back as he stepped out of the doorway and turned to make his way to the double doors. As he pushed his way into the main cafeteria beyond, all Emma could do was follow his movements with her dumbfounded stare.

She could leave, she thought. She could forget what she had seen, and she could follow the tall man's path out past the principal's office and into the night. He would go on to live his life, and she would go about hers.

There were security cameras throughout the school, but based on the snippets she had read about him, he knew how to avoid detection.

Emma didn't.

Once the cops reviewed the footage, it would be obvious that she had been in the same place as the killer.

Thinking hard, she thought through every cop show she'd ever watched.

She had to play this just right.

Just because she knew she *had* to call the police eventually didn't mean she had to dial the number right away. After all, she had just witnessed the tail end of a murder.

Sinking to the floor, she began to wail.

She was traumatized, after all.

35

Noah had been stretched out on his couch when he got the call from Max Osbourne. After he asked Max to repeat himself a couple times, he leapt to his feet to get ready to leave.

Winter was at Autumn's apartment, and he called her on his way out the door to advise that they had another witness.

She had just finished a call with Max, and the SAC had given her the same option to stay home or come to the office that he had offered Noah. Bobby Weyrick, Sun Ming, Miguel Vasquez, Max Osbourne, and Chloe Villaruz were already at the FBI building, and Winter suspected there would be too many agents left to sit around and twiddle their thumbs.

Her assessment was accurate, and Noah mulled over her words even as he sped through a yellow light.

Based on what Max had told him, Sun was in charge of questioning the witness once her parents arrived. On a good day, the woman came across with the same level of hospitality he would expect from a cactus, and on a bad day, her demeanor was closer to a stick of dynamite.

Even if she was in a great mood, that left their only cooperative witness in the company of a prickly desert plant.

Had Levi Brandt already been present, Noah would have opted to stay home. He needed a break from the investigation and the FBI office as a whole. Tomorrow was Friday, but weekends didn't mean much when they had a serial killer to track down. But in Levi's absence, someone had to ensure the cactus didn't get too close to their witness.

With a sigh, he shifted his pickup into park. He glanced up to the rearview mirror to make an effort to tame his hair, pulled the key from the ignition, and stepped out into the parking garage.

"Agent Dalton," Max Osbourne greeted as Noah neared the cluster of desks that belonged to the Violent Crimes Division.

"Sir," Noah replied with a nod. "Where's everyone else?"

"The witness's parents just got here. Come on, I'm headed to the interview rooms now. Agent Ming is usually good in the interrogation room."

Noah wasn't so sure. "She's good at getting information from suspects, but with all due respect, Agent Ming's strong suit isn't talking to witnesses. Or, honestly, anyone we need to cooperate with us. Agent Black told me what happened with Gina Traeger and the Richmond PD, and we can't afford to have that happen again."

The SAC slid him a look. "Go on."

"This isn't a normal case with normal witnesses. We aren't talking to a witness who saw someone like Ted Bundy out on the prowl. This guy, The Norfolk Executioner, or whatever in the hell people are calling him, he's got a lot of sympathy from people in the community. Shit, he's got a lot of sympathy from people in the *bureau*."

"And you think Ming will fuck it up?"

Noah was on a slippery slope, and he knew it. "Again, with all due respect, Agent Ming can't charge in there like her normal self. If she does, she'll fuck this up for us like Detective Olson did with Gina Traeger. We've tried two more times in the past couple weeks to get something from Gina, and she stonewalled us both times. Someone needs to go into that interview room and talk to this kid and her family like they're fellow human beings, not *suspects*."

Max narrowed his eyes, but he nodded. "You're right, Agent Dalton. Good call. You're with Agent Ming, then."

Noah's intent had been to remove Sun Ming from the interview equation altogether, but he could tell by the SAC's expression that he had made all the progress he could. Jaw clenched, he strode into the room behind the one-way glass.

"Evening, Agent Dalton," Bobby Weyrick greeted. "Welcome to the night shift."

"You're the only person here who's actually *on* the night shift," Chloe Villaruz reminded him.

When the agent from Dallas flashed a grin at Bobby, Noah thought he saw a twitch of irritability on Sun's face. As much as he wanted to dismiss the look as a figment of his imagination, he knew better.

Great, he thought. *First Sun's got a chip on her shoulder from the case, and now she's pissy about Agent Villaruz smiling at Bobby Weyrick.*

This was going to be a fun day. Night. Whatever.

He wished Winter was here, and for a split-second, he thought to excuse himself to call and beg for her to drive to the office.

Winter valued her time with Autumn, and ever since the start of the Haldane case, there hadn't been many opportunities for the two women to get together outside the context of work. Plus, there were five other FBI agents present.

Too many cooks, he told himself.

If Winter was here, she would be relegated to the sidelines where she would lose her damn mind.

Instead, he decided he would make a mental note of all the awkward glances and uncomfortable pauses so he could regale the story to Winter later. In the meantime, he needed to study the school footage closely so he didn't walk into that room sounding like an idiot.

"Agent Ming," Max's gravelly voice called out fifteen minutes later. "Agent Dalton. You're both here, and the witness's mother is with her. The rest of you, go look over that security camera footage again and get ahold of Agent Brandt if you need to walk through the scene. He's at the school with the local cops, but he already sent us the two names on the index card. You know the drill, agents."

More phone calls. Damn, it really was a good thing Winter wasn't here.

The three Agents—Bobby Weyrick, Chloe Villaruz, and Miguel Vasquez—nodded their understanding before they let themselves out into the hall.

"All right," Noah said as he glanced over to Sun. "Showtime."

Two pairs of dark brown eyes shifted to the doorway as Noah stepped into the drab room, Sun close on his heels. He flashed the two a smile, and he could only hope the warm look was enough to counteract whatever glare they had received from his fellow agent.

"You're Amber Olmsted, right?" Noah said. "I'm Agent Dalton, and this is Agent Ming."

Sun offered a stiff nod as he gestured to her.

Biting back a sigh, he pulled out a rickety metal chair and dropped to sit.

"Agents," the mother replied. Her posture was stiff, but

there was no hint of malice on her unlined face. She might have been on guard, but she wasn't hostile.

Not yet.

He forced himself to look amiable as Sun took a seat at his side.

Amber kept one protective hand clasped on Emma's shoulder as she and her daughter exchanged glances. "You've got some questions for my daughter?" she asked.

"We do," Noah confirmed.

"All right," Ms. Olmsted said, squeezing her daughter's shoulder. "Go ahead, Emma."

Emma tucked a piece of wayward curly hair behind her ear and nodded. "Okay. What did you want to know, agents?"

As he folded his hands atop the table, Noah offered the teenager a reassuring smile. "Just start by walking us through your day after school ended."

"Okay." The girl took a deep breath. "Well, I, uh, I'm starting my junior year, and my coach, Coach Spring, not Mr. Yarr, he's just the assistant coach. Coach Spring was helping me work on a scholarship to play volleyball at Virginia Tech. I wouldn't have to take out any student loans, and I could study whatever I wanted."

"What are you thinking of studying?" Noah asked.

He could feel Sun's scrutinizing glare on the side of his face, but he ignored the petulant glance. They needed rapport with Emma Olmsted.

With a shrug, Emma took a sip from her bottled water. "I was thinking about actuarial science, but now I'm starting to think more about engineering. I've always been good at math."

Amber Olmsted's stony expression softened at the mention of her daughter's college plans.

"My friend is really good at math too," Noah replied. "But she went to school for psychology. They use a lot of statistics, at least in school. I never knew it, but there's a lot you can do if you're good at math. We even have stats people at the bureau."

Emma's eyes widened. "Really?"

"Really. They do data analysis. You should check it out. Data analysis jobs are popping up all the time, and they're out there in just about any industry you can think of. Law enforcement, medicine, business logistics, even agriculture. Being able to crunch numbers is a good skill to have."

The start of a smile worked its way to Emma's face, and for the first time, Noah thought the interview had a fighting chance. If Sun morphed into a cactus, at least Noah had established some semblance of rapport with the girl.

"He's right," Sun said, her voice icy but still professional. "It's a versatile field. Is that why you stayed after school? To talk to your coach?"

Emma shook her head. "No. Coach Spring is on maternity leave. Mr. Yarr..." She paused and visibly shuddered. Noah wondered if it was because she'd seen the man's body, or from something else. "Mr. Yarr is, was, just the assistant coach, but no. I wasn't there to talk to him, either. I'm a little rusty from summer break, so I stayed to work on my serve."

"Was there anyone else there with you?" Sun asked. "Isn't it against school rules to stay alone that late?"

Emma frowned at Sun. "No, it was just me, and no, it isn't against the rules or I wouldn't have been there. Janitorial staff and security staff are there late, plus there was another girl, but she left about a half-hour before I finished up."

"Do you stay after school to practice a lot?" Sun's intent stare was fixed on Emma.

"Yeah, well, mostly when Coach Spring is there. She helps me figure out what I need to work on, and then she'll help me come up with a plan to get better at it."

"She sounds like a good coach," Noah put in.

Emma's smile brightened a little. "Yeah, she's pretty great."

"But you don't stay late as often when Mr. Yarr is in charge? Why not?" Sun was chomping at the bit, winding up to pounce on the girl. Great.

As Emma glanced to her mother, the woman nodded. "Tell them what you've told me, honey."

"Okay." Emma returned her wary eyes to him and Sun. "We moved to this school district a couple years ago, and at first I thought everyone was just making up ghost stories, you know? Lots of kids in my school like to do that. They like to cause drama, stuff like that. But they said that there was a girl at the school where Mr. Yarr used to teach that went missing."

"Do you know what her name is?" Noah asked.

"No, no one ever called her by her real name. They'd always make something up, like Mary Jane or something. But, well, that wasn't it."

When Ms. Olmsted's eyes went wide, Noah propped his elbows on the table and leaned forward to meet Emma's nervous glance. "What else?"

"I've been on the team since I was a freshman, and there have been some of the girls who quit just out of the blue. And whenever I'd go to ask them about why they quit like that, they'd sort of freak out. The rumors were that Mr. Yarr had sex with them, and that was why they quit."

"What?" the elder Olmsted exclaimed, her hand going to her throat. "He's been raping teenage girls? You've got to be *shitting* me! Where were you people, huh?" She waved an index finger at him and Sun. "A teacher is running around raping high school girls, and, and what? We've just got to wait for a vigilante to swoop in and slit his throat? Is that how the legal system works these days?"

This wasn't good. He darted a fervent glance to Sun, and as he suspected, her lips were pressed into a tight line, her eyes narrowed.

"Ms. Olmsted," Noah said before Sun could butt in. "Please don't take this the wrong way, but we're the Federal Bureau of Investigation and his crimes weren't under our jurisdiction, so we weren't aware of his offenses until he, himself, became a victim. I understand why you're upset. Believe me, it pisses me off too."

Ms. Olmsted opened her mouth to say something more, but instead swiped angrily at the tears that had begun to spill down her face.

Noah went on. "One thing I've learned from doing this job is that guys like Yarr have a really specific method. They use their position of influence or authority to make sure their victims are too intimidated to speak up. And if they do speak up, like that missing girl from Yarr's old school probably did, it doesn't always go like it should. But trust me, Ms. Olmsted, there's a lot more at play in these situations than just the police dropping the ball."

Amber Olmsted's eyes still glinted with a mixture of grief, irritability, and great sadness, but after an agonizing bout of silence, she nodded her understanding. "You're right. I'm sorry, agents. This is just a topic I feel very strongly about. I have two daughters, and I sometimes worry what kind of a world I brought them into."

"I understand completely," Noah replied with another reassuring smile. "Emma, you were by yourself at the gym then, right? No friends or anyone else with you?"

"No, it was just me. Honestly, I wasn't even sure that Mr. Yarr was there until I left."

"All right," Noah said. "Walk us through that, then."

"Okay. Well, I just put the ball away in the crate like I

always do, and then I went back to the girls' locker room to get my backpack so I could go home. I didn't see anything when I went into the locker room, but when I got back out, that's when I saw that Mr. Yarr's office was open."

"What happened next?" Noah prompted after the girl paused for a little too long.

"I didn't even know he was there, so as I was walking by to leave, I looked in the room, and that's when I saw him. He was dead, face down on the desk, just like you guys found him."

"Did you try to do anything to help him?" Sun asked.

Noah swallowed a sarcastic comment and kept his gaze on Emma.

"I, no, I didn't. I mean, you saw all the blood, right? It seemed pretty obvious that he was dead."

"We looked over the security camera footage," Sun went on, unperturbed. "You didn't call the police until the suspect had been gone for close to ten minutes. Why'd you wait so long to call 9-1-1?"

Emma's dark eyes darted back and forth as she shrugged. "I don't know. I guess I was scared."

"Scared of what?" Sun pressed.

"Scared that the guy might come back for me, or I m-mean, I d-don't know," Emma stammered.

"For the love of god," Emma's mother snapped. "She's a sixteen-year-old girl! She saw a man facedown in a pool of his own blood, and you want to know why she didn't call the cops sooner? What planet do you live on?"

Sun ignored the outburst and forged on. "You saw the killer, didn't you, Emma?"

The shadows shifted along the girl's throat as she swallowed. "Yeah." Her voice was hushed.

"What did he look like?" Sun was on the warpath. And apparently, she had never realized they could catch more flies with honey. Or if she had, she hadn't taken the concept to heart.

"I didn't really get a good look." Emma shook her head. "The overhead lights all dim after six o'clock, so it wasn't bright enough for me to make out what he looked like under his hood."

"I thought you said the light in Mr. Yarr's office was on?"

"It was," Emma swallowed hard again, "but it didn't really help me see him."

"How so?"

Emma opened and closed her mouth, but she only shrugged in response.

"You know, Emma," Sun said, her voice deathly calm. "If you're lying to us, we can charge you with obstruction of justice. How do you suppose that'll impact your scholarship to Virginia Tech?"

Before Emma could reply, Noah cleared his throat. They were headed full speed into a brick wall if Sun didn't dial back her hostility.

"Agent Ming," he said, waving a hand to the closed door. "Can I talk to you for a second?"

Sun's dark eyes glinted with malevolence, but she nodded and pushed herself to stand.

"We'll be right back." He offered Emma and her mother a quick smile.

As soon as the door latched closed, Sun whirled around to face him. "What do you want, Dalton?" she hissed.

"I want you to get yourself in check, Ming," he returned. Any semblance of amiability had vanished. He wasn't going to let Sun ruin what might be their last chance to identify and catch The Norfolk Executioner. "This isn't Guantanamo Bay, and unless you think that girl in there can shoot someone between the eyes with a Barrett M98B from almost a mile away, she isn't a damned suspect!"

"She's holding something back," Sun replied. "She's lying. She saw more than what she's telling us. She might know the killer."

"I doubt she *knows* him. You know what happened with Gina Traeger, right? I'm sure by now you've heard about how Detective Olson screwed that whole thing up for us, right? About how he was a complete asshole to the only witness who'd ever seen The Norfolk Executioner and *lived*, and about how she won't say a damn word to us now, right? You've heard that story?"

On any given day, Noah had a long fuse.

He could laugh at his own misfortunes, and he rarely took off-color comments as a personal affront. But as he stared Sun Ming down while he waited for her response, he was close to the end of his fuse.

If she ruined their only opportunity to identify a man responsible for at least twenty murders—none of which had turned up a single, solitary shred of forensic evidence—he would snap.

"She's lying, Agent Dalton," Sun repeated.

He straightened to his full height as he narrowed his eyes. "If you fuck this up, Sun, you'd damn well better believe you won't skate away from it scot-free like you did on the Presley case. You might still think I'm some damn newbie fresh from Quantico, but I've been here long enough to understand how this shit works. We've got one more shot to find this guy, and if we don't, that's going to be on *you*. You understand me?"

Jaw clenched, she glowered at him. "She's facing a federal obstruction charge. She'll cooperate now, Dalton. Trust me. I've been doing this for a while."

There was an unmistakable condescending tinge to her voice, but he could see the shadow of anxiety behind her eyes. She knew she had made a mistake, and now she was trying to convince herself that the act wouldn't cost them the entire case.

"I guess we'll find out, won't we?" With one last scowl, he dropped his hand to the metal lever and pushed open the door. "Sorry about that," he said as they stepped back into the room.

"It's fine." Amber Olmsted's voice sounded like it could cut through a chunk of cinderblock. "My daughter is scared, agents. She watched a serial killer walk away after he slit a man's throat. She's lucky she's alive. I hope you've at least got enough empathy to understand why a teenage girl would be scared to describe someone like that."

Noah glanced to Sun.

Though the motion was stiff, she nodded. He felt the tension ease just a bit from his shoulders. "Yes. I do. Emma, did he say anything to you?"

"Just something about Greek mythology," Emma replied with a slight shake of her head. "About how Artemis was a protector of girls and women and how that's what he's doing."

He barely kept his sharp intake of breath in check. Winter had seen a festival celebrating Artemis in her vision not long ago.

"He was wearing a hoodie, but I think..." Emma paused to look to her mother. When the older woman nodded, she continued. "I think I could probably describe him a little. I don't know how accurate it'd be, though."

"What did he show you on his arm?" Sun asked, but her voice was as gentle as Noah had ever heard it. "We saw him show you something on the video."

The girl swallowed. "A tattoo."

Sun's voice was still gentle. Noah was actually proud of her sensitivity. He hadn't known she had it in her. "Of what, Emma?"

Noah watched the conflict at war on her face. Finally, she sighed, tears slipping down her cheeks. "Artemis."

"Have Emma sit down with one of your sketch artists," Ms. Olmsted suggested. "We can do that tonight, but after this…" her gaze slid to Sun, "anything you want to ask us had better come through our lawyer."

36

W hen Autumn saw the determined glint in Winter's
eyes as she took the call from Noah Dalton, she
half-expected her friend to pack up and dash out the door.
Instead, she thanked Noah for the update and told him she
would see him in the morning. Winter leaned back and
propped both stocking feet atop the stone coffee table.

"You're not going to go in?" Autumn asked, arching an
eyebrow as she took another swig of beer.

Winter shook her head. "Not right now, no. Noah said
they're having the witness talk to a sketch artist, and that
usually takes a little while. Not much I could do there in the
meantime, you know? Even Noah's heading home."

"Got it," Autumn replied with a nod.

"I mean, I guess I could go in and sift through a hundred
and fifty more names and phone numbers," Winter muttered.
"But I'll leave the telemarketing for the daytime."

"How'd the interview with the witness go? Sounded like it
might've been a little dicey."

Winter snorted a laugh. "Noah said he'd tell me about it
tomorrow, but yeah, he said it got iffy as soon as Sun decided

to take over. She threw an obstruction charge out there, and I guess they got lucky. They're doing the sketch artist thing right now, but the kid's mom lawyered up from here on out."

Stretching her legs along the couch, Autumn shrugged. "Even a broken clock's right twice a day."

"Plus, at least we have confirmation that the killer's a man. That ought to cut down on the number of alibi phone calls I get to make every damn day."

"Wow," Autumn laughed. "Is that normal? Do you have to call seven hundred people to check their alibis on every case?"

"Oh, hell no." Winter looked stricken. "Don't get me wrong, there's a lot of tedious work in every investigation, but this one's just a special kind of tedious. I can deal with sorting through databases or searching through old case files, stuff like that, but when it comes to making boring phone calls to see if someone was at the place they said they were at? That's something else. If I could go the rest of my life without making an outbound call to anyone who isn't a friend or family member, believe me, I'd do it."

"So, there's just a wider pool of suspects for this case, then, right?"

"Right," Winter replied. "And I swear, we've looked through every damn law enforcement official in the state of Virginia, and none of them match up with the guy we're looking for. There are a couple who don't have alibis and who we *might* be able to classify as a suspect, but the evidence is still all circumstantial. It wouldn't even hold up in front of a grand jury, much less in a trial. That's the whole reason we're even looking at LEOs, honestly. Because whoever this guy is, he hasn't left a damn *bit* of evidence behind."

Autumn whistled through her teeth before she drained the rest of her beer. "Could be a crime scene tech too. I mean, if there's anyone who knows how not to leave behind forensic evidence, it'd be a forensic scientist."

She expected a chuckle or a sarcastic observation about how Winter would add crime scene techs to her telemarketing list. But as Winter opened her mouth to respond, her blue eyes snapped open wide as a look of sudden realization passed over her face.

"You're right," Winter breathed. "We talked about that in one of our briefings but had relegated them to after we'd finished the law enforcement list, since it seemed more important to find someone who could make that kind of shot first."

Autumn leaned forward. "They keep databases of forensics people, just like they do with cops, right?"

Winter nodded and reached for her bag. "Looks like I've got a new list to start going through." She paused in her hurried movements and faced her friend again. "I really wanted to talk to you about something tonight, but it's going to have to wait. Don't let me forget about it, though, all right?"

"I'll pencil you in," Autumn replied with a grin.

WINTER THOUGHT she should have felt guilty for abandoning her friend out of the blue, but Autumn had become as much a part of their case as the agents in Violent Crimes.

Winter sent Noah a text message before she left the parking lot of Autumn's apartment building, and his response was almost immediate.

It's better than having to call people, his first message said. *I'll help you with it. Sounds like it might be a long night, so I'm going to shower before we head out. We should probably stop at a gas station and get coffee.*

No need, Winter wrote in response. *It's the night shift. Weyrick's got that coffee maker, remember?*

You trust Weyrick's coffee maker? Starbucks, darlin'.

The drive home felt like it took an hour.

At every red light and stop sign, she had to stifle a groan. Her pace was just below an outright sprint as she made her way from the car to her front door.

Though she wanted to change, grab her laptop, and run back out the door, Noah was right.

Just because the forensic techs in the state of Virginia had been compiled into a database didn't mean the work would be any less tedious than the plethora of phone calls they had made so far. No matter how revolutionary their new evidence, the search for the killer would still be painstaking.

With the remainder of the boring search ahead, she slowed her breathing and calmed her racing heart. The killer wouldn't materialize as soon as she and Noah walked through the doors of the FBI office—they would put in hours, maybe even *days* of work before they finally found the object of their search.

The shower relaxed her tired muscles, and by the time she rinsed the conditioner from her hair, clarity had returned to her thoughts.

She could deal with her depressing realization—a realization about which she was reminded whenever she thought of Noah—some other time. She had a serial killer to catch.

She repeated the mantra to herself, but the little voice in the back of her mind was persistent. The idea was faint, almost like a whisper beneath the shouts of another group of people, but she couldn't silence it.

What would she do if he left? What would she do if he found someone? Did she really expect him to put his entire life on hold while she worked out her conflicted feelings?

Were the feelings even conflicted anymore?

She had seen Aiden plenty over the last couple weeks, but the encounters hadn't come with the usual rush of adrenaline. When he smiled at her, there was nothing more than a twinge of something akin to pride in his pale blue eyes.

For the first time in recent memory, their interactions weren't nerve-racking, they were...what? Friendly. Calm. *Normal.*

As she stepped out of the water's warm embrace and dragged a comb through her hair, she mulled over the slow-moving shift in their dynamic. Ever since the start of the Haldane case, Aiden and Noah's pissing match had dwindled to little more than an occasional sarcastic comment. Even then, Winter suspected the remarks were more akin to an inside joke than any actual insult.

Twenty minutes later, leaving Noah in the vehicle, she was walking into her favorite coffee house. And almost got knocked on her ass as she dug into her purse for her wallet.

Strong hands wrapped around her upper arms, steadying her. "Sorry, ma'am. I—"

"I wasn't paying attention," she said at the same time.

The man was wearing combat fatigues. And as her gaze swept up from his sand-colored boots, up his camouflaged legs to his smooth-shaven face, the pulse of pain in her temples took her off guard.

The hands tightened around her arms as she felt herself tilt to her left. Concern etched across the blue-eyed soldier's expression. "Are you okay, ma'am?"

No, she wasn't. But not for the reason this man was thinking.

She forced a laugh. "Of course. Sorry again for not paying attention."

And she bolted for the restroom.

Shit. Shit. Shit.

She didn't have time for a damn vision, but by now, she knew better than to make an attempt to stop the inevitable.

She was turning the lock just as the searing sensation edged its way farther into her brain. She dropped down to the tiled floor. She had bounced her head off the floor enough to learn her lesson. The closer she got to the ground, nasty public bathroom or not, the shorter the fall and any resulting injury.

When her eyelids fluttered closed, she was no longer in the bathroom. The sun's burning heat touched her face, and she blinked repeatedly to clear the dust from her vision as a breeze whispered along the desert.

Aside from the move to New York for college, Winter hadn't traveled much in her twenty-six years of life. Though she had never been to a desert, she knew the desolate landscape and searing sunlight for what it was.

She was on a bluff, and below, a sprawling stretch of sand, rocks, and scrubby plants went on as far as she could see.

Above the wind's mournful cry, she heard another sound. A weary sigh.

The sound had come from a man at the edge of the bluff, and when she spotted his attire, the desert setting made sense.

Tan, digital camouflage fatigues, a matching Kevlar vest, and sandy colored boots. In one hand, he clutched the grip of a matte gray rifle as he ran the other through his black, disheveled hair. Winter wanted to approach him to catch a glimpse of his face, but she was rooted in place.

It was him.

Not the man she'd bumped into moments before.

The man who stood with his back to her was The Norfolk Executioner.

A distant crack drew the man's attention, and as he turned, she squinted to read the insignia on his shoulder. No matter how hard she tried, however, she couldn't focus her gaze on his face.

With a sharp gasp, Winter's eyes flew open as she sat bolt upright. She reflexively dabbed beneath her nose and was relieved when she spotted only a slight smudge of crimson.

She may not have seen the man's face, but whoever he was, his uniform had labeled him as a US Army Ranger. There was no doubt in her mind that she had just seen the man responsible for the murder of Tyler Haldane—The Norfolk Executioner.

After splashing water on her face and pulling herself together, she smiled at the anxious soldier hovering outside the bathroom.

"Are you okay, ma'am?"

She wanted to throw her arms around him. Not just for his obvious concern for her wellbeing, but this man had given her a gift she could never tell him about.

"I'm wonderful. Promise."

And she was.

Because of him, the length of her painstaking search would be dramatically shortened.

Now, she just had to mentally justify taking out a man who proclaimed himself to be the protector of women and girls.

Her stomach soured, and she didn't want her coffee anymore.

A
s he watched Winter step up to the wooden podium at the front of the briefing room—a place he had begun to think of as a second home—Aiden felt his lips curl into a smile.

Though Winter credited Autumn with planting the idea in her head, she had been the one to crack open the case, to put all the puzzle pieces into their proper places. This was Winter's moment, but he had helped her get here.

The path had been twisted and messy, but after all the conflicted feelings, all the spite and irritability, all the bickering, all the pointless competitions, they had emerged on the other side. And now, she was about to announce to some of the FBI's brightest that she had discovered the identity of the serial killer they'd been hunting.

Despite the pressure of the media circus through which they had tiptoed since the death of Tyler Haldane, Winter had prevailed. He was proud of how far she had come, and he could only imagine how much further she had left to go.

She looked so poised and professional as she began to speak. "The Norfolk Executioner is why we're here. Last night, he killed his tenth victim in the state of Virginia, and his twentieth in the country as a whole...that we know of. But last night, he left a witness. Today, just before this briefing, that witness picked this man out of a photo lineup."

What Winter didn't share was that, once she'd narrowed down the list of suspects to Army Rangers with Artemis tattoos, the rest of the investigation had been easy. To put icing on the cake, young Emma did indeed point to their suspect only an hour ago, tears pouring down her face.

The girl was as conflicted about the killer as the rest of them.

But she'd done the right thing.

With a light click, the overhead projector brought to life the image of a driver's license.

"That's him," Sun said. She was seated across the room at the side of Bobby Weyrick, a man she had been close to in almost every meeting they'd had about the case so far. But even as Aiden mulled over the possibility that the two had engaged in a secretive affair, he couldn't bring himself to care.

Winter nodded. "Yeah, that's him. That's Augusto Lopez, a twenty-year veteran of the Army Rangers. He left the military about nine years ago when he was thirty-eight, and ever since then, he's worked in forensics. He was stationed in Fort Hood when he left, which is why he stuck around the Dallas area.

"Not too long before Augusto retired from the Army, his daughter went missing. The main suspect was the man she'd accused of molesting her over the summer that year, her maternal uncle. The cops in Killeen weren't able to find anything they could use to tie him to the crime, but they still tried to push it through a grand jury. The guy denied everything from the get-go, and since it had taken her a little while to come forward about it, there wasn't much physical evidence.

"The grand jury didn't have enough to indict, and about nine months after that, Augusto's wife, Tina Lopez, killed herself. She committed suicide while he was deployed to Afghanistan, and from what I heard from a couple family friends, he blamed himself for it. He took the loss of his family pretty hard, and he became withdrawn. Honestly, I don't think any of us can blame him for that.

"The cops questioned Augusto once his wife's brother went missing, but they never found the guy's body. A year after that, the first rapist outside Killeen was shot in the head with a Heckler & Koch G36 rifle. No shell casing, no footprints, fingerprints, nothing. Then, six months later." Winter paused to glance at Chloe Villaruz.

"Same weapon," Villaruz put in. "He killed three more with the same weapon, and then he left it at the scene of the fourth murder. Same as that Barrett rifle you guys found. No serial number, just absolutely nothing. Our theory was that if he was involved in law enforcement, he might've known an arms dealer affiliated with one of the cartels. That might be where he got the G36 *and* the M98B."

"Right." Winter nodded. "We've handed both weapons off to the ATF. Chances are, they won't get anywhere with them, but the arms dealer that sold them to Augusto isn't our jurisdiction."

Aiden kept the sentiment to himself, but he was glad that they didn't have to deal with the Mexican drug cartels.

Chasing a serial killer was one thing but chasing after someone like Pablo Escobar was an entirely different ballgame. Their office had been thrown into enough of a tizzy when Sun was labeled as a potential suspect for Tyler Haldane's murder. He couldn't imagine work in a field so dangerous and volatile that even other federal agents were untrustworthy.

"Emma Olmsted said that he talked about the Greek goddess Artemis," Winter added, pressing the controller to bring up the next photo. "This is a tattoo on the inside of Augusto's forearm. It's a bow and arrow, and it's a symbol associated with Artemis."

"Good work, Agent Black," Max announced. "We've got a warrant for Augusto Lopez's arrest, and we'll be meeting with the tactical team in about ten minutes to discuss how we'll be executing that warrant. I think by now we all know how dangerous this man can be. We might've found him, but we aren't out of the woods just yet."

Aiden had started to shake his head before the older SAC even finished. "No," he said. "He might be dangerous, but I don't think he's dangerous to *us*. Emma Olmsted told us he saw her, and he let her go. If he was really dead set on escaping, we would have found her dead along with Marco Yarr. Same with Gina Traeger. She might not have cooperated with us, but we know that she saw him too."

"He's right," Autumn put in. "I've been here all morning looking over this guy's information. I'm here for threat assessment, remember? Augusto Lopez is only a threat to the people on his list. He told Emma Olmsted to 'do what you think is right.' Does that sound like a man who's going to open fire on a bunch of cops to you?"

As he glanced over to Autumn, Aiden could hardly keep the self-assured smirk from his face. Nine o'clock had not yet rolled around, but he knew today would be a good day.

WHEN I SAW the black van circle the block the first time, I

knew what was about to happen. I had already made my peace with my fate, be it life in prison or the death penalty.

My advice for Emma Olmsted to do the right thing had been sincere, and the girl hadn't disappointed. It would have been easy enough for her to bury her head in the sand and pretend that nothing had happened, but she had chosen the more difficult path—the *right* path.

How could I fault her for that?

I didn't like to follow the news articles about the men I'd killed. When I crossed out their names, I was done with them. But no matter how hard I tried to avoid the television segments and online news updates, I knew the level of attention I had attracted.

The entire country was fixated on Richmond, and I was the reason for their obsession.

As I straightened the photo of me, Tina, and Evie on the mantle of the fireplace, I paused.

There wasn't a place for someone like me in a civilized society. I had been promoted a couple times in the lab where I worked, but there was only one skill at which I had ever truly excelled.

That skill was death, and there was no place for a killer like me in the civilized world.

Before I lost my girls, I had a family to tether me to reality. But now, it felt like I drifted from place to place like an apparition. My ties to the moral world were gone, and the time had come for me to face my fate.

Even though there hadn't been a BOLO put out on me yet, I'd been doing this long enough to understand what the cops weren't saying…they were coming for me.

But first, I had a few more things to attend to.

Before the door of the black panel van that had just pulled up outside slid open, I shot Greg Winstead in the head and pushed him from the second story window where I'd taken up residence as soon as the chatter on the police scanner grew more excited. I'd already pinned a notecard to the rapist's shirt, listing the names of his victims.

Honoring all six of the girls this man had emotionally and physically destroyed.

Maybe those women might be able to sleep a little better tonight.

I sure hoped so.

Because as I turned and looked into the eyes of the terrified men shackled to the steel pole I'd installed along the wall of the bedroom, I knew I'd sleep a little better tonight too.

I grinned.

"Russell Peterson...it's time to pay for your crimes."

38

Winter's heart slammed in her chest as the sound of a gunshot echoed in her ears.

Before she could respond, she was yanked back into the van, the heavy metal door narrowly missing her sneakered toes as it slammed shut.

Scrambling to her feet, Winter caught the blur of something dropping from the pristine farmhouse they'd just approached.

"Shit," Noah muttered, his fist still holding the back of her Kevlar vest.

Even while he tried to yank her down, Winter fought to look out the window. "Let me go!"

He didn't, but he loosened his hold. "Who the fuck is that?"

Who?

Getting a better look at the thing on the ground, Winter realized Noah was right. It was a who. A person. More specifically, a man.

She shook her head. "I don't know." She looked harder,

trying to see past the blood and gore. "But it's not Augusto Lopez."

Even through the walls of the van, Winter heard a noise that raised the hair on her arms.

Screaming. Terrible screaming.

"What—" Noah shouted.

Another gunshot drowned out whatever else he was going to say. Everyone in the van grew quiet, watching, waiting. Seconds later, another body fell.

This time, Winter noticed the notecard pinned to the front of the man's shirt. She immediately knew what it was.

Shit.

"He's finishing what he started," Winter said before yelling at the driver, "Fall back, fall back," then held on tight as the van spun in the gravel before catching surface and jerking backward at rapid speed.

Other vans, police cars…a virtual army of law enforcement vehicles converged on the scene. Noah grabbed the radio, ordering the others to fall back as well. The next few moments were chaos as the situation was assessed.

"Agent Black, report." She recognized Aiden's voice right away.

Scrambling to get out of the stifling van, using it as a shield, she inhaled a deep breath of air before lifting her mic to her lips. "Black reporting."

But before she could finish the words, Aiden was at her side, sweat dotting his temples from his dash from the second van on the scene. She was about to tell him that he hadn't needed to hurry because, while Augusto Lopez had killing on his mind, she didn't think his targets were on this side of that window.

Another gunshot vibrated through the air.

Another body fell.

"Shit," she muttered. "We have to do something."

She looked around.

The house was a perfect sniper hide, she realized. Sitting high on a hill, the lovely farmhouse had been stripped of all the trees that would have given it shade over the past century. Neat stacks of wood set beside a small outbuilding to the side.

The stumps where those trees once stood looked fresh, and Winter could almost see the soldier cutting them down. Whether it was to take away any tactical advantage law enforcement would gain to access the upper story of the home or remove an avenue of escape for the hostages he held, she wasn't sure.

Probably both.

Noah stepped out of the van, still talking rapidly into his mic, directing the teams.

They would be too late, she knew.

Another gunshot.

Winter whipped her head around, squinting against the sun as she watched another body fall from the upper window. She also saw the shadow of Lopez, but only for the slightest moment.

Pain ripped through her skull, and she teetered to one side.

Hands caught her arms, but she didn't need them to steady her. The vision was gone almost as quickly as it appeared.

"Seven more," she whispered into Aiden's concerned eyes.

Noah whipped around, his gaze flicking between her and the SSA. Annoyance was replaced by the same mask of concern.

It pissed her off.

Ripping her arm out of Aiden's grip, she forced her legs to hold her up, swiping at the drop of blood she felt run down to her upper lip.

"We don't have much time," she said, relieved that her voice held more strength.

She could still see the men shackled to the steel pole. Still see the three sets of shackles that now lay on the floor. The men were terrified, but Winter couldn't find it in herself to feel sorry for them.

Murderers.

Rapists.

Child molesters.

Augusto Lopez was taking out the trash.

While one part of her wanted to cheer him on, she knew he had to be stopped.

No man could be judge, jury, and executioner.

If they let one man get away with it, how many would follow?

Laws were there for a reason, she reminded herself, thinking back to the criminal justice classes she'd sat through not all that long ago. The six main functions of law were to keep peace in a country, shape moral standards, promote social justice, facilitate orderly change, provide a basis for compromise, and to help in facilitating a plan.

Winter had promised to, "Well and faithfully discharge the duties of the office on which I am about to enter. So help me God."

A lawless land was a peaceless land. And more than anything, Winter wanted peace.

Though Winter wasn't sure what she thought of the subject, she muttered, "God, help me now."

Both Aiden and Noah stared at her, concern still clear in their eyes.

Aiden spoke first. "What are you thinking?"

A gunshot.

Winter didn't even turn, just closed her eyes when the body slammed into the ground.

"I'm thinking six. And I'm thinking we don't have much time until there are zero."

"What does Lopez want?" Noah asked.

He was thinking in terms of a hostage situation, but Winter knew better.

"He wants to finish this, finish them."

Aiden was scanning the landscape. "There's no tactical advantage. We'll have to ram the door."

Winter straightened. "That won't be necessary."

Before either man could say a word or grab her, she took off in a sprint, heading toward the covered porch. She feared having another dead body fall on her more than she feared being shot at. But she was on the porch before another gunshot sounded, and the body she feared splattered on the ground well behind her.

Five.

"Winter!"

She heard approaching footsteps but didn't wait, instead opening the front door. It wasn't locked.

Noah burst in behind her, cursing words that would normally make her ears burn, but she was taking the steps two at a time. She was only halfway up when another gunshot made her jump, automatically crouch, if nothing more than from instinct.

"Four," she muttered. A countdown of the worse kind.

Or the best. Winter didn't like the little voice whispering in her ear.

Noah was right behind her now, and she could hear other footsteps running into the home.

Bam!

Three.

Winter wasn't foolish enough to run straight into the room. Lopez didn't appear to be interested in hurting anyone besides the people he held hostage, but she didn't know how attached he'd be to finishing the job, stopping anyone who might get in his way of handing out the justice he so very clearly thought these men deserved.

She placed her back to one side of the door while Noah moved into position on the other side, gun at the ready, daggers of pure anger hurtling her way.

"Augusto Lopez!" she called. "FBI. Drop your weapon. You're surr—"

Bam!

Two.

"Shit," Noah said before adding a few other choice words.

SWAT was coming up the stairs, and Winter knew they'd do their job with deadly force. Even while Noah shook his head furiously at her, she reached for the doorknob.

Bam!

One.

Closing her eyes, she turned the knob and pushed the door in. Still growling under his breath, Noah went in first before she could stop him. She was on his heels, stopping in her tracks at the carnage before her.

Knowing his time was close to an end, Lopez had stopped pushing the men from the windows. Hell, he apparently no longer cared that they were shackled. The last two slumped, only their chains holding them up.

"Drop your weapon," Noah shouted.

Lopez just smiled, kept his gun at the last man's head. And pulled the trigger.

I'D DONE what I'd set out to do. Not all of it, maybe. I could have helped society so much more. But I could leave this earth knowing I'd done the very best I could.

I knew this day was coming, and a part of me wished I'd

thought of chaining these bastards up sooner. One bullet through their heads from a distance wasn't really punishment enough. But luring them to my house—and they were so easily lured—had them pissing their pants like the little pussies they were.

I'd managed to get ten before this day arrived. I'd hoped to have twenty. Fifty. A hundred.

Ten would have to do.

When the agents burst into the bedroom, I'd made my peace with God. I'd smiled up to the heavens, whispering to Tina and Evie that I'd see them real soon.

I was ready.

Well, almost. I had to distribute justice to Amanda Harris, Jillian Sizemore, Amy Rebstock, and Sandra Palmer first. Even as I stared down the barrel of two weapons, I pulled the trigger of mine, wiping the whimpering scum ball who'd raped and molested those innocent girls from the face of the earth.

Then I waited.

Waited for the explosion of pain. Waited for my world to go black.

Waited for the peace of death to remove me from the pain of life.

When peace didn't come, I stared at the agents still pointing their guns at me.

"Thank you for letting me finish," I said, dropping my gun.

Their paralysis broke, and they rushed me, kicking the gun away, taking me down.

This was an unexpected development. I was alive.

As they cuffed me, I began to laugh.

This was unexpected...but good.

I might have run out of targets out in the real world, but

where I was going...prison...was full of men just like the predators I'd killed.

Possibilities raced through my mind as the female agent read me my rights.

Endless possibilities.

39

Autumn had been so relieved to see the stress lifted from her friends' shoulders, she almost forgot that they had captured a serial killer.

In the press conference to announce Augusto Lopez's arrest, the bureau had given Shadley and Latham credit for their role in locating the man. Specifically, the SAC of Violent Crimes had given *Autumn* credit.

Due to her familiarity with the case, she had been assigned the psychiatric evaluation of Augusto, though the interview wasn't for another few days.

The purpose was straightforward and simple enough, but Autumn was loath to admit to her FBI friends how giddy she was to meet The Norfolk Executioner. She had been fascinated by serial killers since she was in high school, but so far, she had never been granted the opportunity to conduct an in-depth discussion with such a notorious offender.

When she was summoned to Adam Latham's office, she assumed the unscheduled meeting had to do with her upcoming session with Augusto Lopez.

As she made her way down a hallway, she glanced out the

floor-to-ceiling windows that composed one side of the corridor. The sun cast an orange and gold halo on the city skyline as it sunk down into the horizon.

Autumn blinked against the glow as she returned her focus to the hall.

Damn, when had it gotten so late?

She was scheduled to meet her friends for Shelby's birthday dinner that night, but she had set an alarm to give her ample time to make it to the restaurant. For good measure, she pulled her phone from a pocket and double-checked the time.

She breathed a sigh of relief when she noted that she had fifteen minutes before the alarm was set to go off.

The glass and metal door to Adam Latham's office was cracked, but Autumn rapped her knuckles against the frame for good measure.

Shadley and Latham boasted dual coast offices. One here in Virginia while the other resided in Arizona. During her initial interview and during all meetings up until now, Dr. Latham had participated via video chat from the Phoenix office. This would be her first face-to-face meeting with this particular boss.

"Dr. Latham?" she called.

He looked up from his desk, and through the glass, she watched him wave her in. "My apologies," he said. "I thought you'd be another minute."

With a practiced smile, Autumn stepped onto the carpeted floor. "No problem."

As he glanced up from his laptop, there was a glint in the man's blue eyes that she could only describe as predatory. She had seen the look before. In the foster care system, on the faces of college frat boys, anywhere someone could exert their power over a weaker, more vulnerable person in their control.

Though her initial reaction was to assure herself she was just paranoid, she had learned to trust her instincts when it came to the motivations of other people. Her sixth sense had saved her from the same naivety that led so many other young men and women into peril. She wasn't about to question it now.

"Did you need me for something, Dr. Latham?" Autumn asked, forcing a smile back to her lips as she folded her hands in front of herself.

"Need? No," he chuckled with a dismissive wave. With a light tap, he closed the laptop and pushed the computer to the side. "I just wanted to congratulate you. I know you're still working on the Augusto Lopez case, but I wanted to tell you how impressed I am at your start here. There aren't many folks we hire right out of grad school who start off quite like you. You got this firm a hell of a lot of publicity, and *good* publicity at that."

She inclined her head. "Thank you, sir."

"At the least, I thought that warranted an in-person thanks. I know I speak for Mike when I say that we're glad to have you on board with us, Dr. Trent. We're both looking forward to working with you from here on out. You bring a lot to the table, and that's not easy for someone your age. Now, if you have a minute, I was wondering if you'd join me for a quick drink?"

Was that even a real question? Did he honestly think she would feel comfortable turning down the offer?

"Sure," she replied as she took a seat in one of the armchairs in front of his mahogany desk. "I have to make it quick, though. My friend's birthday is today, and I'm meeting her and her fiancée for dinner soon."

Latham's grin widened to reveal his straight, white teeth. He was in his fifties, but aside from the touch of silver at his temples, his appearance didn't belie a single year over forty.

Despite the age difference, Autumn could still admit he was a decent-looking man. Or, at least he would be if he wasn't so damn creepy.

"What great timing, then," he commented, ducking down to retrieve a corked bottle of brown liquor.

Before he poured the scotch into two crystal glasses, Autumn had already decided she would watch him take a sip before she followed suit. She didn't know much about Dr. Adam Latham but based on the crawling sensation on the back of her neck, she wouldn't put it past him to drug her drink.

To her relief, the only questions he asked had to do with the Lopez investigation. She wasn't sure she had the mental capacity to offer a polite refusal if he decided to take a more personal approach in their conversation.

"Thank you for the drink." With a light clunk, she set the polished glass atop the desk and rose to stand.

Latham pushed out of his seat at the same time, and he flashed another of those disarming grins as he extended a hand.

Shit.

Autumn gritted her teeth and forced herself to look pleasant as she accepted the handshake. The instant her palm touched his, she wanted to yank her arm away and sprint out the door.

And in that instant, she wished Augusto Lopez was still a free man.

WINTER HUSTLED down the hallway to the elevator. She could still make it to Shelby's birthday dinner on time, but she had to hurry. The doors opened just a few moments after she'd pushed the down button, but she groaned when the cheery ding sounded as she came to a halt on the third floor. When the doors parted to reveal the newest passenger, she stuffed down the flash of annoyance.

"Aiden," she said, keeping her voice level. "You're here late."

She immediately hated herself for saying something so stupid.

She hated herself more when he gave her a curious, slightly concerned glance. For a second, she worried he might reach and place his hand on her forehead to take her temperature. "I'm always here late."

"True. I guess I'm never here late enough to see you here late. If that even made sense."

"Good point." He laughed, but it had an "are you all right" edge to it. He cleared his throat. "You look good. Where are you headed?"

She glanced down to her flowy teal and silver blouse, black leggings, and silver flats. She felt distinctly uncomfortable in something so girly. "Thanks. I went shopping with Autumn last week. Everything I'm wearing came from a clearance rack and at her insistence...I mean, suggestion."

He chuckled. "That sounds like Autumn."

There was a touch of wistfulness in his smile, and Winter was more convinced than ever that he had taken a less than professional interest in her friend. Unlike the times she had noticed the sentiment before, however, there was no pang of sadness or irritability.

"You like her, don't you?" Winter asked, the corner of her mouth turning up in a smirk. When he started to shake his head, she poked him in the chest. "You do. No, don't even deny it. I've known you for how long? Thirteen, almost *fourteen* years, Parrish. Nuh-uh, you can't hide that. Come on."

Even as he rolled his eyes, he had started to chuckle at her vehemence. "We're not talking about this right now. It's been a long month, and I'm going to go home, by *myself*, and sleep for a week. I just wanted to tell you something before I left, so I'm glad I caught you. And *no*, it doesn't have anything to do with Autumn."

She couldn't stop herself from teasing him one more time. "Yeah, yeah."

He ignored her. "You've probably heard it from fifteen different people by now, but you did a damn good job. I know the headaches, or visions, whatever you want to call them. I know they might have helped, but all the real work, that was you. I want to say I'm proud, except…"

He narrowed his eyes at her, and she knew what was coming next. Her ass had already been half chewed off by Noah, the SAC, and the ADD for running into the farmhouse so recklessly. But she'd do it again, even though she'd promised each of them that she'd be more careful in the future.

"If you ever pull a stunt like running into that house again, I'll have your ass back in the BAU before you can say 'serial killer.'"

She rolled her eyes, then smiled as a smile played on Aiden's lips. "You can try."

He crossed his arms over his chest. "Let's not argue. Let me say what I need to say." At her lifted eyebrow, he went on, "I'm impressed. I'm looking forward to seeing what you're going to do at the bureau."

She felt her cheeks grow warm. Aiden didn't offer compliments often.

"And…" he paused to raise an index finger, "this might not be all that professional, but I just wanted to say I'm sorry for all the bickering and bullshit with Dalton. He's a good guy, and I know it doesn't matter what I think, but I think he's good for you. Whenever he's around, you seem, I don't know. Better. Happier."

As her smile widened, she felt the first pinpricks at the corners of her eyes. She had applied mascara for the first time in recent memory, and she didn't want to test the limits of the mid-tier cosmetic by crying right before she left for a public gathering.

"You know," she said, elbowing his upper arm as she grinned. "I could say the same thing about you and a certain someone."

"Oh my god." He raised a hand to rub his eyes and groaned, and Winter only laughed harder.

Winter's decline over the next couple weeks was gradual but no less painful. As much as she and Noah complained about the number of phone calls they had to make during the Lopez investigation, she wished they could go back to those days. At least then, she had a purpose.

Now, she spent her days at the courthouse or at her desk. Paperwork, court testimony, and the occasional training class had become the new routine.

Cyber Crimes hadn't come any closer to discovering the source of the email she received, though they hadn't given up. She could feel her mind as it slipped closer and closer to the inky black chasm of hopelessness and despair, but she couldn't bring herself to burden her friends with her problems. For the most part, she didn't even know what her problem *was*. Not until she skimmed past a news article about the serial killers captured in Richmond over the past year.

Augusto Lopez led the pack in terms of media coverage, but next in line was Douglas Kilroy. As her eyes fell on the man's name—the name of the menace that had plagued her for more than half of her entire life—she realized what had given birth to the yawning canyon of nothingness in her mind.

As she stuffed her phone into the pocket of her leather jacket, she snatched up her keys and walked out to her car. For the duration of the trip to the cemetery, her movements and decisions were carried out by little more than her brainstem.

She'd never leapt off the couch in the middle of a movie to drive to the site where her parents were buried. Over the years, she had been to their graves in Harrisonburg more times than she could count, but this was the first time she'd felt the need to stand on the ground where the damn bastard who'd killed them was buried.

The leaden daylight caught the driver's side window as she pushed the door closed. Her booted feet crunched against gravel, but her steps quieted as she crossed over to a patch of lush grass. In this seldom traversed part of the cemetery, none of the headstones were labeled with names, only numbers. But Winter didn't need to see the man's name. She knew which grave was his.

"Douglas Kilroy," she said to the empty clearing. "You're the whole reason I'm here, you know that? And I guess that means you're the whole reason *you're* here too. You should have killed me when you had the chance, you stupid piece of shit."

She raised her face to the sky when the sun broke through the clouds for a moment. As it warmed her face, she thought of her mother and father, of her baby brother. The brother who haunted her days. Her nights.

Winter had always thought that Kilroy was the ghost in her closet, but she knew better now.

Winter's ghost was her baby brother.

"But you didn't." There was an unmistakable tremor in

her voice, and she glanced around the area to ensure she was by herself. "You didn't kill me, but even when you're dead, you still find ways to ruin my life! You were the whole reason I joined the FBI in the first place. All I ever wanted was to put your stupid ass in a prison cell or put a bullet between your eyes, but I didn't do either, did I?"

The wind picked up, and if she believed in spirits or ghosts, she would have thought he was laughing in her face. The thought made her even madder.

"Maybe I should have just done what Augusto Lopez did. Maybe I should have said 'fuck it,' and just come for you myself. At least then I'd know that *I* was the one who chose my life. But now, was I? Was it me who picked this, did I do any of this for myself, or was it all just for *you?*"

The silence was eerie as she stared down at the unadorned headstone. She felt herself teeter backward, and she wondered how much longer she could keep herself from falling into the dismal canyon. With no one but herself for company, the plummet was inevitable.

"I'm not alone," she said, her voice stronger. "You were alone, Kilroy, but I'm not. You were alone because you were a miserable excuse for a human being. Every breath you took was an abomination to the god you thought you were."

With one trembling hand, she retrieved her phone. A droplet fell to the screen as she typed the code to unlock the device. Though her first inclination was to think the afternoon showers had started early, she realized that she had started to cry.

The tears weren't for Douglas Kilroy. He didn't deserve her tears.

She could only assume they were for her, for the person she might have been if he hadn't taken away her family.

Her mom. Her dad. Her baby brother.

More tears fell as she thought of him.

"Where are you, Justin?" she whispered.

In the distance, thunder rumbled.

She thought that was answer enough.

NOAH OPENED his eyes a slit at the first buzz from his phone, and when it sounded out a second time, he groped at the surface of the coffee table until he found the device. Shit. He hadn't meant to fall asleep.

Blinking to clear the film from his eyes, he swiped at the screen to open the messages. They were both from Winter, and as he read the first sentence, he pushed himself to sit upright.

"Shit," he spat. She was at the cemetery where Douglas Kilroy's ashes had been buried, and according to the second message, she was about to lose her mind. "Shit," he repeated, shoving away a plaid microfiber blanket.

I'll be right there, he replied.

Rather than focus on the reason for her sudden break-down, he focused on how many traffic laws he could break without putting other drivers at risk. For a normal person, the drive to the cemetery at the edge of town took close to twenty minutes. For Noah today, the trip took twelve.

He didn't know where Douglas Kilroy's remains had been put, but the mass of gray clouds overhead meant there were few other visitors. To his relief, he spotted the little Civic after he turned around the second bend past the entrance. The roar of his truck's engine had barely stopped by the time he hopped down to the ground and shoved the door closed.

"Winter," he called as he neared the patch of grass.

With a faint sniffle, she pulled her stare away from the gravestone. The muddy daylight glinted off the glassiness in her eyes as she swiped at her cheeks.

"Oh my god." He was surprised he managed to speak through the sudden tightness in his throat. "Winter, sweetheart, what's wrong?" Before she could respond, he closed the distance between them and pulled her into his arms.

"I don't know." Her quiet voice was muffled as she rested her face against his shoulder. "I don't know what I'm doing here. I don't just mean at the cemetery, I mean, I don't know. Everything. Why am I even in the FBI? Did I really do all this for Kilroy? Because of Kilroy?"

He stroked her long hair, just letting her talk, say whatever she needed to say.

"Noah...I based my entire life around finding that asshole, and I never bothered to stop and think what I'd do once he was dead. Maybe I just thought everything would magically fall into place like some Hallmark movie, I don't know. I just, I don't know what the hell I'm doing anymore."

"Darlin', just because Kilroy's dead doesn't mean the shit he did just goes away. That's the fucked up thing about all of this, honestly. He's gone, but all the people he hurt, they're all still here trying to find their way."

He paused, checking to see if she was even able to hear him through her sobs. When she looked up at him with those blue eyes rimmed in red, it nearly broke his heart.

"What do I do?"

He pressed his lips to her forehead. "You refuse to give him power over you, and you give yourself some time to adjust to this new normal. Be kind to yourself. It's all right to be a mess."

She barked out a laugh that was mostly a sob. "I've got that one down."

Vulnerable like this, he didn't think he'd ever seen anyone so beautiful. He had to look away.

"We've all got to figure out the reason we do what we do, darlin', and sometimes, it just sucks. I've been there, sweetheart. When I got back to the States after being in the military so long, I didn't know what the hell to do."

"But," she sniffed, "you figured it out."

"Yeah," he replied, brushing his fingers through the soft strands of her hair. "And so will you."

She tightened her grasp on the front of his shirt. "I don't want you to leave."

"Leave?" He made a snorting sound. "Who said I'm leaving?"

In a split-second of panic, he wondered if she was privy to a piece of information he hadn't yet heard. Was he about to be transferred? With his luck, he'd wind up in Florida, someplace where even the landscape was hostile.

"What if you find someone?" she managed around a swallow.

"Oh," he said, relaxing a little, "that kind of leave. Trust me, darlin', that ain't about to happen any time soon, either. I can't even remember the last time I went on a real date, and right now, I'm not even remotely interested in tying myself down."

"Isn't that usually when you find someone," she murmured in response, "when you aren't searching?"

"Not if you don't want to."

Her sniffle sounded a little like a laugh, and he took the moment of reprieve to pull away from the despondent embrace. As he tipped up her chin to meet her bloodshot eyes, his grasp was gentle, almost reverent.

"I'm not going anywhere. You'll get through this, and I'll still be here while you work on it."

The seconds ticked away as she held his gaze, and even though he thought an eternity might have passed, he didn't break his eyes away until a fat raindrop landed on the bridge of his nose. On cue, a clap of thunder rumbled in the distance.

"Come on," he said, circling an arm around her shoulders as he turned to face their parked vehicles. "It's supposed to pour today. Seems like a good time to catch up on some TV. We can go to my place and order some pizza. My couch is way better than yours."

With a half-laugh, half-snort, she nodded. "You're not wrong."

As much as he was sure he had stumbled upon an opportunity to turn their friendship into something more, Noah had vowed months ago not to make the first move. The ball was in Winter's court now, and he had sworn he wouldn't renege on his conviction. But when she fell asleep with her face tucked into the crook of his neck and an arm around his waist, he wondered how wise the decision was in the first place.

She had just as much a reason to be scared of a change in their relationship as he. Neither of them wanted to jeopardize their friendship, but at what point did they take the risk?

Now?

Never?

The whirlwind of thoughts had finally died down enough for him to drift toward the start of sleep. In his mind, he walked along a sidewalk. The concrete was smooth and unbroken, but as soon as he glanced up, his foot smacked into an unseen barrier, and he started to fall.

Before he could finish his graceless descent to the imaginary sidewalk, he took in a sharp breath and snapped open his eyes. Winter issued a tired groan and shifted in place, but before he could close his eyes, he heard the buzz of his phone atop the coffee table.

He knew the device was his—Winter had set hers on the carpet.

"Dammit," he breathed after the second buzz. It was a phone call, and at one in the morning, he could only assume it was important.

With as little movement as he could manage, he reached out to scoop up the device. He didn't recognize the number, nor did he recognize the area code.

If this is a wrong number, I swear to god…

"This is Agent Dalton," he answered, keeping his voice low.

"Noah?" a man's panicked voice asked.

Though he hadn't heard the man speak in years, he knew that voice. That voice belonged to Eric Dalton, his biological father.

"Eric…" he said sharply. After all this time, this man didn't deserve the label of dad. Because he had no idea what else to say, he went with the inane. "Do you know what time it is? What the—"

Winter stirred, and Noah closed his eyes, willing his temper to recede.

"Noah, I-I need your help."

He sat up straighter, frowned when Winter murmured in her sleep.

"You what?"

Winter snapped awake, even though he hadn't raised his voice. At least he thought he hadn't, anyway. She rested her hand on his arm, giving him a worried look. He shook his head and mouthed, *my father.*

Her eyes widened, and she shifted positions as he went to stand up, needing to pace off the manic energy that now seemed to clog his every pore. From the corner of his eye, he watched her pick up her own phone, praying to all that was holy that she wasn't about to leave. He needed her, he realized. Needed her here.

"I messed up, Noah," Eric said.

Noah snorted. "I'm shocked." Sarcasm was his most powerful tool in this moment.

"Son..."

Noah gritted his teeth, opened his mouth to tell the sperm donor he was talking to that he wasn't his son. To never call him that again. To...

"I messed up bad," Eric went on, his voice cracking now. The man was truly scared.

Noah turned in his pacing and looked at Winter. She was staring at her own phone. She was pale. She looked stricken, almost like she'd seen a ghost.

But he could do nothing because his own ghost from his past was saying, "Noah, if you don't help me, they're going to kill me for it."

IT HAD BEEN A NICE DREAM.

A nice, normal dream of a nice, normal run through a field of sunflowers, the warmth of the day shining on her face. Noah had been behind her, running too, a picnic basket in his hands.

That was what normal couples did. At least she thought so.

They went on dates. Went on picnics. Held hands. Kissed. Made love.

But Winter was awake now, and there was nothing normal going on inside Noah's apartment.

He looked like he'd seen a ghost when he mouthed, *my father.*

In the time they'd known each other, she was ashamed

that it had taken her more than a few moments to call up a name. Eric Dalton.

The man who had abandoned his son was now calling in the middle of the night. For what? Winter couldn't tell.

What time was it anyway?

Reaching for her phone, she noted the time and something else. A missed text message from her friend in the IT department.

As Noah paced, Winter slid her thumb across the screen. Seconds later, the text appeared. She felt herself pale as she read the words.

Email location confirmed. Origination: Harrisonburg, Virginia

Her hometown.

Her heart knocked in her chest, and her breathing went shallow.

The email she'd received from someone saying he was her brother—*Hey, sis. Heard you've been looking for me*—had come from her hometown.

The place where her parents had been slaughtered, and her baby brother went missing.

The End

To be continued...

Find all of the Winter Black Series books on Amazon.

ACKNOWLEDGMENTS

How does one properly thank everyone involved in taking a dream and making it a reality? Let me try.

In addition to my family, whose unending support provided the foundation for me to find the time and energy to put these thoughts on paper, I want to thank the editors who polished my words and made them shine.

Many thanks to my publisher for risking taking on a newbie and giving me the confidence to become a bona fide author.

More than anyone, I want to thank you, my reader, for clicking on a nobody and sharing your most important asset, your time, with this book. I hope with all my heart I made it worthwhile.

Much love,
Mary

ABOUT THE AUTHOR

Mary Stone lives among the majestic Blue Ridge Mountains of East Tennessee with her two dogs, four cats, a couple of energetic boys, and a very patient husband.

As a young girl, she would go to bed every night, wondering what type of creature might be lurking underneath. It wasn't until she was older that she learned that the creatures she needed to most fear were human.

Today, she creates vivid stories with courageous, strong heroines and dastardly villains. She invites you to enter her world of serial killers, FBI agents but never damsels in distress. Her female characters can handle themselves, going toe-to-toe with any male character, protagonist or antagonist.

Discover more about Mary Stone on her website.
www.authormarystone.com

facebook.com/authormarystone

goodreads.com/AuthorMaryStone

bookbub.com/profile/3378576590

pinterest.com/MaryStoneAuthor

instagram.com/marystone_author

Made in the USA
Monee, IL
19 September 2020